SCRAP

A BARCELONA THRILLER

Marius Stankiewicz

New Europe Books

For Paul

Published by New Europe Books, 2024
Williamstown, Massachusetts
www.NewEuropeBooks.com

ISBN: 9798985756401

Cataloging-in-Publication data is available from the Library of Congress.

First edition
10 9 8 7 6 5 4 3 2 1

Printed in the United States of America

SCRAP

1
Voyeur

When the light came on across the street, the room's dull glow seeped into the rainy night. Lightning bolt fissures ran across the greasy walls, and empty bottles of wine were strewn about like an abandoned game of spin the bottle. A dirty mattress lay reared up into the corner.

From his dark loft in the opposite building, Lucas Brodowski was looking wistfully out the window. After he took another sip of his wine, his eyes roved over the room across the street a second time. He spotted a milk crate holding up a few melted candles, a floor lamp missing its lampshade, and a heavy metal band poster on the door, the band's name in a font that looked like a careless stack of hedge trimmings.

Lucas wore nothing but his underwear, and while he continued eating dinner, a man and woman suddenly burst into the room. He perked up and looked on as he knew the woman, whom he had spotted a few times drinking little pinch-cup coffees at a local *cafetería*, reading some book about vampires.

She had long, black hair with one side of her head zero-guarded, revealing a tattoo that looked like an arrow married with a pagan symbol and some obscure, ancient hieroglyph. Other body art covered her skin like postage stamps on a package. Her face was full of dark makeup, piercings, and labret spikes, though Lucas couldn't tell to which hole metal was attached or from which hole metal was protruding. Her morgue-white skin stood out, as did the shape she was endowed with. Esmeralda was her name, or Esme, for short, and she lived on the fifth floor in the building opposite—Lucas lived on the sixth, the *ático*—yet the broken blinds of Lucas's ceiling-high windows were not always open like hers, which served to expose her raucous romps.

The man who accompanied Esme into the room was slender yet muscular, with spiky hair and frosted tips. One could easily have mistaken him for the soccer star Cristiano Ronaldo, wearing, as he was, a gold chain hanging down to his sternum and a diamond dangling from each earlobe. He was overtaken by uncontrollable lust mixed, it seemed, with the nervous agitation of a coke rush. While he impatiently removed his sneakers, unbuttoned his jeans and kicked them off, and tore off his shirt, Esme seemed more in command of herself. She gently flicked away her stiletto heels, disrobed calmly from her silk black gown and lingerie, and neatly folded and placed them next to her open chest of sex toys. Despite the erotic scene unfolding, and the nascent bulge appearing between his legs, hunger was a higher priority for Lucas, who had not eaten all day.

Half-finished and cooling, a plate of ready-made, ricotta-filled ravioli sat in front of him on what seemed to be a door planking two sawhorses, all items he'd found in the trash. His loft, for that matter, was filled with all kinds of junk mostly picked up from street corners, things like washing machines and books, which he'd already stacked up to form another insulating layer of wall, and about three dozen bicycles hanging from the ceiling. On one side of his plate stood a half-empty carton of Don Simon, a fork, and hard, day-old bread; on the other side, a kitchen knife and a revolver, whose barrel reflected a faint sliver of sodium streetlight coming in from outside.

Esme was now lying naked on the mattress pressed under the weight of Cristiano's body. It was as though the world had fallen silent for the peep show, and someone had turned off the lights in every flat facing the street, spotlighting a curtains-open stage for a solo spectator. The raindrops hitting Lucas's window were a soothing sound effect over their slapping, spitting, biting, and what appeared to be loud moaning.

He took a swig of wine from the carton and watched them change positions, then placed a slathered ravioli into his mouth and took another bite of stale bread. Esme's hands were now up against the window like a suspect being frisked by a police officer. A little condensation formed on the glass. Right when Cristiano buried his right hand into Esme's waist and pulled on her hair, hardly relenting in the act, Lucas received a phone call.

"We had a deal!" Ricardo shouted in the way of a greeting. Lucas put another sodden ravioli into his mouth and ate it noisily. Ricardo was a sly drug dealer from Panama, a fierce ex-*sicario* who was now competing for territory in Spain, worlds away from straw hats, cumbia, and a canal like a belt around the slim waist of Lady America.

Lucas didn't answer him right away, trying to gather his thoughts. "You didn't really bring me to Europe unless you consider Tangier a European exclave," he said, still chewing loudly.

"It was close enough and you owe us."

"Owe you? I still had to find my way to Barcelona. I've paid my debt with you already, Ricardo, by selling all those fake credit cards to add to the time of doing a quick shipment for you." Sauce ran down Lucas's mouth. "I'm not in that racket anymore. I told you so the last time you called." He looked over at his revolver, then back at the spectacle across the street. His eyes widened. Cristiano was taking out a whip and a hammer. Then a man appeared from behind, filming the whole thing.

"Not in that racket?!" Ricardo snapped. "You never had the choice *not* to be in the racket—the racket chose you, as far as I remember, after you left the force."

"Plans have changed," Lucas said with a mouthful of ravioli.

"'Plans have changed'?!" Ricardo's blood was boiling over on the other end of the receiver.

"Change is good, Ricardo. You should consider it—'break good.'" He wiped his mouth with a napkin.

"Things *could* change—for the worse," Ricardo snarled, "and you could find yourself in a back alleyway with a hole in your head."

"I guess any kind of change is out of the question," Lucas said. He was unfazed by the threat. You might even say he was as subdued as before he'd picked up the phone. With the knife and fork down next to the plate, and the phone now squeezed between ear and shoulder, Lucas's hands were free to pick up his revolver. And so he did, like a child playing with a toy gun for the first time. "So, what do you want me to do to get out of your debt, again?" Lucas said, looking over his piece of steel. "To not appear in an alleyway with a bullet in my head?"

He was now blowing hot air on his gun and polishing it with a napkin, whose tail end would have been stuck under his collar had he not been in his birthday suit.

"Nothing to overexert yourself over," Ricardo answered, a bit more relaxed.

"Well, what do you want me to do to get you off my back and—"

"—and for you to remain 'dead or missing' for Lula?"

"I'm taking that as some kind of threat, Ricardo, in a very roundabout way. So, what is it *you* want me to do to keep off *my* ex-chief's radar? And to not be sent back to Brazil in a casket or in handcuffs on a plane?"

"You know *what* I want, Lucas. Or better, *who* I want. The same person *you* want. I want him dead and you want him dead. But I want him alive first, for him to pay me what he owes, before you get to have him. There'll be some money in it for you too … some of what he owes, provided you find him. I heard it's harder to get to him than to the Pope."

Lucas leaned back in his chair and mulled over the proposition while carefully examining his gun.

"So, you want the Catalan?"

"Like I want to drink from the fountain of youth."

Lucas threw his feet up on the table and scratched the tip of his nose with the barrel. He had socks on; he was not entirely naked, after all. He managed to light up a cigarette while aiming the gun at the window, sealing one eye and pointing it at Cristiano, who was now holding a feather and passing it over Esme's thigh. The camera was still rolling.

"You think you're some hotshot drug dealer," Lucas said.

"Same rules apply, Lucas," Ricardo cautioned, "and by that, I mean heads will roll."

"What rules? And whose head will roll first?" Lucas blurted out. "Yours or mine?!"

"Your big mouth hasn't changed one bit, Lucas. Long distance phone call or not. SAME RULES APPLY!"

Lucas was getting irritated that the call had dragged on for too long with empty and humorless threats. He placed the gun down and leaned into the table, holding the receiver out in front of him like it was an old boxing ring microphone.

"If the same rules apply," Lucas bellowed, rage coming over him on an impulse, "then apply the same rules! Rio de Janeiro or Barcelona! Taipei or Timbuk–fuckin'–tu! Apply the same rules!"

No sooner did he hang up on Ricardo than the phone rang once more. He quickly picked it up and let fly another round of curse words.

"If you want him, go hunt him down yourself you—"

"Want *who*? Hunt *who* down?" It was Xavi calling. Lucas held the phone away from his ear and took a deep breath. Xavi asked once more who Lucas was talking about, but didn't prod any further when he didn't get an answer. He then asked Lucas to do a job.

"*Shoot?* What do you mean, *shoot?*"

With murder and wicked endings on his mind, it took him a second to swap mental chips, since Xavi wasn't referring to the revolver that lay on the table but rather the camera that was in Lucas's bag.

Lucas had found an old Leica M-3 in the trash many months ago. He'd taken it home, fixed it up, and even bought film and set up a darkroom in one of the unused bathrooms in the loft. Xavi called it the Trash-O-Matic, a pun that would have insulted anybody whose day job consisted of turning one man's waste into another man's daily bread.

Lucas remembered how to operate analog cameras from the time when he'd taken a forensics class in cadet school. With all the homicides in Rio de Janeiro, he was sent to many crime scenes, and eventually got as good at aiming his lens at dead bodies as at aiming his gun at fleeing bag-snatchers or robbers from the *favelas*; at pressing a shutter as fast as pressing a trigger.

Across the Atlantic many months later, his camera became the object through which he infiltrated the Black Arrow. He documented their mischief-making against the government, ecoterrorism, squatting in old buildings, sit-down protests at banks, all the way to street theater and the charitable work they did with victims from the economic crisis. But gaining their trust and a foothold in the organization was all part of his highly deceptive artifice.

Lucas was gathering vital information from their hackers concerning the Catalan, a drug kingpin whose head was deserving of a bullet. This was the main reason he was in Barcelona—not activism, not selling fake credit cards or drugs, and certainly not dealing in scrap, but to hunt down and kill Barcelona's most ruthless pusher. Lucas's life had been spared during the drug dealer's murderous rampage in Brazil. But Lucas's brother, Thiago, and his father and mother, Gregorio and Rafaela, were all dead, with trails of blood leading back to the crime boss who ran his operations out of Spain's most populous coastal city. The problem was that Lucas was waging a personal war against a specter in the criminal underworld, a man who was as elusive as he was powerful, whose real name was as mysterious as his whereabouts.

The man known as the Catalan ran an impressive cocaine cartel, with cargo routes connecting continental Europe and Africa with Latin America, but nobody could put a face to the name, since his public persona was as plain as water. It was rumored that he was a family man who owned a nice house in a suburban, gated community; attended church on Sundays and swam every day to keep fit; had a dog which he walked daily and a few buddies he played pétanque with. Word was that he supported Barcelona FC during El Clásico matches. Maybe he was even a diehard supporter of an independent Catalonia.

The only way to find him was via a trail of dirty money laundered through various cash-flow businesses like brothels and nightclubs, then pumped into a vast network of shell companies. This could explain the urgent task of an anonymous collective of proficient hackers who abhorred capital flight, corruption, and stealing from the poor.

Though his getting to the Catalan was the settling of a personal vendetta, Lucas convinced everyone at the organization to target him and steal millions from him to help hundreds of evictees from bank-owned homes get back on their feet. For Noguerra, Barcelona's police chief, there was something in it, too.

Lucas's job was like killing two rats with the same poison pellet. In order for the city's top cop to continue turning a blind eye to his blood revenge, Lucas had to agree to an off-the-books mission consisting of obtaining evidence against the Black Arrow and getting everyone locked up. With a foot in both worlds, the fine line separating both realities had to be tread carefully so as not to get too much evidence right away on the Arrow, which in turn would dash his hopes of getting to the Catalan.

The prime suspect of the case against the Black Arrow was Laia Requena, the organization's leader, who also happened to be Lucas's girlfriend. No small feat this "special friendship" was, as it had taken Lucas months of deepening his cover as— and this was how he had sold it to Noguerra—"a politically conscious *chatarrero* suffering from Robin Hood syndrome."

Lucas and Noguerra secretly called their clandestine operation Maze in a Black Arrow, labeled as such since Lucas had to find his way in the dark by himself without anybody's help. As for the Catalan, Noguerra had given that aspect of the case no title, and not much care for that matter, as long as it was an outside job by a rogue cop and not anybody connected to the local force, so as to avoid a war between the mafia and Barcelona's police.

"So? Will you come to the bar in the next hour with your—?"

"Whose mugs need capturing?" Lucas said, rubbing his brow with his free hand, wanting nothing more than to punch Xavi square in the face.

"Bile Helmet," Xavi answered.

"Bile Helmet?"

"That's right," Xavi said with unnecessary pride. "The main ticket for the Break the Banks Festival."

Considering the recent call from Ricardo, Lucas wanted to tell Xavi that he was tired, or that he was privately enjoying himself, or that Xavi could go fuck himself. But in the end, Lucas agreed. "*Hijo de puta,*" he muttered under his breath after ending the call. He looked down at his plate, where the last remaining ravioli was staring up at him. He forked it and wiped up the last bit of sauce and finally popped it into his mouth. He looked down at his plate again and gave himself a mental pat on the back. It was Paco who had once taught him the proper technique of mopping up ravioli: *"fare la scarpetta,"* his partner in crime had explained.

Paco was an Andalusian at heart, though very fond of Italy. He especially liked Italian mafia movies like *The Godfather*, *Donnie Brasco*, and *Goodfellas*. To Lucas, who had a Polish father, the word *scarpetta* sounded like the Polish word for sock, *skarpeta*, reminding him of his childhood and of being punished for having too many holes in his socks. The thought of wiping up his dinner plate with a dirty garment and then stuffing it into his mouth improved his mood, especially since the story of how he and Paco had met almost ended in tragedy.

2
Paco from Huelva

He met him on a highway overpass on an unusually cold afternoon a few months into hunkering down in Barcelona. By that time, Lucas had smashed his old cell phone to bits, procured a fake Portuguese passport and driver's license, and let himself go with the way he looked. Back home, he had kept himself clean-looking, earning the nickname Babyface; in Barcelona, his hair had grown a few fingers thick, and a scrim of beard quickly sprang into something of a Chia Pet. He even dyed his hair blond to look more like his Polish father, to fit in as a "European."

Rather than take the subway, Lucas decided to cross the overpass to catch the bus on the other side. When he reached the middle of the walkway, he saw a man sitting on the railing. The man was talking to himself nervously, using strange and unwieldy hand gestures. An old acoustic guitar, a bowling ball bag, a potted plant, and a pair of muddy soccer cleats were placed neatly in a row next to him.

Lucas stopped, lit a cigarette, and approached the distressed man. He leaned forward against the rail and gazed steadily at the cars speeding underneath, wondering where everybody was heading, and about the height of the overpass, as well as Gibraltar, probably the farthest point this highway reached.

"So?"

"So, what?" the man said coldly.

"Are you just here to make friends with passersby or are you gonna … ?"

"I'll do it when you get out of here, pal," the man snapped. "I don't need an audience."

"You won't get one," Lucas replied. "But what about your funeral? Will you want an audience there? Will people come to pay respects? Here's another one: When you get up *there*, if you ever get up *there*, what are you gonna say to the Man at the front gates? You ever thought of that, buddy?" The man's forehead crimped up into small little folds, and he looked obliquely at Lucas. His mouth tightened and he balled up his fists so much that his knuckles went white. "Thanks, big guy," Lucas answered for him, "it was great, but I think I overstayed my time on earth." Lucas's insensitive approach, which was a poor attempt at reverse psychology, seemed to be working. "I don't believe you'll jump, anyway. Will you really do it?" He exhaled the cigarette smoke, fishing with his eyes for sports cars zooming under them.

"You don't believe me, huh?!" the man sniffed, wiping crocodile tears. "I'll do it! I swear I'll do it!"

"Fine. Suit yourself." Lucas straightened up, flicked away his cigarette, and put his hands in his pockets. He started walking off, no longer showing any attention to the man's mental plight.

"Wait, stop! Can I have that cigarette?"

"I never offered you one," Lucas answered.

"Just give me a cigarette, will you?"

Lucas smirked, turned around, and removed a cigarette from the pack, but he kept his hand at a certain distance so that the man would have to get off the rail to accept it. Seeing that he wasn't into playing games, Lucas gave in and got closer. The man grabbed the cigarette with his mouth, and Lucas offered his lighter, but he moved his head away. On the brink of death and the bloke was trying to be cool to the end, choosy as to how he would light up his last one on planet earth. He put his hand inside his jacket pocket and pulled out a Zippo lighter, then stared at it, at the engraved initials. It had been a gift from his girlfriend, or ex-girlfriend as of a few hours earlier.

"You ever wonder why we still haven't made contact with aliens?" he asked, out of the blue. Anticipating the direction of the conversation, Lucas lit up another cigarette—wishing it was a joint instead—and approached the rail, now looking at Agbar Tower in the distance, Barcelona's most prominent building, which looked little like an edifice and much like what Esme had in her treasure chest of sex toys.

"We've been trying for decades with satellite technology, shooting radio frequencies up the ass of the universe and nothing. You know why?"

"Not a clue, brother."

"It's because the people who work at NASA or the Atacama or wherever those star people congregate are mostly men—and aliens are women." Lucas looked over and wondered what drug he had consumed earlier in the day. "I'm serious. We just don't understand women. At least I'll never get them." He finally lit his cigarette and snapped shut his Zippo. He brought his hand down and let out a weary breath, then rapped the lighter against the railing out of frustration, acknowledging the epic screw up that involved him and his ex-girlfriend's sister.

"I met a girl from Norway a few weeks ago, and your story just made perfect sense to me." Lucas paused, took a puff of his cigarette, and exhaled thoughtfully. "I'll never forget the way she looked that night: a solid ten, blond and curly hair, a perfect handful, tender and soft to the touch. She wore these heels, the kind that should be prohibited on transatlantic flights—"

"Where did you meet her?"

"I was chatting with her at this bar, really smooth-talking my way back to her place." Lucas paused for a toke and glanced over. The man was already hooked on the story and not fretting nervously anymore. "We were ordering drinks, having a great time, when suddenly she got on my case for lighting a cigarette from a candle that stood right in front of us, telling me that every time somebody lights a cigarette from a candle, a sailor dies tragically in a rainstorm."

"That sounds very Nordic," the man said, chuckling. "Could definitely ruin the night."

"It could. But then I said something about her being too superstitious. She said something about destiny, and soon after, rather than us parting ways, she opens up and starts telling me about a high school trip to some forest when she was a young girl."

"Uh-huh. Keep going. This is getting good."

"She and five of her classmates went camping for the weekend. And after a whole day on those cute nature walks with her friends, she decides to pick mushrooms like her grandmother used to before the war. She picks these large mushrooms with nice white stalks." With the cigarette still between his fingers, Lucas gestured the size of the mushroom. "So, she's picking mushrooms and saving more than a batch for later because she had plans of cooking up a soup on the campfire. But after she makes soup and serves it to her friends, they all end up dying later that night. But get this: She didn't even eat the soup! Can you believe it? I mean, they were found green and stiff as boards in their sleeping bags inside their tents."

"Unbelievable!" the man exclaimed.

"She told the judge during the trial that she didn't eat the soup just because, for no reason at all."

"You gotta be kidding me!"

"So, as she's telling me the story, I'm bursting out laughing. I mean, I had tears in my eyes, not out of sadness, of course, but that's how funny it was. She, on the other hand, was so offended by the way I reacted that it looked like she wanted to take the fancy candle holder and smash me in the face with it. When she finally calmed down and asked me why I was laughing, I told her that, yeah, someone somewhere gets hit by a truck, succumbs to a malignant form of cancer, gets beaten to death for not paying back a few cigarettes, but where I'm from, people die every second from drugs and murders and gang violence—I mean, every day! Hundreds! Thousands! Innocent or guilty, doesn't matter! I tried to explain to her that it was so ridiculous to die in such a stupid way that the only thing you could do is laugh and wonder how absurd life is." Lucas now applied himself and got serious. "I don't know what your problems are with your lady or the reason you want to cause so many people around you so much grief, but people in my neighborhood are just trying to live day by day, pure survival mode but without the optimism."

Lucas punctuated the story's denouement by throwing down his cigarette and putting it out with his heavy boot, a pair he'd found in the garbage. A long, pregnant silence ensued.

"My name's Paco," his distraught bridgemate finally said, reaching out his hand.

"Lucas." He firmly gripped Paco's hand. "How about a *caña*? Maybe some dinner?" Paco nodded, grateful for the intervention. He got down from the railing and started gathering his belongings.

Lucas could now see that Paco was tall and lanky with thinning, shoulder-length hair and bushy sideburns. His long face, a planet of craters and wrinkles, looked like it was being sucked in from inside as he bore a perceptive yet sad look, creating the impression of living a life of hard knocks. He looked like a slob and seemed artless in his behavior, bored but ready for excitement in whatever shape or form, good or bad. The words "conflicting" and "unpredictable" easily sprang to mind, conjuring the essence that was Paco Fernandez from Huelva. And even though he seemed much better in temperament, his previous state of mind lingered about, as though it were a permanent part of him.

"I know a good Italian place that serves terrific ravioli," Paco said, staggering onward with the acrid smell of booze as his aura. He cradled the potted plant and held the bowling ball bag in the other hand. "Once you walk in, you'll think you're walking into God's kitchen."

Lucas nodded and helped Paco carry the guitar and cleats. "By the way, can I buy this guitar off you?"

"Buy? I'll tell you what, you can have it—for saving my life. You a *chatarrero* or something?"

"Something like that," Lucas answered.

3
Scrap

hatarreros were scrap collectors. Most of the time they were undocumented migrants with no legal job options or spiritually bankrupt scroungers from some war-torn country. Those Lucas knew were drug-fiending vultures who picked apart the electronic innards of televisions, printers, and paper shredders to sell whatever they could to score dope. They lived off of whatever they could get their hands on, and their empty stomachs and bad habits propelled them into the night's ether. Some scrappers lamented the throw-away society in which they lived, but celebrated with Don Simon whenever they found perfectly functioning yet obsolete microwaves or fridges left by the wayside by capricious consumers who preferred brand new rather than fixing old. Some scrappers were so good at locating reusable materials from some far-off Xanadu, it was as if pings from these dying devices were signaling their location to their poor satellite ears. Thirty-five percent of new gadgets got cyborg transplants, parts gutted from old devices yet melted and molded into something new. Some scrappers managed to remove a day's wage worth of parts like it was a game of Operation. One pound of copper got you four euros and one pound of aluminum cans, twenty cents. Prices per metal the *chatarreros* memorized like pithy verses from the Bible, turning them into unscrupulous street hawkers pandering useless goods in the streets like zealous preachers selling faith.

"Strong euro currency makes it expensive for buyers from abroad to buy in bulk," explained Javier, the corpulent, toothless, and mangy looking worker at the scrapyard. The stereotypical ugliness of a junkyard dog stuck like motor oil to his tank top. "No demand!" was Javier's mantra—and justification—to pay less than the other scrapyards. "No demand! No demand! *Amigo!*" But the scrappers continued plowing the streets of Barcelona for a pittance, hoping to find a wallet with a few forgotten notes or some family photos inside, which they could get temporarily sentimental about.

One scrapper, Usama, even found a fake Louis Vuitton bag with ten thousand euros inside. After the big score, he sat in the park on a bench, drinking and wondering why he deserved to have good fortune smile down on him. His theory was that it had been a drug deal gone wrong that got the pigs on the pusher's tail, causing the pusher to dump the evidence in the bushes at Ciutadella Park. Last the local scrappers heard, Usama had returned to Syria to try to rebuild his home and start a new family, since everyone had died in the war that had been raging for thousands of days.

But all that wasn't Lucas's life, not the least bit. Though he lived in a neighborhood where most people eked out a living this way, he was forced to pretend living hand-to-mouth. Apart from penetrating the Black Arrow, he had also put himself at the center of the scrapping community and made friends with some of them, without anybody knowing exactly who he was or how he had ended up in Barcelona. Nor did the police force from back home know, or would even think he would go rogue, when he cut all ties with his homeland and quit reporting back to his supervisor, Lula Oliveira. For all they knew at the precinct, Lucas could have been found out by the Catalan and long ago given a Mediterranean Sea burial. This version of his disappearance worked in his favor, because he could continue keeping his ear to the streets and tabs on certain dealers who exploited the addiction problems of some *chatarreros*. He hoped, by following this trail of pushers, that it would lead back to the Catalan's den or to some distribution point. And it seemed to be paying off because piece by piece and with every lead, Lucas was inching closer, and doing so outside the realm of the corrupt police force he had no more respect for. The gutters, where he found all his reusable goods for resale, would soon run red with blood. For having to bury his entire family just weeks apart, he had ice in his veins, blood in his eyes, and hate in his heart. Love? What took its place was a computer glitch of brutal images he couldn't erase—playing back and forth, out of his control and without end—of a cold-blooded murder on a hot, tropical day during the Galo da Madrugada procession.

4
Recife

The sputtering scooter meandered through traffic at the outskirts of the historic port city that sees the biggest Carnival parade in all of Brazil. Sitting astride it and weighing down its fragile suspension were two young men. The one riding pillion was pressing his phone to his ear, listening to funk music and bobbing his head to the beat. With the other hand, he was busily coiling a lock of hair that had escaped a cornrow. Closer to the hub of all the festivities, the rider began honking his horn and shooing away idling festival-goers from under a large tree. The tropical heat was unbearable, and the sun was blazing, and for this reason, everyone tried to claim whatever shade they could. Or maybe they were saving a privileged spot for a ruthless duo of contract killers.

After clearing out just enough "cattle"—what the pillion passenger called them, seeing how slow they were in surrendering their foot space—the rider finally stopped, killed the ignition, and got off. They both looked around with a wild glare in their eyes, but quickly got to discussing important matters, like deciding how to split the lump sum of money between them, as there was a huge payout for the job. The conversation became intense, with the rider drawing the exit strategy with his finger on his palm, giving directions and commands like a quarterback in crunch time. The passenger listened attentively, showing that he understood everything with careful head nods. The rider then pulled out a few photos from his back pocket. They both looked them over and selected which ones to use before the rider put them away. Their eyes finally twinkled greedily at the prospect of their fortunes turning. They joked and playfully shoved each other as they merged with the party revelers, ignoring those they had evicted who were looking at them from the corners of their eyes. But nobody dared to wag their tongue at the favela boys, as some had spotted a handgun in their waistbands when they alighted from the bike.

Speakers loaded onto trucks were blaring, and the atmosphere was electric. In the full glare of television media, colorfully costumed dancers and their lightning-fast footwork would be broadcast nationwide. The boys entered the parade teeming with sweaty, half-naked bodies, cheering, laughing, and shaking their hips. They copped a feel and a quick, intimate dance from whichever girl entered their hula-hoop space. On the pretext of grabbing beads from one girl and moving them to another, they repeated the very same tactic, even stealing sips of their new dance partner's Cachaça or cold beer. The favela boys enjoyed every minute of Carnival, but they were there for business, not for pleasure, despite it not being very obvious.

When they saw the sign that said Hotel Americana, they pushed through the crowd in a hurry and rushed into the lobby. They drew their guns and asked the hotel attendant where room thirty-one was. After bounding up several flights of stairs, they kicked down the door and walked up to Gregorio, who was watching the parade on TV in front of a fan on the terrace. He fell off his chair, eyes wide from panic, and started screaming for help, pleading with God and begging them not to take his life. They both stood over him and emptied their clips. Then, as per the orders given, they dropped a bunch of photos next to his bloodied and lifeless body. A noise in the bathroom alerted them to Rafaela, who was hiding in the shower. They played a single game of rock-paper-scissors. The winner ripped the fan out of the socket, undid his belt, and went into the bathroom.

* * *

"Good evening," said the tall silhouette of a man shading his eyes from the strong porch light with a folder. "My name is Detective Hector da Silva and this is Agent Barbosa." Lucas peeked out through the door's crack. He looked over the man's sports jacket, trimmed beard, and short dark hair. His movie-white teeth flashed when the folder in his hand slipped to the side. Next to him stood a uniformed officer, a burly man with a strong jaw and a smug look on his face.

"Not home," Lucas said. He began closing the door when da Silva reached his hand through the iron bars and held it open. The officers exchanged knowing grins. They could understand the boy's paranoia and why he wasn't open to the idea of having lawmen as company in Rocinha.

Detective da Silva's eyes dropped down to Lucas's stomach wrapped in a bandage. Since the door concealed the rest of his body, they couldn't see that in his hand was a pistol cocked and locked should the men decide that playing niceties was over and that violence would be the best way to gain entry.

"What do you want?" Lucas asked. "I've never seen you before on the hill. Don't think it's very safe right now ... turf war still going on after my brother's death." Lucas wondered if *they* knew who *he* was—the most hated cop in the city, who happened to live in the most dangerous neighborhood whose guardian was Christ the Redeemer in the distance with His arms outstretched to the world.

Lucas stood up on his toes to look behind them. He saw a military police vehicle at the foot of the deep, concrete stairs, the kind BOPE did rounds with. Two policemen walked out of a shadow with large assault weapons. Their lit cigarettes' ember tips flew around their faces like fireflies. Lucas cut his eyes over to the used mobile phone shop, where two more policemen with guns just as big stood around chatting, oblivious to the possibility of being ambushed by gangs fighting to control the favela. Lucas was reluctant to cooperate. It was not good to see so many so-called men of law around. Anything could pop off any minute.

"Are you Lucas Brodowski?" asked da Silva, unshading his eyes with the folder and now moving it to his hip.

"Yeah, so?" he said. "I wasn't a part of my brother's gang."

"We're not here for that," Barbosa said.

"We are looking for the next of kin to a—" da Silva raised the folder. He moved his head back so the porch light could reach the document on its cover. "—Mr. Gregorio and Rafaela

Brodowski." Lucas let out a long sigh. He knew very well what was happening: another death notification.

"Just tell us if you're the son of Gregorio and Rafaela and we'll be on our way," said Barbosa, evidently in a bad mood, looking back at the men standing near the jeep.

Hearing the names of his parents a second time had a different effect than the first. His spirits sank instantly and he almost wilted. A freezing chill ran up his spine. He felt like he couldn't breathe. Try as he might, he couldn't stop his head from spinning, and the sudden change of pressure in his heart felt as though blood and oxygen were leaking out. Soon he couldn't feel anything at all, and so Lucas wondered if he'd heard right. Maybe his pain medicine was causing him to hear things.

His brother had known his days were numbered because of the choices he'd made in his life, but his parents? What had they done? No sooner did the words settle, than the corrosive misery started flowing through him once more. Da Silva and Barbosa were there to bring him renewed misfortune, bring back that agony and those wretched feelings of a lacerating guilt. He could not even scream or smash his fist into the wall as he was still in pain—physically as much as emotionally—from the day his brother was killed, from when they got stopped by the corrupt cops who had been lying in wait.

Lucas didn't unlock the cage right away and kept the door's two chains semi-taut. The pistol was getting loose in his hand. He just stood there waiting for something. Secretly, he wanted the cops to storm the house and shoot him dead. He'd had enough of murders and bodies piling up weekly. Perhaps he was waiting for guidance about what to do, how to react, a message from the Redeemer in the distance, or a message from deep within. He wasn't even religious, but he'd been brought up in a Catholic household—by a father who now lay in a morgue zipped up in a black bag next to his mother.

Lucas disappeared from the doorway and placed the gun inside a drawer. He let them in, immediately snapped three bolts shut after closing the door, and limped to the kitchen, revealing that he'd also suffered a leg injury. He offered them a glass of water, which they refused, and leaned against the counter, crossing his arms, watching them closely, holding back the tears welling up in his eyes. There was tension in the room thick enough to choke him.

Da Silva was readying paperwork while Barbosa perused the dimly lit living room, poking his nose in family pictures, if not simply enjoying being in the home of a recently deceased drug lord, one whose murder had rewarded the precinct with a loud, booze-filled fête. The living space was scantily furnished with an old sofa, an older box-shaped television, and a small coffee table on which sat a glass bowl full of mints. Barbosa stopped at a shrine of Lucas's brother, Thiago, who had carved up the city in recent years at will. He didn't even suppress the angry look that came over his face. He thought Lucas would now have to add more votive candles and another two sanctuaries for his parents.

"That was all of them," Lucas said, keeping his eyes down at the floor. Thiago had gotten what he deserved, they thought, and the thousands of little Thiagos in the making needed to be rubbed out before they got too brave with guns and master plans to take over the city.

"No more shoulders to cry on," said Barbosa in a crass, repugnant tone. He turned around from admiring all of Thiago's soccer trophies on the shelf. "We've all suffered our losses." The cop was referring to all his colleagues who had died carrying out their duties in the very slum Lucas lived in.

Before Lucas could ask what exactly had happened, da Silva asked him to sit down but Lucas refused—he didn't take orders from cops anymore. After a brief moment of awkward silence, he finally told Lucas the horrible tragedy.

"During Carnival?" Lucas said. Da Silva nodded. "I didn't even know they went to Recife."

"These were found at the crime scene." From one of his folders, da Silva pulled out a dozen six-by-eight color photos of rolling landscapes hewn with delicate rows of soil and vine.

"I've never seen this place before."

"Any reason they were next to your father's body?" asked da Silva.

"Next to my father's body? He is a soccer coach—"

"Yeah right, and I'm the pied piper," butted in Barbosa. Before Lucas could put him in his place, da Silva calmed them down, bringing some civility back to the visit.

"In this photo there is an old, small chapel made out of stone," da Silva said. "It is sitting on the crest of a hill near a vineyard. There's also some inscription over the entrance. The style is very unique and we are trying to locate it. We consulted a professor at the Federal University of Rio de Janeiro. We believe it is Spanish."

"Spanish?"

"From Spain," the detective said.

"So, you're suggesting the person who killed my parents might have fled to Spain or is from Spain?"

"That is a possibility," said da Silva. Lucas shook his head. Unable to accept this bizarre theory, he limped back to the door and undid the bolts. The length cops will go to further tarnish a good family name because of a single criminal outlier, Lucas thought.

"I'd like you to go now," Lucas said, trying to keep his composure, placing his hand on the door handle as a gesture to get them to leave. He glanced over to the drawer where the gun was. The effort of keeping himself from opening the drawer and grabbing the gun and shooting them dead was demanding tremendous self-control.

"I heard there are some *other* dark shadows in your family, Lucas," said Barbosa, keeping Lucas wound up and off-balanced. "Maybe your father was doing some business with the Spaniards? Maybe he got into some gambling debt? Maybe drugs?"

"Get out of my house!" Lucas shouted.

"Treat us like this?" da Silva responded, restraining his anger. "No sense of camaraderie, partner? You are one of us, no?"

"*Was*," Lucas answered, "but not anymore."

Da Silva and Barbosa gave each other a conspiratorial glance and left without saying a word. A few minutes later there was a knock on the door. Lucas opened it, not caring if he'd be met with a hail of bullets.

"On behalf of myself and the other officers from the precinct," da Silva said with a voice full of sorrow, "we're really sorry for what happened to your parents." Lucas stared right into da Silva's eyes, ready to unleash on him. "As for your brother," da Silva added, "we only wish we could have killed him sooner."

Barbosa was already in the car at the bottom of the concrete stairs talking on the phone. He didn't care about condolences, or expressing sympathies, or anything that would put him at the feet of a drug lord's kin, because he was indeed one of the officers who had taken part in the operation that killed Lucas's brother. Since they'd all worn masks that night, Lucas never found out the identities of the men, or which of them were suspended. But those involved knew who Lucas was, and were not very happy about how the young cop fresh out of police academy excoriated the force up on the stand.

Right when da Silva turned around to take his leave, one of the photos fell out of his folder and landed on the concrete step. He didn't notice as he was eager to get out of this "shithole"—how he once described the favela in a press conference.

Lucas didn't call him back to let him know he had lost a vital piece of evidence. Once they drove off in different directions, he opened the door, crept outside, and grabbed the photo. It was the one with the stone chapel sitting atop a hill, a comely landscape full of swaying passages of dirt among grape vines.

Later that night, Lucas received a strange phone call from Lula Oliveira, his superintendent at Division Twelve, informing him that he would be put back on the squad. But instead of keeping the peace locally, Lucas would be sent on assignment to where many Brazilian football players dream of going to play for the best team in the world. The chief sold it like a promotion, but for Lucas it was the strangest and most suspicious instance of climbing police ranks: Lucas had been a civilian cop straight out of the academy, then he was fired for taking the stand at his brother's murder trial, and now he was being hired back as a special agent. What was going on? Something was up, this he was sure of, but he went along with it anyway. From that day on, he couldn't distinguish the good from the bad, the honest men from the murderers.

5
El Barrio

Lucas took another swig of Don Simon. Even though he felt bloated afterward, the antifreeze-tasting wine never disappointed as it was cheap, bold, and went straight to his head, giving him the sensation of stewing in an outdoor Jacuzzi in close-to-zero Fahrenheit. He poured himself another mugful—he drank from mugs, not wine glasses—walked over to the window, and sat on the sill. Apollo, one of two felines that lived in the loft with him, and which belonged to his ex-girlfriend, jumped up onto the sill. Lucas brushed him off with his hand, wishing he could kick him instead—he hated cats as much as they hated him. After giving Neymar, the cat's brother, a swift whack to stop it from joining him, he looked out the window once more.

Esme was now clothed in an outfit that didn't match her dark demeanor: a pink robe, white headband, and bunny slippers. She was sitting on the edge of the mattress with her legs crossed, bouncing her foot nervously. She was smoking a long, thin cigarette and looking at her phone. Cristiano and the filmmaker were looking into the viewfinder screen—they were neither auteurs or amateurs—but were still diligently reviewing parts of the recording and giving it the kind of scrutiny that if done right, would result in millions of views on snuff platforms.

Lucas grabbed the dishes and threw them into the sink. He picked up the pile of soiled work clothes he'd been wearing all day and stuffed them into one of the three washing machines lining the wall, two of which were in need of parts he was still looking for in the streets. He pressed a few buttons and the washing machine began to tremble; foam appeared in the window. He then walked over to the mattress, which was in no better shape than Esme's. He lifted it with one hand, while with the other, he pulled out the pressed pants he'd been flattening—he had no iron. He put them on with a fresh shirt and socks, walked to the window, and closed the blinds. Grabbing his camera bag and coat off the rack, he left the apartment, but didn't get very far. He froze when he saw a note taped to his door.

"WANT TO TRY PLEASING ME INSTEAD, YOU SLEAZY PERVERT?"

Lucas was surprised. He ripped the note off, crumpled it in his hands, and threw it into the hallway. A sense of unease came over him, and so he wondered: If he was being watched, were they seeing as much as he was seeing? Also, did they know as much about his past life as his present life? He was on edge for the remainder of the night.

Only a year out of Rio de Janeiro's Superior School for Police Cadets, the young Brazilian who'd appeared on the streets of Barcelona seemed mature for his age, and surprisingly capable of going undercover. He wore a blond and messy undercut with a lazy stubble, and had a strong build thanks to many years boxing at a club called El Mundo. He was quiet and calm, though easily riled up, with a hard-to-read smile that he sometimes made a matter of public interest. A set of dark eyes sat above cheekbones you could sharpen a dull knife on. Indeed, it seemed way too many knives had found some utility on his face over the years: a scar above one eye could be attributed to an attack in primary school by a rival gang of kids, and the one behind his ear—a robber he was able to stave off one night walking home from a dance club. His ex-girlfriend once told him, after running her finger over it, that the wound behind his ear felt like a string filled with knots. The stitch mark on his chin was not from a knife wound but a hard tackle on the soccer field when he played with his brother back in the days. His rugged look, sufficiently tarnishing good features, amounted to a discernible face that was a mix of Slav and *pardo*, the outcome of having a Brazilian mother and a Polish father. Despite bursting with the kind of energy that could hardly be contained, there was a grace to his behavior and a charming side he sometimes had to show to get what he wanted.

Lucas locked the heavy door and walked over to the elevator. He pressed the button and waited, but the elevator didn't come—it was out of order, again. Even at the best of times it worked for one trip a day, but for a second trip it would stall between the third and fourth floors. Out of frustration, he kicked the elevator door and headed for the stairs. He passed two high school students sitting on a step and making out or, as his father used to say, drinking each other's spit. He greeted a man standing in a doorway, smoking a joint. The man returned the greeting with an unfriendly nod. Even though the building was in a disreputable state, Lucas felt at home there, as he had his own personal space and, so it had seemed to him until recently, privacy and a sense of anonymity.

When he got to the first floor, he was surprised to see Doña Álvarez, his neighbor, making an effort to hold the main door open for him. The groggy pensioner had been walking her dog, Juanita, but just managed to escape the sudden downpour. He grabbed the door without acknowledging her as he was still mulling over what the note meant. She might have asked him if he had his umbrella, but he didn't hear and hadn't brought one anyway, despite having more than a dozen in his loft somewhere, anywhere; throw a coin into the loft's vast space and it was bound to hit something that could protect you from the rain.

He stepped out of the heavy doors and lit a cigarette under the arch, then stood there listening to the crescendo of rain. People were running down the street with newspapers over their heads. Some huddled under first-floor balconies, waiting for the downpour to end. Amid a neighborhood of empty and weed-filled lots, the building opposite, in which Esme lived, was bedlam. Some would describe it as a Barcelona-styled brownstone as it was erected by hand, brick by brick, in the modernist style, and not made of poured concrete like Lucas's building. Its façade was pockmarked from rock-throwing protesters, and some of its windows were boarded up or fitted with iron bars reminiscent of an old prison cell. Adding to its look were weeds bursting through the cracks of the plaza in front. But this never stopped the local teenagers from playing soccer in the plaza. Every day after school, fierce matches were held between youth from rival neighborhoods, fighting for nothing more than bragging rights. Most of the teenagers were either Algerian, Moroccan, or from the Dominican Republic, and when they found out that Lucas was Brazilian-born, and that his father played pro, they invited him to play. Lucas would get the better of them with tricks and excellent dribbling, but soon after, invitations fizzled out as he took the games too seriously.

As Lucas stood there, staring out at the rain, he recalled bustling through the streets of this shabby warren, pushing his burdened shopping cart full of copper wires, a toaster, and a rust-punctured muffler. He remembered the abandoned car last summer with its tires stripped and stolen. Rather than seeing it rot with mold and rust, the neighborhood kids had dumped dirt over the chassis and planted flowers inside, beautifying its mangled skeleton. This improvised potting shed, with its aromas and vibrant colors, attracted more children with paintbrushes and surreal imaginations. After they painted its flaky fiberglass canvas, their mothers would urge them to wash their little hands and faces in the water that flowed from an old fountain nearby. By the end of summer vacation, an abandoned car was transformed into a flying garden with angel wings and the head of a unicorn painted on what remained of the hood.

This was the street Lucas lived on, and its wide, spacious sidewalks and chamfered street corners were always full of mothers pushing strollers and fedora-wearing seniors cavorting on park benches. But there was also a darker side to this neglected subdistrict wedged between La Rambla, Barcelona's major tourist haunt, and Montjuic, the flat and verdant hill on which sits an old, castlelike fortification and an arborous vista of the Mediterranean Sea. In these streets, one could find rampant prostitution, drug dealing, and a shifty nightlife happening next to day cares, playgrounds, and cathedrals frequented mostly by the older and faithful generations.

In the rain everything was muted, and Tamarit Street looked like a dark tunnel without a hopeful glimmer at the end. Looking up into Esme's window, Lucas saw that the lights were turned off. He lit another cigarette and reached his hand through the heavy door, feeling around in his mailbox. While sifting through grocery store flyers and escort advertisements, he found what he was looking for: a pamphlet calling for another protest at the music festival the Arrow had organized. He flicked the cigarette away, braced himself for the weather, and finally stepped out toward the apparition parked in front of his building. He grabbed the rainproof sheet and pulled back a slit big enough to put a key into the ignition. It was a Honda motorcycle he had bartered at a scrapyard for three washing machines and four televisions, then fixed up himself. Though he never had any problems starting it, the recent weather was giving him trouble. After giving up on cranking the engine, he pulled the sheet over the piece of junk and gaped at it. Disappointed, he went on his way, putting his hands into his pocket and nuzzling his chin into his chest.

Metal shutters clattered from the wind, and the few trees lining the street bent and swayed like in a tropical storm. Lucas looked into his camera bag to make sure he had his Trash-O-Matic. He flipped back the cover and pulled up the collar of his worn-out leather jacket. Catalonian flags waved erratically in the wind.

The *chatarreros* weren't collecting salvageable rubbish. He walked by a few of them standing in the entranceway of a grocery store called Consum (so bold they tell you what to do, no marketing, no persuasive language), watching the street flood in front of his eyes. Lucas knew the *chatarreros* personally because he did rounds with them in search of car part treasures or loose banknotes in thrown-out jeans. They were waiting for the torrent to die down. One of them, a Peruvian named Diego, yelled out as Lucas walked by. "How about some cash for that air conditioner?" Diego was referring to an exchange that had gone in Lucas's favor, but Lucas hadn't shared the profits from selling the unit to another scrapper. "Oh, yeah," Lucas answered sarcastically, "millions are just rolling in, let me call my agent and he'll transfer it over today." Diego waved him off boorishly.

Their shopping carts were chained up to traffic poles or bike lock stations. The scrap they had amassed over the last few days was covered up with blue tarps or whatever suitable fabric they could find to use as rain cover. On any other day you'd see the *chatarreros* hastily filing down the streets, even hear them a mile away as the wheels of their carts grated against the concrete pavement. Sometimes they advanced in groups like hunter dogs; other days Lucas saw only the lone collectors, those who'd recently landed in Barcelona and had not yet become acquainted with the other *chatarreros*. What stopped everyone from working that day was the stream of water running through the streets, filling the deep gutters and escaping into the sewage canals. Everybody watched it like watching their dreams wash away.

Lucas ducked under a shop sign. A man was sitting on the step next to him. When the man looked up, Lucas noticed out of the corner of his eye the familiar face, but pretended not to know him. Capitulating to the sad greeting, Lucas pulled out a pack, removed a cigarette, and dropped it into the upturned hat that sat in the man's lap.

"You got any more of those fake credit cards to sell, *rubio* [blondie]?" he asked. They finally acknowledged each other, as they had had dealings in the past. The man's name was Barthos, a Greek with a bald and shiny pate and a thick bird's nest of a beard. He used to run a resort on Crete, but after the collapse of the economy and the subsequent dissolution of his marriage, he followed a trail of money to Barcelona that soon ran dry. Though Lucas was just a middle-man for Ricardo, he operated a small swindle of selling fake credit cards. Barthos was one of the first guys to get him customers. Lucas would pocket some cash and the rest would be funneled back to Ricardo. Barthos, of course, would get his cut, too.

"Not anymore," Lucas replied in broken Spanish. "I could make some phone calls."

"We got a guy that's been asking about you. He's a new guy around the block. Never seen him before. Asks a lot of questions, stupid ones, about you." Lucas screwed his face on hearing this bit of unexpected intelligence. "We call him Polaco because he's Polish. He's right over there."

Lucas looked across the street, where a man was sitting curled into himself on a huge trunk next to a guitar case. He was wearing a funny hat and staring blankly at the curtain of rain coming down. Lucas had never seen him before, not even at Plaza Orwell, where all the musicians busked.

"Polaco, huh?" Lucas asked, his gaze fixed and hostile.

"Yeah, Solidarity, *pierogis*, and beautiful women—a Polaco."

"You should be a comedian," said Lucas, dropping another cigarette and some loose coins into Barthos's hat.

"Don't even have a pot to piss in, my friend," said Barthos.

"See you later," Lucas said, stepping off and merging with the rain.

Lucas walked across the street to the ATM next to the bank entrance. He pretended to be withdrawing money while looking over the guy and the large trunk he was sitting on. Noticing the sudden attention, the man became self-conscious and straightened up. Lucas looked at the man's shoes and the guitar case at his feet. Though his beard, unkempt hair, and trench coat projected that forlorn, down-and-out look, his shoes were way too shiny, not to mention a strange, rich-looking gleam in his eyes. Lucas pulled his gun from behind the waistband of his pants, grabbed him by his collar, and yanked him up off the ground, throwing him against the wall.

"What are you doing?" the guy whimpered. "Let me go, man!" Lucas held him with a tight grip and pushed the gun's barrel into his Adam's apple, causing him to choke and cough. The rain was pouring, slapping against the concrete, muting his frenetic gasps and shrieks. No witnesses around, Lucas thought, I could just blow him away.

"Have we met before?" Lucas asked, looking fiercely into his eyes. The Polaco, avoiding Lucas's stare, was silent. "Do you know me?!" Lucas asked again, raising his voice. The man shook his head, frightened by the encounter.

"I just wanted to … I heard that … maybe I could score some dope … or some fake credit cards?"

* * *

En route to the Arrow's headquarters, a dive bar in Plaza Orwell, Lucas spotted broken store windows and old ladies roiling in their worried states of mind while sweeping up the floors or putting up tarpaulin covers to stop the rain from flooding their shops. The melted garbage bins that had been set on fire the week before stood off to the side of the street. A sidewalk normally full of tourists looked more like a battleground after the first barrage of shells. A charred vehicle was flipped on its back like a helpless beetle. Fences and some traffic signs were bent out of shape. Walking by this devastation, Lucas felt a mix of emotions. In Rocinha, people fought every day for basics like water, electricity, and shelter, but Laia was bent on getting the banks to admit they were the devil's spawn.

He walked by the building in question, the one that had been turned into a community center by squatters, then repossessed and returned to the bank. Lucas recalled what had happened the previous week. Crowds of protesters in the street and helicopters circling overhead. Journalists everywhere. Sirens blaring and police loudspeakers booming loudly, telling the squatters to leave the building immediately. The police always gained the upper hand and broke through their barricades, always beat the *okupas* to shit. Laia, Xavi, and the many others who were defending the community center were going to be stomped on, no matter how much of a fight they were willing to put up. The building would eventually be reclaimed and given back to Azure Capital, a bank with way too much power, since it could get all the illegal occupants forcibly evicted just as it wished. Not even Xavi chaining himself to the front door in front of the countless press photographers would stop the police—he was freed with bolt cutters. Never mind Laia dropping herself by rope from the roof of the building—her publicity stunt finished the moment she was cut down.

Lucas wondered how long before street cleaners went back to work, since demonstrations and nihilism are bad publicity for a city parasitically dependent on the tourist dollar. This was exactly the first social ill that sparked Laia's monkeywrenching and street tactics. Residential apartments were rented out to tourists as short-term accommodation, causing an increase in rent and prompting Laia to engage with the municipality to control this Internet-driven phenomenon. Then there was gentrification. This form of displacement was spreading like a malignant tumor, resulting in residents being kicked out to the city's periphery. "Tourism is terrorism" was Laia's first trademark graffiti spray-painted all over the city under the cover of darkness. This minor act was soon followed by a more serious urban upheaval: The Black Arrow staged a protest during one of Barcelona's last bullfights, calling for an end to the murder of sentient beings. They ran into the dusty arena and dumped liters of red paint onto themselves in defiance of the macabre spectacle. After her arrest, Laia's next move was even more controversial: protesting Christopher Columbus's legacy, demanding the removal of the *Mirador de Colón*, which stood at the end of La Rambla. She handed out flyers calling the *conquistador* "a bloodthirsty megalomaniac who decimated half a continent," and attacked the Spanish monarchy for never calling into question the Spanish conquest of half the world.

Botero's fat cat stood in the downpour as Lucas walked through his favorite part of the city, *Raval*. He called it Little Turkey for all the times he'd eaten kebabs at 3:00 A.M. after a long day of scrapping. The Algerian tea vendors had packed up their tents, putting off hawking their treats for a drier day. Lucas walked by a group of prostitutes chatting with each other under fancy, wide-brimmed umbrellas. There was no sign of business that evening, but at least in the absence of Juans and Joses, it seemed the perfect time to catch up and see how their families were doing, if they were receiving the remittances, and if the money was being spent wisely.

He passed by Cagalell, or "Stream of Shit," named for being a sewage canal that had run around the medieval city walls. Nowadays, the busy boulevard was called La Rambla, and received thousands of tourists from all points of the compass. Russians, Chinese, and Indians paraded up and down this walking street, fashionably dressed, holding bags full of souvenirs, sampling foods at La Boqueria, or buying squares of grass turned into plaques that honored the great soccer heroes who ran up and down Camp Nou. La Rambla was the hub of the city, and Barcelona was the vibrant and cosmopolitan capital of the world.

6
The Black Arrow

ucas entered a narrow side street before turning onto a
hidden cobblestone footpath. He walked farther away from
the tourist artery until he stopped at a nondescript door,
where he was greeted by Antonio, an Italian ex-soccer player
who, after his unsuccessful tryout with Fenerbahçe S.K. in
Turkey, had put on way too much weight. Lucas threw down
his cigarette and shook Antonio's fat hand. He looked the
sickly doorman up and down, his glare stopping at Antonio's
cirrhotic face and jaundiced eyes. Antonio nodded and moved
to the side to let him in. Before entering a dark and narrow
staircase that descended to the Black Arrow, Lucas felt an
odd feeling of apprehension—like he would be found out
that day.

The air in the dim and vacant bar reeked of smoke.
Pictures of revolutionary leaders like Mao, Che Guevara, and
Malcolm X hung on the walls, along with neon beer logo signs

and dartboards. Guy Fawkes masks hung off the corners of picture frames whose black-and-white images retold the stories of the Spanish Civil War, much like the Stations of the Cross on church walls narrated the struggles of Jesus. A Sex Pistols song was playing quietly in the background.

Laia was working like a dog; in the days leading up to the Break the Banks Festival, her duties consisted of making inventory and placing orders on vodka and whiskey. Beer, too, was the drink of the dissenters, and while counting up all the kegs needing to be replaced, she was chatting with Xavi, who played the role of bar manager when not her sidekick on political matters.

Reed thin with a sprouting ponytail and a receding hairline, Xavi was as short-tempered as he was short. In fact, he was a hand's width shorter than Laia, making him vertically challenged in front of Lucas, who himself was no giant. Making up for his stature, however, were his fanaticism and combativeness. Like Lucas, he was liable to explode like a firecracker. The two charged positives, whenever they went head-to-head in words, often ended up in blood, bruises, and late-night *urgencia* visits. Xavi's butterfly knife would "come out and sing," an expression he would use when anger pushed him to the point where he would carve up pictures of traitorous local politicians pinned against the dartboard.

When Lucas walked in, Xavi was leaning against the counter and drying beer glasses with a cloth, telling Laia a story about the judge from his last trial, the one at which he was charged with forging government documents and possession of stolen goods. Laia had gotten many laughs out of the joke before. It was about the judge wearing nothing under his frock, perfect attire for when he met with those he protected in the corporate world. It was a stale joke but she, as always, pretended to be humored by it, which angered Lucas even more.

Lucas weaved through unoccupied tables on which stood turned-up stools pushing aside clean ashtrays. He proceeded to the stage to unpack his camera gear. He greeted Bile Helmet, who were sitting at the only table with its stools down.

"You the camera guy?" yelled out one band member.

"Yeah," Lucas said. Suddenly, the stage lights went on, blinding him. He nearly flipped, knowing Xavi had probably hit the switch on purpose. The legendary frontman from Tipperary, Ireland didn't even react to the shock of LED that burst inside the basement bar. The forty-year-old singer with an immature face was as pale as a ghost. He was stoop-shouldered, with a close razor shave and a head that was shaped like a match. Frank the Machine—he insisted on being called by his full name—had prison tattoos that looked like water dripped on paper filled with inky chicken scribbles. Round the clock he possessed a deranged and drugged-up look, unlike his bandmates Moco (booger) on guitar and Charro, the drummer, who seemed averse to heavy drinking despite it coming with the territory. They were all waiting for Lucas while chatting among themselves and smoking cigarettes. They invited Lucas over with the offering of a cigarette, yet he preferred to recover his sight and ready his Trash-O-Matic.

The members of Bile Helmet were all dressed in black; they were going to pose in balaclavas in front of a black banner that Charro started unfurling behind the drum kit. On it was printed their band name, the anarchy symbol, and, ironically, several of the festival's sponsor logos. Moco and Charro were going to use the bar's house instruments during the photo shoot. Frank the Machine, however, had other designs on how the session would proceed.

The Irishman pulled out a red bandana from his back pocket, folded it up, and slowly tied it around his head, as if he were reenacting some kind of sacred, samurai ritual. He then took his cigarette from the ashtray, plugged up his lips with it, and walked over to an adjacent table. He slid a duffel bag out from under it, unzipped it, and pulled out his prop: an M60 machine gun, the kind made famous by Rambo. Lucas was blown away by the sight, yet for the guys, it was just Frank the Machine being Frank the Machine.

Mr. Machine sashed the gun's bandolier over his shoulder with a ridiculously sinister grin before looping his neck with its strap. He took a step back and braced himself for the make-believe massacre, panning the heavy gun side to side, making cack-cack-cack-cack sounds with his mouth as if he were an incorrigible stutterer, his teeth pinched down on his cigarette.

"Is that thing even real?" Lucas asked, stupefied by the sight of a man with a war machine hanging off his neck.

Frank the Machine began eyeing his weapon insanely, blowing hot air on it and polishing it with the sleeve of his ripped sweater. "You bet it is," he said, the smoke from his cigarette making him squint his eyes. "Wanna see?" His bandmates laughed. "Wanna see?!" he yelled out over their laughter in a crooning voice, like he was singing one of his belligerent choruses.

"Have you ever shot it?"

"Of course I have," Frank the Machine answered in his Irish accent. "Not at people, though ... at trees, cows, stop signs … the sea." The band members convulsed with laughter. His brogue made the idea of shooting down traffic signs and farm animals even more ridiculous.

"You should see him transport that thing on his bicycle," said Moco. Everyone burst out laughing. "Of course, in his duffel bag," he added. "Even as far as the Eiffel Tower."

When Frank the Machine finally put the machine gun down on the floor, Lucas showed him the photo of the stone chapel. "You ever see this place before?"

"Looking to get baptized late in life, my son?" Frank said, his mock serious face concealing another burst of amusement. Moco and Charro sat up to have a look at the photo and started laughing. Everything was a source of comedy for these lowlifes, Lucas thought. Nuclear holocaust, *hehehe*; AIDS, *hee hee hee*. Lucas wanted to provoke a brawl but couldn't think of anything to say to get them enraged. They'd probably die of laughter if he were to pull out his revolver.

"Here, drink this and take this," said Frank, sticking out his hand. On it sat a tiny purple pill with a smiley face. Frank poured Lucas a shot of vodka and told him to lighten up, since he seemed too serious for the job of a "photo-taker, shutter-presser, *artiste* with a lightbox." Lucas hesitated, but took the pill before slugging back the vodka.

Laia's and Lucas's eyes finally met, but she quickly looked away. She had every right to greet him coldly for what had happened at the picnic. Lucas got his Trash-O-Matic ready and went to the bathroom to escape the smoke and relieve himself, but hardly had he entered when the doors swung open.

Laia walked in, lit a cigarette, and leaned against the door jamb. She exhaled smoke through the side of her mouth, keeping her angry eyes locked in on Lucas, who was bent over the sink with soap on his face. Ignoring her, Lucas continued washing. Hot steam rose up, hitting the spongy ceiling full of brown leak stains and exposed pipes. He finished and ran his hands through his blond waves, then caressed his beard in a slow and relaxing motion, trying to imagine being taken away from there.

"So, what happened?" Laia finally asked, pulling on her cigarette. They hadn't seen each other since planning out the attack.

"I told you I don't know what happened," said Lucas. He looked down into the sink and saw in the faucet's reflection an enlarged nose but eyes the size of pin pricks. He looked at himself in the mirror and wondered if he was a fugitive. He wondered if some special agent had been dispatched to Barcelona to kidnap and bring him back to Brazil, kind of like what Mossad agents did when they kidnapped Nazis in Argentina and took them back to Europe to stand trial.

"What do you mean you don't know what happened?!"

"I don't know," he said. "I'm not a bomb-making engineer or whatever." Nausea started climbing up his throat for saying words he never thought in a million years he'd be saying. He spit into the sink.

"Let's just hope they don't trace it back to us."

"Let's hope not," Lucas replied sarcastically.

"They're starting to say you're not down for the *cause*, and Xavi keeps saying that you lack political engagement ... that your interest in social justice seems 'schizophrenic,' in his words, and that your actions with the organization are noncommittal and unfocused. I'm always defending you, but—"

"The *cause*?" said Lucas. "I'm not too fond of that word. Too distracting."

"I tell them you're one of us. Aren't you?"

As far as Lucas was concerned, the *cause* for him was a triple homicide, and the *effect*—him being "sent" on an "international manhunt."

Lucas didn't answer her question. He was still mourning in private and very often was at war with himself. He'd often sit in the dark of his loft and wonder when he would finally find the Catalan. And during those low points, a maniacal clarity would appear in his thoughts, coming in the form of a surge of strength born out of anger so vile and profound that he'd go from complete self-abandon to vividly imagining himself killing the drug lord. But in public, Lucas didn't give away any clues to his mental state as he was very good at hiding his feelings, perhaps existing like every other person who felt pain, sadness, anger, fear, joy, and indifference.

He looked down at the counter, at the puddles of water drowning lighter burns and the carved initials of the many patron-punks who had come through the bathroom doors. Wet toilet paper lay piled up in the corner looking like a fresh mound of glue. If not for chips, smears, shatters, and long hairline cracks, then a miscellany of stickers and random graffiti tags filled the entire mirror. There was, however, a clean and untouched aura around the face of whoever looked into it, a part spared from destruction, as though vandals sympathized with the need to see just how messed up you really were after taking copious amounts of drugs. He glanced above the mirror. On the wall under the ceiling, someone had written in bold letters with a thick-tipped marker, "REAL EYES. REALIZE. REAL LIES."

"So, what are we going to do now?" Laia asked. "The next corporate picnic put on by Alba and that corrupt bank of hers is next year."

Irritated and overwhelmed, Lucas fitfully jerked away from the counter's edge and began pushing through steam filling up the bathroom like a sauna. "I'm not running this organization—you are!" he yelled. When his fingertips touched the wall, he reached up and slid the ceiling window open. A rush of steam escaped into the night. "I did everything you told me to do," Lucas said, returning to the sink. "I placed the bomb in a knapsack, placed the knapsack by the trash can, walked away, and detonated it—no kaboom!" He looked down at his feet, then up at the mirror, then back down at his feet once more. *The bank employees did nothing to me. They didn't kill my parents, so what do I care? All I had to do was take out the battery, these dumb revolutionaries.*

With the tap still on, brown water was now slopping down to the floor's broken tiles reared up like spikes. The bathroom was filthy but so was the dive bar, the one where Lucas and Laia had met many months ago. Lucas had been a regular customer, drinking bad beer on the cheap and listening to metal music from the headphones that hung down from the ceiling over every stool. Laia had served him until dawn. The rest was history, and his plan was set in motion.

He finally shut the tap and watched the sink's water subside. He rolled his neck to relieve the tension building up. Too tired to say anything, he lit a cigarette and stared at himself in the mirror, completely bewildered by who he was and what had become of him after his parents' death. He tasted the acid of revenge on his tongue and started spitting into the sink.

Laia was watching him the whole time and saw that he was high or unwell or just going crazy.

Lucas took a few more tokes and butted his cigarette out in his face in the mirror. He tried to light up another but threw it at his reflection when he couldn't. The cigarette ricocheted off the mirror and fell onto the wet countertop.

"It's much bigger than you and me put together," Laia said. "Soon Barcelona will start to look like Rio, with massive palaces built right next to favelas. The higher the fortress walls the rich build to protect their property, the greater the wealth inequality. If not for the *cause*, then for what, Lucas? Tell me? For what?!" Laia stopped and lowered her head. She looked exhausted and, surprisingly, seemed to have run out of words on the subject. She looked away and sighed. She knew he was right, that he shouldn't have to commit to the *cause* for another person but for his own beliefs.

"We have another protest tomorrow," Laia said, throwing down her cigarette. "I hope to see you there." He glimpsed her in the mirror. "It will be civil this time," she added. "I promise."

"You said you had something for me," Lucas said. Laia paused and turned around. She pulled out a piece of paper and handed it to him.

"His name is nowhere to be found on company registration documents," she said, "and even the bank accounts are linked to unknown third parties." Lucas grabbed the paper and scanned it. "But we know this nightclub or brothel or whatever you want to call it is owned by him. He's got many establishments like this … but hey, next time you want more information, you have to prove yourself. I can't keep on defending you." Laia walked out, leaving Lucas to himself.

Agitated and lost in the moment, Lucas started making faces that covered the entire emotional spectrum. He started jerking his body, trying to duck his own reflection in the mirror. He slapped his cheeks and tried to snap out of it, but only after sticking his head under cold water was he able to recover sobriety. He went back outside and took a few pictures of Bile Helmet.

"For the *cause*," he'd say to himself. "Do it for the *cause*."

7
Meet the Partagases

In the kitchen there were only two people in their own worlds of love and longing, yet the room was surprisingly abuzz with a variety of sounds. Josefina was humming at the stove while preparing a homemade and hearty breakfast known as *Tres Golpes*, a meal she had learned how to make as a child back home in the Dominican Republic. Plantain was bubbling in a pot, and the pan was crackling from the fried eggs and salami, sounds which combined to be a notch louder than Amelia's amorous giggling.

Sitting at the table, the Partagases' only daughter was eating a small pre-breakfast snack of a gluten-free muffin and drinking a *cortado* with almond milk and a dash of brown sugar. To the frustration of Josefina carrying out the morning's routine all by herself, Amelia was messaging her fiancé on the phone while flipping through the pages of Bridal Guide. But Josefina wasn't angry, since it was the plump maid's job to prepare all meals in the household. In fact, she was privately amused looking over at Amelia taking little nips of her adulterated coffee—to Josefina, coffee required no other additives for it to take effect and launch a person into the day.

On matters of keeping culinary traditions alive, Josefina was also the only purist in the house who championed the most primal of cooking methods: throwing food items on the fire or dumping them into a pot of boiling water. She was also of the belief that, "If it existed one hundred years ago, then it is good for your body, but if it's processed, packaged, and painted, then with every bite you are taking days off of your life."

Nobody needed to rag on Amelia on her day off from work, and nobody did, as she permitted herself to disconnect in a comfortable pair of house pants while letting her fiancé know how much she loved and missed him. The financial channel was playing at a high volume on the television. For Miquel, Amelia's father, who would be up any minute now, the blender was blending peaches and bananas for his morning smoothie, a mix Amelia thought was disgusting. The moka pot was gurgling on the stove for Alba, Amelia's mother, who had just walked into the kitchen in her robe with a rested look on her face. She was thin with long brown hair, and was a very attractive and intelligent woman in her late forties. Though she was of average height, her willowy shoulders were delicately pulled back, adding an inch to her stature along with a confident and absolute aura. She had been married to Miquel for twenty years, seven of those years as the CEO of Azure Capital, better known as AC to shareholders.

Alba entered the kitchen, said her good mornings, and rushed straight to the stove, turning the burner off with the flick of a wrist. She picked up the moka pot and carefully poured herself a tiny cup.

"I've been thinking," Amelia said, "maybe you and father can stay a few days after the wedding."

"Sounds good, but the summer house needs a decent cleaning." Alba pulled out a box of crackers from the pantry and a block of cheese from the fridge. She cut herself a slice and placed it on a cracker. "Josefina, would you happen to know somebody who'd want to make some extra cash cleaning up a summer home in Calella de Palafrugell?" Alba bit into the cracker.

"Yes, Señora, of course," Josefina replied.

Alba didn't hear her maid's response as her attention was suddenly drawn to the television, where she caught the tail end of a comment made by a reporter she knew personally. Crumping on her crackers and cheese, she walked over to the flat screen on the wall and turned up the volume. She shushed everybody, even though nobody was talking, and listened carefully to the reporter's economic projections and thoughts on what was needed to revive an ailing financial sector. Alba began cursing, rebuking him, saying things neither Josefina nor Amelia had a clue about. She knew what would happen with the economy, and so her stubbornness made her sound more convincing, especially since she was about to put a hole in the screen with her fist.

With her morning mood already spoiled, Alba walked straight to the cupboard and took out some plates. Seeing that Josefina was laboring by herself over a breakfast that was meant for four people, including herself, Alba set the table, and afterward she turned off the television—she was fed up with people talking about profits, margins, funds, and percentages these last few days. She didn't want to be reminded anymore that her bank was taking a huge hit in the crisis. Particularly good was she in blocking out other pertinent details that had become a hot topic in the news lately: those of her own inaction to a corruption scandal at the center of which she had found herself. Pancho, the family's pug, waddled in and started licking his empty bowl, taking Alba out of such dire thoughts.

"Have you fed the dog?" Alba asked Amelia. Amelia wasn't paying any attention to her mother as she was still looking at her phone. *A generation glued to screens*, Alba thought. She removed a bag of meaty bits from the pantry and sprinkled some into Pancho's bowl.

"We should be eating food that is free of hormones and antibiotics," Amelia said with an impassioned tone, eyes still on the phone's screen. "We should be checking labels and buying organic. That's what this clip says that just came up on my feed." Amelia raised the phone and showed her screen to Josefina and her mother.

"Amelia, we have this conversation almost every morning," Josefina said, calmly and patiently, with that Caribbean laissez-faire attitude of hers.

"Oh, stop it, both of you!" Alba exclaimed, pouring herself another shot of espresso. "Neither of you are experts on health and nutrition, so put all that to rest." She finally sat down at the end of the table across from her daughter. "Have we talked about catering?"

"Dad said you were going to take care of that," Amelia answered.

"He did?" Alba leaned back in her chair, bothered that she was always doing everything around the house.

"Mom, the wedding is in a few weeks!" Amelia cried out. "Did you at least place the order on the wedding dress?"

"Not yet."

"What?! And the music?!"

"I haven't talked to your father about that yet," Alba said. "Why don't you call up one of your DJ friends from Ibiza?"

"Mother!"

"You *do* know what's been going on lately, do you not?!" Alba admonished her daughter, but her bid for sympathy fell on deaf ears. Josefina, in her own world, was still at the stove humming songs from her childhood; Amelia had gone back to replying to Martin.

"We need beautiful photos to remember the wedding," Amelia said, her eyes still stuck on her phone.

"Of course, the memories," Alba said dryly, sipping on her espresso while reading the paper. Suddenly she got up from her chair, walked over to Amelia, and ripped the phone out of her hands. She opened the window and launched it outside into the water fountain.

"Ma! What are you doing?!" Amelia cried, mouth gaping and eyes widened from shock. She looked over to Josefina for moral support, but the maid continued cooking with a smirk on her face, pretending not to have seen anything.

Miquel finally walked into the kitchen. "What is all this noise about?"

"Dad, Mom just threw my phone out the window."

"Well, tell him you love him in person," he said. Sulking, Amelia crossed her arms and kept quiet. She finished the rest of her *cortado*, then continued flipping through the magazine without saying a word. Her good mood quickly returned as she saw a beautiful dress that would suit her perfectly for walking down the aisle.

"What's this most important day people are talking about anyways?" Miquel said. "A wedding? Don't be silly. There'll be plenty more."

"Daaad!" Amelia whined.

With puffy eyes and sleep still on his face, Miquel took to correcting his tie while reading the newspaper that was spread open on the kitchen table. The tie was the last accessory to tend to as his watch, ring, and bracelet gleamed from a fresh morning polish. His black hair, slicked back, made his crisp white shirt look even whiter. His tan, once fresh and orange, was now a fading mix of salon and sun. Miquel's belly protruded cantilever over his belt, preventing him from noticing that his fly was undone. This lightened the mood and attracted a few giggles from the ladies.

Alba slid a plate of *Tres Golpes* to where Miquel normally sat. She reached across the table and borrowed Amelia's spoon, then began spooning some *mangú* into her mouth. Seeing how Miquel was struggling to get dressed, she staked the spoon into the *mangú* like an ardent explorer marking territory, got up from her seat, and walked over to help him zip up his zipper. She moved her hands up to his tie, playfully knocking his hands out of the way, and corrected his attempt at adjusting its length and appearance. With a coy smile spreading across her face, she whispered in his ear, "Good morning, *cariño*," then asked, "Did you sleep well?"

"I prefer more of a rooster's breakfast," he said in a whisper, followed by a quick kiss on her lips. Alba looked into his eyes and smiled while continuing to wrangle with the stubborn knot. She was the only one who knew what he meant by "rooster's breakfast," and knew that its "ingredients" were reserved exclusively for after the eyes opened and before the duvet was thrown aside.

"I think you should look in the mirror," Amelia said, "before attempting stage two of getting dressed."

"I have my gracious and most loving lady to look after me when I'm not as prim and proper as usual," Miquel said.

"So, who is our band, Mr. Prim and Proper?" asked Alba, sitting down. "I don't want it to be some folk band, please. I had enough of them last year at Adriano's birthday party."

"You very well know I'm just the money man on this matter," he said, pouring himself some of the fruit smoothie. "You both are the deciders, very critical ones, might I add, because I don't want to fall asleep like last year at the table when they played the Macarena with a fiddle. Maybe this year will be the year I break out and show my salsa steps. We've been practicing quite a bit." He brought his glass up to his lips and finished the whole smoothie in two gulps. After placing the cup down in the sink, he swayed his hips spontaneously and after a few moves, deferred to his wife for confirmation of his smooth footwork.

"There have been significant improvements, I have to say," Alba said.

"In my country, they'd dance circles around you," Josefina interrupted, walking back and forth between the stove, the fridge, and the cutting board, knife in hand, ready to slice and dice.

"Spare me the thought of Dad dancing with his two left feet," Amelia said. Josefina started giggling.

"What's so funny, Josefina?" Miquel asked. "You don't think my love is Latin enough?"

Josefina gave him a wry smile. "You look like a diseased cow on the dance floor," she said. "Like mad cow disease or something." Everyone burst out laughing.

"I agree, Josefina," said Amelia. "I think you should focus on getting that hip fixed instead, Papa."

"For the wedding's dance-off, I'll be fine, don't worry about me," he said, still dancing.

"Ah, a dance-off, huh?" asked Alba.

"Well—"

"I'm always the last one to find out about these things," Alba said. "Like both of you have some sort of *cosa nostra* thing going on."

"Yeah, and I'm the hitman for hire," Miquel joked. "Besides, it's just a dance competition. No big deal. Every wedding has a dance-off."

"I just want to be in the loop about things, even if they're little things."

"We were talking about my future," burst in Amelia, like a teenager wanting to change a boring topic. "Full of more hope and less of your hip problems and hospital stays," she added.

"Whatever the age difference between your mother and I," Miquel said, reaching into the bread bin for a gluten-free muffin, "you have to know that, with bad hips or not-so-fancy dance moves, we still love each other very much." He looked over at Alba. She was now glancing through a financial magazine and picking out grapes from the fruit bowl. "I think, given that you haven't even crossed any sort of milestone yet, you should be planning our … what? Nineteenth anniversary? Next year?" Miquel looked at his wife again for confirmation.

"No, *cariño*," Alba replied with a plain face, still looking at the magazine. "The twentieth anniversary is next year and our daughter shouldn't be organizing such an event—you should!"

"Oh, okay. But another important milestone," he said, trying to redeem himself, "would be that your mother, my beautiful wife, hasn't touched a cigarette in … how long?"

"Hmm, eight months," Alba said, looking over at Miquel spooning yogurt into his mouth.

Miquel finally sat down at the table and turned the television back on with a remote. "Hey, are you hearing this?" he said. "No arrests?" The television was playing a newsreel from the protest. It showed a garbage bin on fire, a squatted building that had been taken back by Alba's bank, and protesters throwing Molotov cocktails. "Not the kind of news to wake up to," he added. "I tell you, this country is going to shits! People nowadays rely too much on the government, lacking creativity and the will to take control of their own destinies. Makes me sick! A return to dictatorship is what this country needs." Everyone stopped what they were doing and looked at Miquel, hardly in shock as they were quite used to him making such off-color remarks. He grabbed the fork and looked down at the plate of *mangú*, eggs, and salami. Rather than digging in, he hesitated for a moment. He got up in a hurry and stole a nutrition bar for the road from the fruit bowl. Alba got up with him, grabbed his briefcase, and walked him to the door.

"Have you figured out how to deal with those criminals yet?" he said quietly, looking at himself in the mirror in the hallway.

"We own the building, and there's nothing more to it," she said matter-of-factly. "We, as in, *we*, and not the bank."

"And what about the bomb they found at the picnic?"

"The detective called me last night and told me they found no fingerprints on it despite the sloppy work put into making it."

"Well, we'll just have to be careful," Miquel said, opening the door. "It was only a small device and it didn't even detonate … still, no need to worry Amelia. Better not say anything."

Alba grabbed the umbrella leaning next to the teak door and slid her feet into Amelia's rain boots. She lifted her robe with her left hand, maneuvered it into the crook of Miquel's elbow, and walked him outside.

"So, Barça stuff today?" she asked sarcastically, opening the umbrella over his head as they walked to his car in the driveway. "Or getting the Chinese to finally buy our best vintage?" He gave her a tired look but she fired back. "When are you going to start distancing yourself from doing work you know nothing about and start selling wine?"

"*Cariño*, please," he begged. "I don't need a lecture on how to run a business." Miquel stopped at the door of his Mercedes and turned to face Alba. He wedged his briefcase between his knees so it wouldn't touch the wet concrete and caressed her cheek with his hand. "And what about the invitations for Amelia?"

She assumed a startled look just to irritate him. "Relax," she said. "I placed the order with Adriano a long time ago and will be picking them up today."

"Out of all the things not taken care of and the invitations were first on your list?!"

"They're important," she said. "For our marriage we didn't even have any … nothing to celebrate … we just gave her up, our own daughter."

"That was years ago, and it's still bothering you, Alba?" he said, already angry at where the conversation was heading. "When are you finally going to put the past behind you? We were young and stupid and wanted to live a little before we became tied down to—"

"To life?" she interrupted.

"Tied down to life," he agreed, with a sad note in his voice. "You're always on the ball with things, and that is why I married you, but you've been acting really weird these last few weeks."

"A lot has been going on," she said. He checked his watch and saw that he was running late, so he kissed her again, said that he loved her, and got into the car. He turned on the engine and looked at her standing there, then slid the window down.

"Maybe when this rain dies down," Miquel said, "we could call the landscape architect to take care of this yard. Would be a shame to see it go to waste."

She looked up and watched him reverse out of the driveway. After the high gates of the property started closing, she went back inside. Josefina had gone back to her room to watch Venezuelan soap operas, while Amelia was running on the treadmill so she could fit into her wedding dress, the one she didn't have in her possession just yet.

In the kitchen, Alba sat down at the dinner table and removed a pack of cigarettes that she had kept hidden in her robe's inside pocket. She pulled a cigarette out and lit it up with great pleasure. She leaned back in her chair, completely relaxed, her mood changed in a span of a few seconds. She inhaled and exhaled the smoke like a beginner fully enjoying the novelty. She didn't even care that she was ashing into her palm. And she didn't have to worry about the smell of cigarette smoke in the kitchen—Josefina promised to take the fall in case Miquel would find out. In this case, she was also okay with the fact that Amelia was often in her own world, and wouldn't notice the smell of smoke.

In complete repose, Alba looked over the kitchen. Josefina had left it immaculate. The *Tres Golpes* she had made for the entire family sat in the middle of the table, cold and untouched, and would probably go to the trash.

8
Social Protest Poetry

Amid the crowd of angry protesters at the main entrance of 56 Avenida Rocafort, a sea of placards jostling the air spelled out what many would believe to be a city on the brink of collapse. There was "Stop Corporate Greed" and "Tax the Rich," as well as "End the New World Order," "The Community Is Ours," and "Capitalist Banks Steal From the Poor." There was also "Down with Alba Partagas!"

Laia was standing on a garbage bin with her arm wrapped around a traffic pole, holding the bullhorn's microphone to her mouth. She occasionally made a fist and beat the air with every syllable of her short yet powerful protest song. Lucas was next to her holding the bullhorn high in the air, while Xavi held the umbrella over her head, purposely keeping it away from Lucas, who was getting soaked in the drizzle. Laia turned her face away from the microphone, leaned into Lucas, and whispered in his ear, "I know that shameless bitch is somewhere in there."

As Laia continued chanting and agitating the crowd, Lucas looked up at the building. He didn't know who she was or even what she looked like, but he knew the "shameless bitch" sat somewhere at her office desk, probably leafing through papers or making important phone calls, or stealing millions from pensioners who required thick glasses and a good money sense to read over and scrutinize their own bank statements.

Laia was the protest leader, as she had been for the last few months, holding a certain kind of magical aura over the crowd, a form of collective and tractable hypnosis. However much of a voice she gave back to the voiceless, however much power she wrested from the elites, there were always forces in society that worked against her and her cause. After every protest, all the pictures in the media would function to portray her as a "hippie with a PhD," a "social misfit," or a "nuisance hindering resolution of the crisis." But the self-proclaimed Marxist was inured to all the attacks in the online as much as offline world.

Laia Requena was rough around the edges. In her tattered black band shirts and frilly jean skirts, she was a symbol of a movement and a leader of a generation left behind. Apart from being worse for wear in appearance, her wardrobe was also of drab colors, except for her stockings, which were usually garish and of a wildly psychedelic pattern. She had fair skin, blue eyes, and a bullring piercing that on any beast of burden would allow for easy control and manipulation. Her friends often joked about that piercing, saying that she was too strong to be pushed around and too stubborn ideologically to be influenced in any way. It was at an alternative, French lyceum where she'd first started rolling joints and setting her blonde hair into dreadlocks, adding bleach-tips and beads as part of her bohemian style. A *keffiyeh* wrapped around her neck was a permanent fixture, along with *hecho de mano* bangles worn as a reminder of her trip to Bolivia in support of some indigenous cause, where she started looking at the history of Latin America from a revisionist perspective. Underneath it all, you couldn't tell that Laia was wearing herself to a shadow from all her protesting, campaigning, and revolutionary fervor, as she was slim but cut from yoga and her daily routine of push-ups, pull-ups, and sit-ups. Apart from a steady diet of Marx, Tolstoy, and Mandela, her vegan lifestyle kept her mind in check and body balanced on the scale. As sappy and clichéd as the motto went, Laia was all mind, body, and soul, but when it came to making a change in society, she was hardly civil and rarely obedient.

She invariably rejected the idea of violence until one day at a meeting she proposed the idea herself, that the Black Arrow start growing its power base by robbing from the rich, donating to the poor, and selling drugs to yuppies, as well as extortion when the perfect opportunity came up. Eventually this would turn the Black Arrow into a criminal organization high up on Noguerra's list.

Whoever at the Arrow was opposed to the idea could have left the meeting that day, but surprisingly everyone stayed to hear her out. Lucas walked out, not because he rejected their plans of graduating to more sinister crimes, but because he was following a lead on the Catalan, which unfortunately turned out to be a dead end. From the moment of his walk-out, the tension between Laia and Lucas started to mount, putting a strain on their already frayed relationship.

In fiery arguments Laia often told Lucas that he was completely lost to the world and to himself, and that he was helping with the organization only as some kind of moral cheerleader. She pressed him to play a more serious role, and blamed his halfhearted participation on his bad attitude more than his ideals. As far as she knew, they shared similar political sentiments, though with unequal fervor: hers, a burning flame of conviction; his, a firebrand that needed stoking.

Laia Requena was the adopted daughter of an ex-member of the Basque nationalist organization, ETA. Lucas Brodowski was a rogue cop moonlighting as a scrap collector, a revenge killer pretending to be a concerned member of the public, a con artist who dropped clues to steer the Black Arrow away from prodding into his past. It was Lucas who convinced Laia and Xavi that he was an economic refugee, a victim of the system who blamed society's ills on the likes of the Catalan. If only they knew he'd once sworn an oath to serve and protect his country, and that he wanted a man dead and not defrauded, then his days would have been numbered at the organization.

As the riot squad now formed a barricade around the protesters, Lucas couldn't help but be transfixed by their weapons. They were a cloned army of Robocops, wearing protective helmets, specialized armor, truncheons, and large, combat-ready polycarbonate shields, each of which had the word "*Guardia*" written on its face. Behind this formation was a battalion with rubber-bullet rifles that would unleash havoc on protesters should they receive the right message trickled down the chain of command at just the right moment.

* * *

There was soft music playing in the background and an air purifier humming in the corner. A knock on the door came, and Alba Partagas took a break from looking over the expenses from a company picnic. She removed her reading glasses and looked up. Seeing that it was only Valentina, her secretary, who had meekly entered carrying an espresso on a tray, she put her glasses back on and looked over another invoice. Valentina put the espresso down on her desk and placed Alba's mail next to a picture of Miquel, Amelia, Martin, and Alba in Calella de Palafrugell at their summer home. Not lifting her eyes from the invoice, Alba handed Valentina some papers and offered a curt, "Thank you," signaling that that was all and that the secretary could leave.

After taking a sip of her coffee, she got up from her desk and walked over to the window. Looking over the entire square, she was surprised to see so many protesters in the rain. Perhaps more protesters had come out this time, she thought, when it was announced in the media that another residential building would be taken away by her bank, threatening the lives of thirty-six more families.

Alba went back to her desk, turned off the purifier and the music, and returned to the window. She brought her face closer and instinctively turned her cheek over where two panes of glass met. Holding her breath, she could barely hear the muffled cries coming from outside. She vaguely made out what they were shouting, that the people wanted her to step down from her position, and that she should get ready for a retrial as new evidence emerged that would incriminate her. She also heard them yell that she should get "hard time," a prison sentence. For all the horrible things wished upon her, not a single emotion came across her face. Alba exhaled, then inhaled deeply, and then checked her watch. Is it time for lunch? she wondered.

She returned to her chair and plopped her elbows down on the desk's hardwood. That was when it finally hit her. Alba dropped her face into her palms and began thinking. *There is no way this will break me,* she thought. She refused to disavow the years of hard work she'd put in to get where she was in life. Regarding this crisis, blame too could be attributed to the global economy and not just to her actions, however blameworthy they were. Though she could always empathize with the victims of those evictions, she had absolutely no compassion for those who broke the rule of law. The irony was that she herself had broken the law, but she also believed that she was above the law. Alba didn't care that some of them would rot in prison for years, be given thousands of euros in fines, or that they would be put out on the streets. In her mind, she had a duty to fulfill in keeping her shareholders' best interests at heart, as the crisis would most certainly deepen, contrary to what many economists were saying. If not her, then somebody else would have taken her position and started returning properties to the bank, just like in a game of Monopoly.

To try to shake herself out of this strange malaise, Alba got up and went back to the window. She didn't know why she did this, only that she felt it necessary to show herself to everyone, to present an image of a confident and strong woman. This, despite most of the protesters unable to see her standing there or not even knowing what she looked like.

No sooner did she come right up to the window, than a Molotov cocktail smashed into the glass a few feet from where she stood. The sound of the bottle shattering pushed her back and reverberated in her thoughts. Everything suddenly appeared in slow motion. She looked down near the building entrance and saw the police moving in.

The officers with truncheons swung at protesters who were trying to escape via the avenues that fed into the square. A journalist captured an officer with his boot pressed down on a man's face. It would make global headlines. A battering ram affixed with a cannon appeared from out of nowhere and started charging and shooting pressurized water at whoever stayed back in the square. Alba looked on in shock, yet a little part of her was pleased to see things were finally happening.

* * *

Laia, Lucas, and Xavi all dispersed and were separated in a matter of seconds. Panic overtook Laia when she couldn't find Lucas. She was just as concerned for him not being by her side as Xavi was concerned for her and the other members of the group who took off running.

When Xavi and Laia found each other, they soon took refuge in an abandoned flat previously established as a safe house in case things were to get out of hand. Lucas bolted from the square in the other direction, as he didn't want to bring the two officers on his trail back to the safe house. Whether or not he threw the Molotov cocktail, it didn't matter—they'd selected him as their target, so he was going to pay for it dearly.

He turned into an alleyway and soon realized that it was a dead end. After looking back to see where the cops were, and not knowing where he could escape to, he took a gamble and hid in a darkened alcove. Taking a few deep and nervous breaths, he stuck his head out from behind the wall and saw one *guardia* turn into the alleyway, while the other continued running down the street. After passing a few dumpsters, the cop came into Lucas's view. He crept forward, keeping close to the wall, looking around for clues of where the degenerate punk could be hiding.

Lucas was desperate and panicking. He looked around and saw a metal pipe on the ground. He picked it up and receded deeper into the alcove. He braced himself, holding the pipe like a baseball bat, gripping it tightly, breathing in and out, deeper and louder. The cop had a death wish, and Lucas was ready to jump out and deliver it by swinging the metal pipe at his head.

A few feet from the alcove, the officer stopped. He looked around, listening carefully for any suspicious sounds, but soon turned back, thinking that the suspect he was chasing had gotten away. For Lucas, it was a relief yet a miracle the cop hadn't noticed this blackened alcove that could have concealed in its shadow a young man holding a metal pipe.

Lucas dropped his hands and breathed out a long sigh. He smiled when he passed the pipe to his other hand and wiped his face with the back of his palm. Sure that the ordeal was over, he let his weapon fall onto a garbage bag, fixed his jacket, and leaned back against the door. He pulled out his necklace from under his sweaty shirt and kissed the cross given to him by his mother. He looked at it and thought about her. He raised his collar and was ready to come out when suddenly, out of nowhere, the cop appeared in front of the alcove with his gun out.

"Hands up!" the cop yelled. "Come out of there! Nice and slow!"

Lucas was taken by surprise and unable to think. He came out with his hands up. He felt his heart beating against the cage of his body, a pulsating hum in his ear, strenuous and rhythmic breathing burning off at the mouth. His fists ceased being fists and became heavy steel balls, as in the heat of the moment he reacted on a nervous impulse. Only afterward did he realize that it was the stupidest thing he had ever done because the cop, overwhelmed by fear, could have fired his gun. Luckily, he didn't, and Lucas took the chance and knocked his gun away. He then began throwing brutal punches into the cop's face. Not expecting hand-to-hand combat, the cop fell back but managed to get in a few strikes. In the end, Lucas overtook him with a pummel and left him in the alleyway, unconscious.

Right when he was about to run off, a door swung open from the alcove, pouring bright light into the alleyway. It startled him as much as the man exiting with his arm around a lady. This was a brothel; he remembered he had been there many months before. The man and woman didn't see the cop lying on the ground as he had fallen into a pile of garbage; they didn't have a good look at Lucas running away, either.

When he exited the alleyway, Lucas took on a different pace, a casual stroll, as if nothing had happened, as if it was all over. Little did he know that his problems were just beginning.

9
Horst's World of Antiques

"Łukasz Brodowski."

Right before Lucas turned the handle, a man called out his name, except not in the usual way, the way he was most familiar with. Lucas had grown accustomed to the stiff, bare, and boring intonation of "Lucas," but for some reason, hearing his name in the version more Slavic and sonorous, he froze, lost in a trance. The sudden and unexpected pronunciation of "Łukasz" triggered the Polish half of his identity in the exact way a hypnotist might snap his finger and cause an audience member to behave like a farm animal. The floodgates to a world of long-forgotten memories were suddenly opened, a mental roller-coaster ride back to his childhood.

* * *

"Łukasz!" Gregorio called out, slapping his son on the back as he sat at the dinner table. "No woman wants a hunchback!" Feeling his father's warm hand thud between his shoulder blades, Lucas bolted up and corrected his posture. He smiled and continued eating his soup, but when his parents started arguing about how Gregorio was raising him and his brother, Thiago, Lucas's mind escaped and he floated away through the kitchen window to his friends, who were smoking weed and kicking the ball around on a small dusty field near his house.

"There's a way of teaching your kids without the smacking and slapping and hitting," Rafaela reprimanded. Lucas would return to the dining room whenever his mother would brave his father's harsh words and defend him. "No woman wants a man to be so violent in the house!"

"If that's violence," said Gregorio, "then stick your head out the window at night and tell me how many gunshots you hear."

"What does that have to do with it?"

"The boy needs to man up," urged Gregorio, slurping his soup. "Shoulders back, chest out, head high! If he can do that, then he earns respect. On the field, off the field—in life!"

* * *

Lucas turned to see who it was and saw the man whom Barthos had pointed out to him—the Polaco who played the guitar and drank beers with his former Eastern Bloc musician friends. Lucas studied him in hostile silence. Next to his feet stood his guitar case and an ancient and massive trunk, the one he was sitting on at the bank the day Lucas roughed him up good. It was evident the Polaco had been hauling the trunk around with him everywhere he went.

"What do you want?" Lucas asked rudely, consciously flipping into his father's mother tongue.

"Just relax, comrade. I don't want any trouble."

"Comrade? I'm not anybody's comrade," Lucas said. Hearing such communist-era argot raised his suspicions even more, especially since his father had escaped Poland during martial law.

Horst, hearing a funny language spoken outside his shop, one he had never heard Lucas speak before, closed the antique catalogue he was holding and shuffled over to the window. He took off his glasses and got on his toes as there was a large phonograph in his way, one he'd been trying to sell at a bargain price even though it had once been owned by a Third Reich civil servant during World War II.

"A friend of a friend told me you asked about somebody," the Polaco said. "About a man named the Catalan."

The words caught Lucas unawares and his mood suddenly changed. With sideways glances he stepped down from the door and crossed the sidewalk.

"I'm listening."

"Well, I don't know him personally, but I—"

"Are you messing with me?"

"No, wait, listen," the Polaco said, bringing his hands up defensively, expecting Lucas to unleash on him again. "I used to clean yachts at Port Vell and, well, I have information … about where he is, what he does."

"So, where is he?" Lucas asked impatiently. "Who is he?! What does he do?!"

"Well, I know how strange this may sound, but I have a proposition for you. Let's meet tomorrow and I'll tell you."

Lucas lunged at him, bunched up his suspenders, and began strangling him. "Listen here, son-of-a-bitch! If you only knew what I've been through—"

"One of the yachts I used to clean was his," said the Polaco, pushing Lucas's hands away from his face, finally showing a bit of frustration. "I remember because inside he had a gold plate of his name in the captain's room. *'El Catalan,'* it read. Some real narcissism, huh? But he's not in the city now. I can lead you to him—" Lucas shoved him to one side, knocking over a few garbage bins. "What are you doing, comrade?!" Hearing this form of address once more took Lucas's ire up a notch. He tossed the Polaco and kicked his trunk against a fire hydrant. The trunk broke open, instantly cutting off Lucas's rage. Spilling out onto the pavement were gold bracelets, silver watches of the highest quality, and a few wads of bills. There was also a gold plate with *"El Catalan"* engraved on it in a fancy, cursive font. Lucas looked up at the Polaco. "I stole it from him," he said, shrugging awkwardly. "Yeah, I did. So what?" Lucas, seeing weakness and vulnerability in his eyes, calmed down. "You really gotta get a hold of yourself," the Polaco said, scrambling for his loot in the trunk. He fixed his hat, which had gotten rumpled in the scuffle, and put it back on. "You looked like you were about to kill me." Horst was still looking out the window, wondering what this was all about. "Well, if you want to find out where he is," the Polaco said, standing up and straightening his wrinkled shirt, "then meet me tomorrow at the Algerian tent at three. There, we can have tea and talk like civilized human beings."

The Polaco grabbed the trunk and guitar case, and right when he started walking away, he stopped and turned around. "You help out here, right?" he said. "Like a volunteer or something?" Lucas didn't say anything, as he was too embarrassed for having taken his rage too far. "Here, take this." The Polaco opened the trunk and pulled out an old, shiny hourglass with black volcanic sand inside. "This might be worth something, not only because it's old but because of its quality—if it could resist the strength of your kick. It was sitting on his desk in the yacht."

Lucas grabbed the hourglass, scrutinizing its three-legged stand and its ornate, leafy pattern. It was made from gold but was unusually dark in luster and looked very expensive. It was an object the Catalan at one point held in his hand. He flipped it over and watched sand sprinkle down. *Time is passing,* he thought, *and he's still alive.* Lucas walked back to the shop, and right before opening the door, the Polaco called out.

"Szumski," he said. "Stachu Szumski is my name." Lucas paused, leered at Stachu, then opened the door. The little bell over the threshold chimed and he went in.

Horst hastily reopened the catalogue and pretended to be looking for an item. "What happened to your face?" he said, turning around. The retired professor took off his spectacles and let them hang on their strings. He squinted his eyes and looked over Lucas. "And what was that all about?"

"Some guy who owed me money, so he paid me with this." Lucas stood the hourglass on the old history books stacked on top of the fifty-percent discount table. Horst grabbed the hourglass, put on his glasses, and examined it carefully.

"From the Duchamp Mariposa collection," Horst said. "It's very impressive. Only a few dozen left in the world."

"You can have it," said Lucas, exhausted. A look of confusion clouded Horst's face. He knew the item would sell for a few thousand euros. In fact, he'd just seen a similar item in the catalogue he was holding. "Laia will be a little late today," Lucas added, taking off his coat and hanging it up on an old wooden coat rack.

"Well, thank you for letting me know, Lucas, and thank you for this. In the back there are some books I'd like you to sort. Oh, I've also set aside those for Laia; you could take them. Sun Tzu, Clausewitz, and some Che Guevara book, the one about that famous motorcycle trip he did around South America, the one turned into a movie."

10

Wedding Invitations

The door swung open and toppling forward before catching herself was Alba, along with a spray of rain and a gust of wind.

"Door!" Adriano shouted from his office chair as he scrambled to contain a few rolls of poster board that flew off his desk and landed on the floor. Alba quickly closed the door, shook her sleeves, and to rid her coat of rainwater, stomped her feet like a Flamenco dancer. She caught a glimpse of herself in the glass. She had made an effort to look good that day, but with the downpour, her makeup had started running and her hair had frizzed.

Looking around the shop, Alba noticed Adriano had made many changes since his son, Marco, had started working for her at the bank as a junior financial analyst. She also noticed that he had taken down several newspaper clippings, medals, and photographs of himself playing basketball for the national team.

Since Adriano was watching television while eating his *bocadillo* and drinking his coffee, he wasn't paying any attention to who had entered the shop. Otherwise, he would have stopped watching last night's sports highlights and greeted Alba as the close friend from their college days and loyal customer she had been for well over twenty years.

Adriano's print shop was on a side street next to La Rambla. This time, rather than the usual order of designing and printing large format banners for special events like company picnics, Alba was dropping in to pick up Amelia's wedding invitations. Seeing that she couldn't get any work done at her office, and that the entire business district was to be evacuated, she'd left unnoticed and driven across town to pick them up earlier than expected.

"*Buenas tardes*, Adriano," she said, walking up to the counter.

Adriano shot up from his springy recliner chair, spilling coffee on his trousers. He bolted to his feet, cursing himself while looking over the stain on his crotch. Noticing that his hands were still occupied, and that he couldn't remedy the mishap just yet, he stuffed the rest of the *bocadillo* into his mouth and quickly drank the last bit of coffee to wash it all down. Seeing a roll of toilet paper sitting on the counter, Alba picked it up and handed it to him. He grabbed the roll from her hand and tore off a few leaves.

"Alba!" he finally said, vigorously wiping his crotch area. "Great that you came as I was about to close up." She looked him over from top to bottom and started chuckling. "Alba, sweetie," he said, "I'm usually ready for your visits, but I guess today, well, our stars don't seem to be aligned."

"Well done, Adriano," she said. "Always playing it cool and averting embarrassment like the sly fox you are." She placed her hands on the counter and looked at him intently. "And that's how you almost had me back in college," she said, trying to be seductive, biting her lip. Adriano blushed. Contrary to her reputation of being a tough, headstrong woman of action, Ms. Alba Partagas was in fact very personable, sensitive, and even flirtatious. "Then again, you athletes were never my type," she added. "I chose brains over brawn, but I do remember that you could always worm your way into any girl's bed ... and sometimes get yourself into trouble as their boyfriends would be there sleeping next to them. Who would have thought?"

"Alba, please, my blood pressure has been mortal these last few days. Such talk could not only give me an ulcer but a heart attack." Adriano's playful mood suddenly shifted to one of concern. "I heard the news. It's all over TV. Are you okay?"

"Which is why I had to step out," she said, hardly emotional. "I am fine, and sorry for interrupting your ... lunch?"

"No problem, Alba." In a last determined effort, Adriano finished wiping himself. He crumpled the toilet paper into a ball and tossed it at the trash can in the corner, missing it by an inch.

"You lost your touch, huh?" she teased.

"Once upon a time, Alba," he said, placing his hands on the glass counter, facing her and pretending arrogance, "I was great at everything, believe it or not—and not only on the court but at courting, as you just said. But then I got married, you see, which is why I'm wondering why your daughter is making that leap of faith. I suppose I have no right to ask."

"You have every right to ask as I know you're probably a bit upset that she isn't marrying Marco. Your son always wanted to take her hand in marriage."

"That was a long time ago, yes. He *was* madly in love with her. I'm just happy that they were able to talk again at the picnic. Okay, um, I bet you're here for your invitations." Adriano took off his glasses and looked up at his cubbyhole sorter. "Where could they be? Hmmm, plain cardstock paper, Classic Belluccia font in black ink, pearl-butterfly shimmer envelopes ... they are ... right here!"

Up high, about an arm's length away, he located a small cardboard box with a pretty ribbon on it. He stepped on a stool, reached up, and knocked the box right into his arms as he adeptly stepped back into his slippers. He returned to Alba and placed the box on the counter, then began untying the bow to show her the invitations but stopped when her hand gently touched his. "How beautiful the bow and ribbon are," she said. Adriano quickly confessed that this job was his wife's. Alba took over the untying, then picked out an invitation and examined it. "And the envelopes?"

"Ah, yes, of course, right over here." He reached under the desk and pulled out a small stack. Alba placed the envelopes into the box, put the lid back on, and fished out her credit card from her purse. "So, what's the damage?"

"Ah, your husband is a fantastic man as he unburdened you of having to pay."

"Well, that's why I married him, and proof positive that marriage doesn't make you throw away everything that makes you great."

Alba grabbed the box, told Adriano to give her best to his wife, and started walking toward the door. She grabbed the door handle but stopped when Adriano called out, "Alba, no umbrella?"

"Ah, it just broke! But I parked close by. I'll place the cards under my coat and make a run for it."

"But you're wearing such a nice coat! Well, just be careful, okay?"

"I will, Adriano. Have a good night."

11
Crash

Alba heaved the door open but a heavy gust of wind pushed it back in her face. Bracing herself a second time, she turned up her coat collar and thrust herself into the downpour. She lowered her chin into her chest and held her lapels together with her free hand, the one that wasn't carefully tucking the box of invitations into her body. She set off at a swift pace, but hardly did she step foot onto the wide sidewalk when the wind started having its way with her svelte and light frame. And the more she tried to hurry, the more it tauntingly challenged her to remain upright.

Miniature whirlwinds sucked up wet leaves while the rain drummed against the pavement. Shop signs swung on their rusted hinges, and pedestrians scrambled toward any place that would offer any sort of temporary shelter. Alba wondered how much longer this weather would keep up, hardly subsiding in intensity for what seemed to be about a week straight.

While making her way to her refuge on wheels, she started thinking. She didn't have to lie about her car being parked close by and her umbrella being broken. Saying that the only available parking space was a block away and that she didn't have an umbrella would have been a good enough explanation. But, for some reason, she couldn't bring herself to say such a thing. Her expensive clothes would get damaged, but this would prompt a shopping spree. Maybe Alba loved getting out of wet clothes in the comfort of her own home and stepping into a hot and foamy bath after staring at her naked body in the mirror. Maybe she didn't care about anything else at that moment, not clothes or umbrellas, not her husband or her work. The box of invitations was what mattered to her the most, what she held close to her like a newborn baby, like the baby she'd given up after birth. She thought about Amelia and Martin's wedding day, about bringing her friends and family together. And despite how her marriage was progressing after so many years—or perhaps not progressing at all, in a state of stagnation—she still wanted her daughter to remember her big day as the best day of her life. This was not how she remembered hers so many years ago, when they had put on a fictitious celebration for her closest loved ones only to conceal the heavy heart of having given up her firstborn.

She took the corner sharply and spotted her car through the heavy downpour. Reaching into her coat pocket, she deactivated the alarm and picked up the pace. She caught a glimpse of the ribbon on the box changing color from the rainwater. The ink on the sample invitation glued on top of the box was starting to run. Her stockings were getting wet and her heels were almost fit for the rubbish bin. Her coat was drenched and she felt the rain's cold soak through like an unwelcome touch.

While she was skimming over puddles a few feet from her car, a burst of wind suddenly caromed her off a passerby, who was lumbering with a stack of books wedged between his arms and chin. Losing control of the entire burden, he fell onto the wet pavement, cushioning Alba who then fell right on top of him, without the fancy box of invitations in her arms.

"No!" she cried out, turning her head and brushing her wet hair out of her eyes. The box had broken open and ended up in a puddle, and the wind was already blowing away the envelopes and invitations, which were taking flight like a flock of white birds.

"Jesus Christ!" the man said in Polish before switching back to Portuguese. "Can't you see where you're going, lady?" Lucas wiggled his way out from under her, as she had pinned him like a wrestler. He dragged himself up from the ground, put his hands on his hips like an angry parent, and took in what had happened. He looked her over, stopping his eyes on the footwear that hadn't mitigated against the crash and fall. "How do you expect to keep yourself upright in this weather wearing those?" he said in broken Spanish, looking down at her heels. "You can get yourself a pair of Wellingtons, no?"

"Yeah, it's you who should learn how to walk in the rain, not me!"

"Yeah, and you look like you were pulled from the throat of a dog." Lucas translated the phrase from Polish literally, which didn't make much sense at all in Spanish.

Alba scowled at him while getting to her feet; she started wiping her coat sleeve despite it doing nothing but rubbing in the humiliation. "You think you look like Prince Charming right now?"

"Probably not," he agreed.

Roused by the sudden flight of a few photos used as bookmarks, Lucas gave chase, fighting the wind and the rain. While gathering the items that had fallen out of her handbag, Alba looked toward him and said sorry for knocking him over, but he didn't hear. She tried again and yelled it since the rain was still pouring hard. Lucas caught the last of the apology and paused, looking back with a bewildered expression.

"You rammed into me and you're not even helping," he said.

Lucas soon realized that it was no use, no point in running after the photos. He bent over, placed his hands on his knees, and tried to catch his breath. He looked over at Alba. The sight of her fragility awoke in him a pitying and protective feeling. He straightened up and walked over and asked her rather coldly if she was okay. She didn't hear him, or maybe she pretended not to. He turned back with renewed enthusiasm, and in the form of an apology, decided to run after her invitations blowing down the street, trying to secure as many as he could by stepping on or catching them mid-flight. He combined the task with peeling off as many soggy envelopes as he could from the puddles. A curt smile etched itself on Alba's wet face: she knew that shoe prints and water stains would damage the paper, yet his effort to catch and preserve whatever he could was impressive. She shifted her eyes over to the heavy books just lying there with their pages turning wildly in the wind. Lucas finally came over and picked them up.

"You're about as light as a feather," he said, half-joking, half-serious. Alba, embarrassed, didn't say anything. "My name is Lucas," he said, shifting the books over to the other arm to offer a handshake.

"Alba," she said, giving him a light shake with her wet fingers.

After taking in all of Alba, Lucas caught sight of a big red stain on her knee. "That doesn't look very good," he said. She looked down to where his eyes stopped and suddenly got nauseous. She always felt weak seeing blood, even her own, even if the blood was diluted by the rain and partially covered by her drenched stocking.

She grabbed her head as a wave of dizziness hit her. Lucas noticed that she was about to faint and offered her his elbow for support. She reached her hand out and leaned on him instead, forcing Lucas to rebalance himself and come closer. He walked her over to the steps leading to his building's entrance. He put the books down and sat her next to them. She leaned back against the old and faded door and grabbed her leg in pain. Her head was spinning and she turned white as a ghost. "I feel like … what just happened?" she muttered, resting her right elbow on the books.

"I'm just up there," Lucas said, pointing up to his balcony. "You see the broken washing machine, exercise bike, and flowers that look like … broomsticks?" Alba's head was still spinning, but she managed to fix her gaze at where he was pointing. "Okay, the flowers might be dead," he said, "but I can run up and get a bandage for you?" He was attempting a bit of humor and trying to help her not think about the blood or the accident or the ruined invitations. "Or maybe a wheelchair? An umbrella? I'm sure I have a wheelchair. I had four just last week." Noticing a smile on her face, he added, "Or maybe you can come up and dry yourself off? Drink something hot?"

Alba looked over her wet body. She placed the back of her hand on her cheek and then moved it to her forehead. She suddenly remembered why she had visited Adriano. "What happened to the invitations?" she asked, in a slight stupor. She looked up from the pavement at Lucas's hands.

"I'm usually great at salvaging things," he said, holding a few damaged invitations. "Apparently, not this time."

"They're ruined," she said sadly, still out of it.

"There's a really good print shop just right around the corner," Lucas suggested. "The owner's name is Adriano, and he'll give you a good price. Just tell him you know Lucas." She looked up at him and tried to smile. "Just be careful, he tends to be very flirtatious with the ladies. He always used to hit on my girl—" he stopped to correct himself, "—ex-girlfriend who had her flyers printed there."

Though she was still feeling faint, Alba's mood improved upon hearing they had a mutual friend. Her eyes roved over him indecisively. Would she really go up? In this neighborhood? She looked at her bloody knee, then at her car parked right in front of the building, and grabbed his outstretched hand. After helping her stand up, Lucas picked up his books. They turned around together and slowly climbed the last step.

"Hey, relax, I'm not a serial murderer," he said when Alba glanced over. She held onto him as he walked her through the heavy doors. He could see in her face that she was having doubts following a stranger up to his apartment in a bad neighborhood. Somehow, she managed to convince herself it would be better to go up than go back to Adriano's shop or get into her comfortable, luxury car.

12
Triage

Alba could have turned back but chose not to. Even after seeing the walls filled with graffiti, the garbage bags scattered about, or the cockroach streaking along the floor, she kept holding onto him, her protector, her good-looking Good Samaritan. The verminous ground floor, steeped in the dry smell of urine, should have been where she drew the line. Or maybe the collapsing ceiling, flickering lights, and missing floorboards. For some reason, though, she stomached the assault on her senses coming at her from every angle, and focused on keeping down the nausea working its way up her throat.

With books in hand, Lucas nodded towards the mossy and dank well of stairs, sighing when he saw the elevator's "broken" sign. "The landlord of this building," he moaned while leading the ascent. "Such a cheap bastard."

"I don't think I can ... climb these stairs," Alba said, looking up at him after taking a hesitant first step.

"It's okay, come on." He shook his elbow for her to hold on tight. "If you fall down," he said with a smile on his face, "at least it will be onto soft wood eaten by termites and not onto pavement."

After making some progress, Lucas stopped at the second floor landing and placed the books off to the side. Alba handed him her purse just for a moment, as she too needed to take a deep breath and massage her leg. While examining her bloody knee, Lucas glanced inside her purse and saw the items she had gathered from the fall: a wallet, a Mercedes Benz car key, and a fancy, silver cigarette case. She straightened back up and said, "Looks like you have quite the experience with temporary invalids." She unhooked the purse from his hand and continued up the stairs.

"You're not an invalid," he said.

"Maybe I'll become one if you live on the top floor."

He didn't admit that he lived on the top floor. Instead, he said, "You're doing great!" with a disarming smile on his face. After a few more steps she found herself stealing peeks at him. Their eyes always missed each other by a narrow margin of time. He seemed genuinely concerned about her knee and determined to help her up the stairs.

On the top floor, Lucas let go of Alba and sprang forward, fishing out his key from his pocket. As she struggled holding the banister, she watched him insert the key into the keyhole but saw that he was unable to open the door. He swore again, bolder and louder, and shoved the door, pulling it toward him, grabbing the awkwardly positioned handle in the middle, wiggling it side to side. Finally, the latch gave way and he pushed the door open. He wiped his brow with his coat sleeve and returned to her.

"What about your books?" she asked.

"Nobody reads books in this building," he said, reaching out to her. "They're all old."

"Hey! Seniors read books too, huh?!"

"I meant the books," he said, backpedaling on a bad joke. "They're old and dusty and..."

"Okay, you don't have to walk me in like I'm your grandmother," she said with a wry smile. "I could carry myself. By the way, you could've told me that you lived on the top floor."

Lucas went ahead first, taking off his coat and throwing it onto the couch. Apollo perked up, but on seeing that it was Lucas, he rested his head back down on his favorite pillow, not worrying about the coat nearly smothering him.

"I'd like to apologize in advance," he called out with his head in a cupboard, hurrying to accommodate his unexpected guest. He put on the kettle, then unwrapped cookies and placed them on a plate.

"Apologize for what?" she asked, walking into the apartment with a limp.

"My housekeeping crew is off duty today," he said, taking a few swigs of Don Simon. Alba hobbled into the living room and saw what he meant.

"And your building-keeping crew too, I noticed," she said.

"What was that?"

"I *said* they'd been doing a great job lately." She stretched out her hand and leaned against the wall as though she were holding the place up but instead was trying not to fall over. She took three more cumbersome steps forward, took off her coat, and dropped down onto the couch next to Apollo, who finally sprang away in terror. She lobbed her leg up onto the coffee table, knocking over a stack of old magazines.

"Make yourself comfortable," he yelled out. "You can put your foot on the coffee table if you'd like for elevation and rest … ice and compression coming right up." She looked at the magazines that had fallen onto the floor: B&W photography, World War II, Anonymous Action Magazine. Ignoring the odd mélange of reading material, she started petting Apollo, who had returned to his favorite spot, even putting his head on her thigh.

With all the stockpiled odds and ends, a big and spacious loft apartment had been converted into a dusty and full-to-capacity storage house. Windows facing the street comprised one entire wall—not a plant in sight soaking up whatever sun appeared in recent days—and the remaining white walls, if they were even visible to the eye, were either stained, laced with flaking paint chips, or had cement fissures, which she could imagine ran as far down as the building's foundation.

Stacks of boxes matched stacks of books in height, filling up every nook and cranny. Judging by the many and varied items such as chairs, microwaves, and old stereos in innumerable quantities, Alba quickly guessed Lucas's line of work. For all these hoarded items crammed into this living space, there seemed to be a spatial symmetry and appeal to the chaos, as though a science existed behind every object's precise placement, and that their disorder was, in fact, some semblance of order. What made this theory even more convincing were the dozens of bicycles hanging upside down from ceiling hooks—old bikes with banana seats, French unicycles, children's tricycles, and even new Tour de France racers stolen from the local cycling club.

The kitchen was in the corner, and if not separated by a small brick wall sloppily put together, and a long Japanese divider filling in for whatever material ran out, then the place where Lucas made his ravioli daily would have spilled out into the loft's living area. Other objects the eye easily spotted included a slatternly armchair, two old grandfather clocks, and two cuckoo clocks that all chimed together at 4:00 P.M. A bunch of shelves that groaned under the weight of more books. A couch that was covered with an old, gaudy woolen blanket, on which rested Apollo now joined by Neymar. The lamp standing by the bed was the only item Alba recognized; she had the exact same one in her home office. Hers was purchased at a boutique furniture shop; Lucas found his in the trash in Bonanova, a rich part of the city.

"You like beating up people?" she asked, clearly in a better mood.

"What? Oh, the punching bag," he yelled from the kitchen. "I used to do a little boxing, but I had an accident and stopped."

In the corner of the loft, attached to the ceiling by a heavy-duty steel chain, hung a tattered and overused punching bag. A homemade stress-reliever, the bag was nothing more than a large sack filled with old clothes that had ceased living out their hand-me-down days. Every time he came back from scrapping, Lucas would unhook the bag and add a few pieces to increase its weight, resistance, and punchability.

"Ah, yes, I do have a wheelchair," he said, spotting one next to the old guitars. He rounded the corner and handed her an ice pack, then went back into the kitchen.

"In case I need to be wheeled to the doctor's while learning how to play guitar?" she remarked. He didn't hear her.

In front of the coffee table was an old and broken television surrounded by black and white photos stuck onto the walls. The photos were of the local children, and of the pensioners in the neighborhood who sat around on benches and talked about the good old days. Alba was amazed how each photo revealed an emotion from the entire spectrum in the human condition. There was sadness, joy, indifference, despair. Collectively, they represented a shrine to the resilient, everyday heroes, an ode to humanity that suffered a great deal but found happiness in the smallest of things.

"Are you a photographer, too?" Alba asked.

"No, I'm not," he yelled out from behind the dividing wall.

"No?"

"Well, I found an old camera in the garbage, and I managed to repair it." Alba could hear only the clatter of dishes and water running. "I took it out one day to take some photos of the local people and it became a weekly thing. When I developed the photos and gave them out as gifts, they liked them so much that they kept calling me out to the plaza to take more photos—of boys playing soccer, mothers talking with each other, children painting that old car out there ... just normal, day-to-day stuff. That plaza may look barren, but it's always brimming with life."

"They really are beautiful," she emphasized.

"I also got some chemicals and started developing them myself," he continued. "My darkroom used to be a bathroom. It's next to the bookcase." She turned around and saw a thick black curtain hanging over the space of a door. At that moment, Alba's phone started ringing. She struggled to reach the armchair where her bag sat, but managed to answer the phone in time. It was Amelia.

"Yes, I got them, but there's a bit of a problem," Alba said into the phone. "Adriano got the date wrong, so he said he'll redo them." She was still looking around the flat like it was some visual obstacle course, when she suddenly felt something unfamiliar and warm over her knee. She turned and saw Lucas sitting on a stool in front of her about to dab a swab of cotton on her wound. "I will ... um ... be late today, sweetie," she said, staring at Lucas. "I have another errand to run. Tell Dad not to wait for me." Alba said goodbye with a cracked voice and hung up. "That was Amelia. She's twenty and getting married," she said, trying to diffuse the awkward intimacy.

"Wow! Pretty young to be tying the knot," Lucas said, still treating her wound. "I'm twenty-three years old, from Brazil, and I've never been married." They laughed.

"So, down on the sidewalk you swore at me in how many languages? Three? Four?"

"I swore at you but now I'm pampering you—isn't that a strange and unpredictable twist of fate?"

She saw in him something strangely attractive, a hale and hearty young man, whom, in a sudden flash, she envisioned embracing and kissing ... but then the kettle began to whistle, taking her out of the thought, and she flushed red from embarrassment.

"Well, thank you for your help," she said, standing up too quickly and almost repeating the fall onto Lucas. She grabbed her bag and coat and limped toward the door.

"That's the bathroom," said Lucas, still sitting on the stool, surprised to see her taking her leave so soon. She turned the other way, the door slammed, then the kettle continued whistling while Lucas was left wondering if he'd ever see her again.

* * *

When Alba stopped at the second-floor landing to take a breath and try to get a hold of herself, she noticed the books that Lucas had put down on the step against the wall. Something was sticking out from under the cover of the top book, *Motorcycle Diaries*. She bent down, flipped it open, and saw one of the black and white photos that Lucas had managed to recover after the spill. She pulled it out and looked at it.

It was a photo of a girl's face in profile, somewhat unrecognizable due to the damage it had suffered from the rain. Or maybe it was a chemical stain, Alba thought, one of Lucas's earlier attempts at developing film. Regardless of its quality, and despite not being able to fully see the girl, Alba was captivated by it. She sat down on the step next to the books, wholly perplexed. *A familiar face,* she thought. Where had she seen it? She even held it up and observed it at different angles, trying to discover in it something new, a clue of some sort, but the lighting on the landing was too dim. Then something strange happened to her. Inexplicably, from the pit of her stomach, she felt a warmth spreading throughout her whole body reaching as far as her fingers, and through this warmth, a strange connection was happening between Alba and the girl in the photo. She realized that the girl's eyes and hair were very similar to hers when she had been younger. She looked down at the book where she'd found the photo and flipped through the pages to see if there were any more—there were none, only a business card used as a bookmark with the shop's name on it: Horst's World of Antiques. Alba slipped both the photo and the business card into her purse. She didn't know why, but she felt it was the right thing to do.

* * *

Lucas got word that a company's whole department would be dumping all their old electronic devices in the morning, so he prepared himself for an early night. He boxed, ate ravioli, showered, and lay in bed staring at the ceiling. There was a glow of a distant streetlamp leaking into the dark living room, but this time, Lucas decided to keep his blinds open so the early dawn would wake him up instead of his alarm clock. Even when Lucas kicked them off the bed, Neymar and Apollo would come back and wrap themselves in curls of fur at his feet. Cobwebs were starting to form between the spokes of one old mountain bike hanging right over his head. After he stared dazedly at the ceiling, his eyelids got heavy and he fell asleep, then had the strangest of dreams.

* * *

It was summer and Lucas was walking in a meadow, feeling long blades of grass running between his toes, watching grasshoppers springing up and taking flight. He came to a clay pit filled with water. It was the kind of pit once used in the industrial extraction of fine-grained rock, but this one had been converted into a beach. Despite the dull appearance of the clay pit, dozens of families would usually bathe in it at weekends to while away the hot days and to enjoy a bit of leisure on the cheap, not far from their village homes.

Lucas reached the beach and saw that it was empty, not a person in sight. In the water's still reflection, he saw clouds passing overhead, and even a few birds soaring in the sky. He took a few steps, sinking deeper into the clay, until he decided to dive in instead of getting mired. He began swimming and looked across and saw an old stone chapel. After a few more strokes toward the chapel, he opened his eyes underwater and saw something shimmering in the depths. He came up for air and looked around to see if anybody had thrown something in. He submerged himself once more, and with every blink, the distance between the bright, shimmering object and himself was cut in half until, right before his eyes, there appeared a dolphin staring at him. The animal was as curious to see Lucas as Lucas was curious seeing it. And the last of the dream was of him reaching his hand out and stroking the dolphin's face.

13

Disintegration

Alba parked her car in the garage of their luxury townhouse. When she turned off the ignition, she sat still and listened to the engine tick three times until it went quiet. A whirlwind of thoughts came over her: the protest, the rain knocking her down, and her ruined invitations. Of course, there was Lucas, who had already settled in her mind, populating the place with pieces of himself, like his scent and smile and rugged charm. She looked over at her handbag in the passenger seat and remembered she had taken a photo of a girl who looked like her.

When Alba glanced at her knee, she wondered what she would have to say to her family. In the end, she decided she would say nothing. That is, nothing close to the truth—she would lie, like she often did, to get herself out of awkward situations or unnecessary interrogations. But maybe she wouldn't have to lie this time. After all, it was a brief exchange, a compassionate gesture and nothing more. Guilty thoughts might have flashed in her mind, yet she hadn't broken her marital vows, so why the worry, she thought.

She got out, grabbed her handbag and shopping bags, and went in through the laundry room, limping as quietly as she could so as not to make any noise. She entered the corridor, placed the bags down, and looked at herself in the mirror. She thought about what Lucas had said, that she looked like she was pulled from the throat of a dog. It was funny and she smiled. She took off her heels and rubbed her feet and checked how wet her stockings were. Pancho waddled in from the living room with his tongue hanging out of his mouth. He greeted her with a lick on her ankle and a friendly wag of his cashew-shaped tail. She gave him a few scratches behind his ear.

"Ma?" yelled Amelia from her bedroom upstairs. "Is that you?"

"Yes, *cariño*," Alba answered. She straightened up and winced, accidentally putting some pressure on her leg. She took off her coat and hung it on the coat rack. She faltered into the kitchen, dropping her handbag on the table.

"So?" Amelia yelled from the top floor.

"He said he'll have them tomorrow."

"Can I see?"

"I returned them right away, *cariño*." Alba flipped through the mail and discarded the flyers into the wastebasket. "How was your day?" she asked, eyes glued to some court documents.

"What happened?!" Amelia said, walking into the kitchen. "Your knee?! There's blood everywhere!"

"Nothing," said Alba. "Just a spill in the rain."

Josefina passed the kitchen holding a heavy load of laundry, but upon seeing Alba's bloody knee, she placed the basket down and ran over in a panic.

"Señora!" she said. "Are you okay? That looks bad."

"It's fine, just get me a bandage, will you?" Alba was irritated by all the unwanted attention.

"I'll get you some ice and—"

"It's nothing, Josefina. Don't worry about it."

"Maybe you need stitches?" asked Amelia, kneeling to get a better look, about to wipe the blood with a kitchen cloth.

"Don't use that on my knee!" Alba reprimanded. "What are you doing?!"

"I just opened it. It's clean," Amelia said, shrinking from humiliation.

"And you're getting married in just a few weeks! Use your head!"

Amelia got back up and pitched the cloth into the sink, then sat down in a sulk at the table. Josefina returned from the laundry room. She put on latex gloves and pulled out a pair of surgical scissors from a first aid kit. She wanted to cut through the stocking to clean the wound.

"I'm fine!" Alba shouted, fed up. "I just need a bit of peace and quiet. Jesus!"

Josefina and Amelia froze, then glanced at each other. To stem the torrent of excessive concern coming her way, and to avoid any further reminders of all the good and bad moments of her day, Alba threw the mail down onto the table, grabbed her handbag, and stormed out of the kitchen with a limp. She was bothered that they were bothered that she was not taking her injury seriously.

Upon entering the bedroom, she dropped her handbag onto the vanity and began carefully slipping out of her wet clothes. She sat down on the edge of the bed in her underwear and bra with her leg held straight, assessing just how serious her injury was. She looked over at her handbag sitting on the vanity. She hobbled over to grab it and went back to sit on the bed, where she pulled out the photo she had taken from within the pages of *Motorcycle Diaries*. As she was looking at the photo, she heard Miquel enter the front door. Pancho's collar jangled and his nails scratched against the ceramic tiles in excitement. Alba put the photo back in her bag, burying it deep under cosmetics and her wallet. She stood up in front of the mirror and looked at herself, stretching her arms out, trying not to think about the photo or her knee or Lucas. She struggled into the bathroom, put on the water in the tub, and sat down on the toilet to pee.

"Ah, you startled me," she said as Miquel walked in. "I thought you were out with Fernando and Duarte?"

"I was, but they flew to Manresa to check up on the grapes. I heard your boardroom meetings are getting violent."

"A total bloodbath," she said.

"Here is some antiseptic and a bandage courtesy of Josefina. She told me to place them on the floor, nice and slow, and then to run out as fast as I could." Alba tried to smile. Miquel placed the items next to the sink and started undoing his tie and belt buckle. "You look stressed and tired. Are you okay?"

"The wind just felled me to the ground, but I'll be fine," she said. He took off his shirt and pants. "There was this guy who helped me."

"Oh, really? There are still nice people around?" Down to his underwear, he stood in the bathroom mirror looking over his hair, wondering if he should just get it dyed again. "Send him one of our bottles left over from the wine-tasting event."

"He lived in the area and was nice enough to pick me up and walk me over to my car." Miquel sat down on the rim of the bathtub and began taking off his socks. "He said I was as light as a feather—"

"—and as beautiful as a rose."

She tried to smile again, but she was bothered that all those sweet fawning words amounted to hot air and nothing at all. She had long ago finished peeing but was still sitting on the toilet bowl, thinking. She began applying some antiseptic to her knee.

"I was thinking that maybe we should sell our summer home," Alba thought out loud.

"The one in Costa Brava?" he asked.

"Yeah, we don't always have to be there. We could raise some money for the legal fees."

Miquel thought for a moment and said, "We'll have money for the legal fees." She scoffed, pitched the cotton ball into the toilet, and flushed it. The hot water was almost at the tub's limit when she began throwing bath salt inside. Miquel got up, embraced her from behind, and kissed her neck. She shuddered.

"Are you sure everything's okay?" he asked again.

"I had an awful day."

"I bet," he said, moving his lips down to her shoulder. "Is there anything I can do to help?" He worked his hands around her thighs and up to her hips and felt her breasts. She pushed him away. He grasped her waist and helped her into the tub ever so gently. She sat down, and he stepped in after her, and they both submerged themselves into a white cloud of foam. After a short while, Miquel leaned forward—challenging his flexibility and the pain scale of his hip and his belly's dimensions—and tried kissing her, but she turned her cheek.

14
Botero's Fat Cat

In the early hours of the morning, at the time when *chatarreros* started rumbling down the street or drunken tourists stumbled back to their rented apartments, Lucas awoke to his cell phone ringing by the bed. Having been in a deep sleep and unable to summon the energy to pick it up, it wasn't until six rings later when he finally stuck his arm out from under the sheet and groped around on the night table, knocking the phone down to his pillow. It was Stachu Szumski, urging him in an anxious voice to get dressed and to meet him in fifteen minutes at the Fat Cat instead of the Algerian tent. "Come quickly. I'll explain everything," Stachu said.

* * *

Standing in front of Botero's cat at 6:25 A.M., looking up into the dawn sky, Lucas noticed it had stopped raining. The cool air passed under his nose, and he shivered in the sunless morning. A few of his bones ached from the seaside humidity and the vigorous punching bag session he'd had the night before. He placed his hands into his coat pockets but impatiently removed his left one to check his watch. Just then, from behind the kebab shop, he spotted Stachu bounding over. Judging by the ease with which he carried his trunk (the other day he'd seemed burdensomely lopsided), Lucas figured that he had sold off the loot or put it in a safe place. He gaped at him and wondered if everything he had said the other day was true, if he had indeed been the Catalan's boat cleaner.

Rather than stick out his hand for a greeting, Stachu gently grabbed Lucas's elbow and walked him around to the other side of the cat's fat abdomen, where its rear left paw was planted. He was behaving as if someone were following him, or perhaps this paranoia existed inside his head only. He placed his trunk down and they looked at each other, Stachu with a look of imminent doom, and Lucas, one of irritated perplexity.

"Good morning, comrade," Stachu said, breathing heavily. Lucas looked him over and saw how out of shape he was. "As you could tell by the look on my face, I'm in a bit of a pickle."

"What the hell is going on?" Lucas demanded. "This better be good. I'm missing a huge payload for this." Stachu grabbed Lucas's sleeve, pulled him closer, and, shooting suspicious glances to both sides, whispered, "Listen, Łukasz, we're in a lot of trouble."

"What do you mean, *we're* in a lot of trouble?"

Stachu pulled out a piece of paper from his pocket. It was a police bulletin with a picture of Lucas on it. Lucas tore it out of his hands and examined it with forensic thoroughness. His eyes widened seeing his name next to his face. The photo was from the day of the protest, and though it was of a poor, pixelated quality, it was him.

"Where did you get this?" Lucas asked.

"Took it down from Orwell. Actually, I took down all the ones I could find in the area." Stachu reached into his pocket and pulled out a handful of papers, all with Lucas's face on them and the words *"Se Busca"* [Wanted] in bold at the top. "But not only you, comrade." Stachu pulled out a wanted picture of himself.

"The burglary?" Lucas asked. He wondered why the Catalan wouldn't just find him and put a bullet in his head instead of notifying the police. The whole thing reeked of suspicion if not entrapment, but Lucas went along with it anyway.

Stachu gestured with embarrassment to the trunk. "Which is why, comrade—"

"Don't call me *comrade!*" Lucas snapped.

"Which is why, brother," he corrected himself, "I need to get out of this country, and fast!"

Stachu nervously lit a cigarette and offered Lucas one out of the pack. Lucas shook his head and huffed; he felt he'd been dragged into this mess for no reason at all. He wasn't thinking about the consequences of a police brawl, but rather regretting having met Stachu and involving himself with a man whom he hardly knew.

"So, what do you want from me then?" Lucas asked.

"I want you to help me get out of this country," Stachu answered in a lowered voice.

"Maybe I should be making a run, too?" Lucas joked.

"Listen, Łukasz, this is serious. I have cash, lots of it. Everything has been sold, and I know where he is. I received news of him today." Lucas looked at him with suspicion, gritting his teeth and feeling his eye twitch. He was starting to feel this was some game Stachu was playing. *This time it better lead to the Catalan,* he thought.

"I have no passport," Stachu said, "and I'm in a hurry! This is going to sound absurd, but I need you to take me back to Poland."

"To Poland?"

"To Poland," Stachu repeated. "I need you to take me there."

"How?"

"On an airplane."

"On an airplane?!"

"Yes, on an airplane." Stachu gestured to his trunk.

"In that thing?" Stachu nodded. "Let me get this straight—you want me to take you as a passenger in your own trunk on an airplane to Warsaw?"

"The flight is only two or three hours; I could handle it. I used to live in a—"

"You've been drinking way too much of that antifreeze wine."

"I'll give you five thousand euros," Stachu said, desperation tinging his voice. Lucas was now listening, but he didn't answer just yet. "Seven thousand euros?" Stachu implored, making Lucas laugh. "Ten thousand big ones?!"

"You're a funny guy," Lucas said. "You live out of a trunk but have that kind of money to hand out like hot meals at a shelter."

"I'll help you if you help me, brother."

"Listen, *brother*," Lucas spat, nostrils flaring like a wild animal. "Europe is open. International travel is easy and cheap. There are no borders. Just drive yourself over there or get someone to drive you."

"It will take a few days and I need to get there now! They're closing in on me, brother!"

"Well, that's not my problem, *brother*! And thanks for informing me about my wanted mug in the neighborhood. For now, I'll manage to hide until things simmer down." Lucas side-glanced and flipped his sweater's hood over his head. He put his hands into his coat pockets and walked away.

"Yeah, go on and hide yourself in a pile of garbage!" Stachu shouted.

"It's an honest day's work," Lucas shouted back, without turning around.

15
Break the Banks

The alleyway leading to the Black Arrow was so narrow and full of people that there was no way to pass through but to plow ahead forcefully. When Lucas finally worked his way to the entrance, Antonio nodded him in, the bouncer's body still surrendering to gravity. The concertgoers would normally be directed to the cash box managed by Angela, a member of the Arrow. Seeing how Lucas was a "high-ranking" member of the organization—he once quipped with Noguerra that such titles reminded him of Communist China—he was waved in preferentially and exempted from paying any sort of entrance fee.

It was Saturday night, the Break the Banks Festival, the Arrow's much-anticipated all-weekend blowout of binge drinking and dissenting. Heavily publicized in Barcelona's seedy underbelly, the event hosted punk bands from all over Europe. The first big act was to start at 11:00 P.M., but some lesser-known bands were opening, already contributing to the ebb and flow of tattooed bodies oozing adrenaline and scabrous facial piercings.

Buzzing and well over capacity, the Arrow was Barcelona's dark decompression chamber. Once inside the cavelike and smoke-drenched venue, the world of subversion and subculture replaced the mundane and the mainstream. One of the acts, called Dirty Knuckles, was performing on a tight and low stage, a disorderly Belgian crew of four "handicapped" musicians whose drummer was the least "handicapped" as he couldn't play the drums. The statuary of amps and speakers on both sides of the stage howled feedback amid the lead singer's grungy, distorted riffs. He struck out middle fingers between songs and spat beer into the crowd when not spewing punk-rock plasma from his grisly voice box. The bass player growled out barely legible yet harsh antiauthoritarian slogans. This motley and mental crew transformed the appalling into appealing; made complete ugliness into grotesque beauty. The performance was an onslaught but also a particularly engaging neurosis.

Lucas eased through the manic crowd until he reached the bar. The floor under him was sticky, and the rub-rail's padding was carved up in some places while in others, it bore cigarette burn marks. These festering wounds from the many years of neglect—justifiably atmospheric and characteristic of dive bars—had never healed in the sewage pipe of society, where not only human waste wound up but the resentful anti-Capitalists.

When he placed his elbows on the bar, a familiar sight from the countertop caught his eye. He cleared away an empty beer glass and saw a flyer with his promotional photo of Bile

Helmet. He spotted Frank the Machine's machine gun in the photo and wondered if he had brought his toy with him that night. He hoped not.

Laia, who was adeptly pouring vodka into a line of seven shot glasses, called out Lucas's name from the other end of the bar, and with how the room was shaking from the din, it seemed like pure luck her shouting even reached his ears. He looked up and returned the greeting with a blank expression. He turned around to face the crowd and see what the night's fuss was all about. He lit a cigarette, privately scrutinizing all the degenerates and wannabe rebels. Before the tall glass of beer touched the coaster, he turned and grabbed it from the bartender's hand. To manage his big crowd anxiety, he took out a pill and popped it into his mouth, following the pill with a long swig from his beer. He then removed earplugs from their packaging and inserted them into his ears.

Frank the Machine poked his head out from the brooding scrum and managed to push through. He approached Lucas, greeted him with a head nod, and claimed a small fragment of bar next to him with his broad shoulders. He leaned forward, trying to get the bartender's attention with a, "Hello, Sweetie! Hello, *Sen-Yo-Rita!*" in his drolly Irish accent.

"Place is nuts!" he yelled in Lucas's ear.

"What?!"

"Nuts!"

"No, just a beer is fine," Lucas yelled. Frank chuckled.

Frank finally ordered and leaned back against the rail. When the drinks arrived, he glanced mischievously at Lucas, removed a vial, and dropped one small pink pill into his glass. He then nudged Lucas, put on a big, fake smile, and handed him his drink. Lucas grabbed it with pleasure, clinked glasses with Frank, and took a huge gulp. He turned back to see a man crowd surfing over the mosh pit as if he were Jesus on the cross carried over a sea of people.

"The Ebola Offensive is up next!" Frank the Machine shouted.

"What?!" Lucas yelled. Frank rolled his eyes and didn't repeat himself. "Did you bring your machine gun, General *Franco?*"

"My what?"

"Machine gun?!" Lucas yelled.

"No way, man! Stoolies!"

"What?"

"Probably head-banging in the crowd! Informers!"

"Informers?"

"Yeah, informers!"

Lucas heard only "informers," but it was enough to make him worry. He spotted Laia in the distance standing in the door frame of the bar's back room. She called Lucas over with a wave of her hand. Lucas nodded goodbye, finished the last of his beer, and began pushing through the crowd in her direction.

In a small closet filled with mops, brooms, a sink, and chemical detergents, there stood a table under a naked light bulb. Seeing Lucas appear in the door, Xavi stopped talking, turned his chair around, and sat down straddling it. He placed his arms on the chair's back and looked over Lucas as if he had done something wrong. Laia leaned back against a shelf full of rolls of toilet paper and unused beer glasses. Her right hand was cupping her left elbow; her left hand was holding a cigarette. She was taking nervous pulls from it while eyeing Lucas.

Sitting across from Xavi was a girl Lucas had never seen or met before. She wore long dreadlocks, a black handkerchief wrapped around her neck like a cowboy in a Western, and a black Dead Kennedys T-shirt. Standing over her, he was immediately drawn to the tattoo on her right forearm, a familiar design he had seen somewhere but couldn't remember where.

Lucas dropped into an empty chair. It felt like an interrogation was imminent. In that moment, he felt a surge of strength within him that needed to be released through movement. His knee started bouncing and his fingers started tapping against the table. He didn't know where this feeling came from, since he hadn't seen Frank the Machine drug him prior to being called to the meeting.

"This is Anastasia," Laia introduced. "She's from Germany and leads the sister wing of the Arrow in Berlin." Lucas greeted her with a handshake, gripping her hand a bit too firmly. After releasing it, he noticed that his fingers and palm were clammy and warm. He glanced down at her forearm and looked over the tattoo. She, too, curiously looked down at where he was gazing. He felt something not right happening inside of him.

"We're going to plant another device," Laia said matter-of-factly. Lucas didn't say a word. He looked at Anastasia, then at Xavi, then back at Laia. "We decided to scrap doing it at their annual corporate picnic gathering," she added. "We want to target her specifically. We know she cooperates with the police, that she paid a nice bribe for the police to take back the center; and of course, let's not forget the fraud case where millions of account holders' savings disappeared into thin air."

Lucas grunted and leaned back in the rickety wooden chair, clasping his fingers over his head as a look of surprise crossed his face—the body language of an uncomfortable listener hearing something that was too dangerous, difficult, and doubtful, not to mention stupid. Anastasia lit a cigarette and fixed a few beads in her hair. As Laia continued speaking, Anastasia kept her cold aluminum eyes fixed on the ashtray in front of her, silently sculpting the cigarette's ash into a cone, a sullen look on her face.

"With the help of Anastasia's hackers," Laia continued, "we found out that she drives a Mercedes Benz, license plate number—" She stopped, wedged the cigarette in the corner of her mouth, squinting her eyes from the smoke. She pulled out a piece of paper from her pocket. "—B 2744 HN. She parks the car in Basement 3, section E45. Here are the surveillance photos we stole from their security database."

"Wait a minute," Lucas interrupted, leaning forward and placing his elbows onto the table. "We're going to plant a bomb on her car? And how do you plan on getting into the Rocafort Building? There is security everywhere. The entrance is even guarded by two men with assault rifles. This appears to be one of your foolish plans again, Laia."

"Guarded now," Xavi said, leaning in, also planting his elbows on the table, "but before you fucked up, anyone could have slid in there and ratcheted her in the driver's seat. There was no security there a month ago, Lucas! And we could only assume it's because they found the undetonated bomb at the picnic." Lucas was ready to turn Xavi into his flesh-filled punching bag, but he didn't say anything

"We have an inside person," said Laia, calming both down. Everybody turned to her, surprised that this information wasn't made available earlier. "It's Angela."

"Angela?" Lucas asked. "Angela at the door?"

"She works in the Rocafort Building as a cleaner," Laia said. "Actually, she works right on Alba's floor and sees her every day."

"We have her security access card," Anastasia finally spoke. "Angela's going to drive in. They won't suspect anything because they know her face. Once inside the parking lot, the bomb will come out, be activated, and stuck onto her car. Our hackers will erase the security footage right after. No sign of us coming in, no sign of us leaving."

"Let me guess, the gas tank, right?" Lucas remarked, trying to be funny. "Like in the movies?"

"Shut your mouth, Lucas!" Xavi yelled, pointing his finger at Lucas from across the table. Lucas was enraged and his knee started knocking anxiously against the table's leg.

"So, who's going to stick the bomb on the gas tank?" he asked. Xavi, Laia, and Anastasia exchanged curious glances.

"Who do you think?" said Xavi. "You're the newest member of the Arrow, and you still need to prove yourself. You're gonna go in with Angela."

"Me?" Lucas exclaimed. "You've gotta be kidding me! No way! I did it last time. This time I'm not doing it. It didn't even go off!"

"It didn't go off," Xavi grated, "because, as I said—you fucked up! You sabotaged the attack!"

"You're the one who forgot to put a battery in the detonator, dumbass!"

Lucas and Xavi stood up and got into each other's faces. Laia threw down her cigarette, thinking, *Here we go again.* In the end, neither of them checked his ego at the door, and no one could stop the brawl from erupting in the closet.

Xavi picked up a broomstick, swung it, and broke it over Lucas's head; Lucas reeled from the blow but flipped the table at Xavi. He then swung a punch and hit him the same way his trainer had taught him many years ago. Anastasia fell back in her chair. Laia jumped in once again, this time succeeding in separating the two men from each other.

"Enough!" she yelled, grabbing Lucas's shirt collar and pushing Xavi back with her free hand. Lucas stepped away and brushed himself off. He was looking past Laia into Xavi's eyes, arms hanging and fists balled up. He was twitching and eagerly wanting to beat him, once and for all, to a bleeding pulp.

Anastasia, the only one in the closet who was calm and collected, got up from the floor as if nothing had happened. She picked up her chair and dusted the seat, then sat down and waited for the meeting to resume. Laia put the table back where it was and returned the ashtray to its rightful place. She offered Anastasia another cigarette to replace the one she had lost in the fracas. Anastasia was ready to say something, but was visibly gathering her thoughts while lighting her cigarette. She trained her eyes back on the ashtray and began rapping the table with her knuckles. Everybody watched her movements, anticipating harsh reprimand. It was evident she was the brains behind Berlin's operations and saw how Barcelona could use some too.

"Lucas," Anastasia said, calmly and thoughtfully, "in the interest of finding out your parents' murderer, I'd buckle down and get the job done." Lucas looked at her with a confused look, wondering how they'd found out. "We have personal details of the man you are looking for," she continued, "name, address, unofficial 'workplace.' I must admit, it wasn't easy finding this drug dealer of yours, as he does a better job hiding himself than an Italian Camorrista wanted for extortion and murder. But we have everything on him, from his shoe size down to whom he fucked yesterday, and we will, unfortunately, work on a quid pro quo basis—that is, you plant the device, and we hand him to you on a platter. Then, you do whatever you want with him." She finally said what she had to say and leaned back in her chair with a sadistic grin on her face. "Defraud him all you want...or maybe torture him." She pulled greedily on her cigarette and removed a shred of tobacco caught in her teeth. "Even in this room, if you want. I'm sure Xavi won't mind. Maybe even kill him, which is what I assume you want to do considering what he had done to your—"

"Don't even utter their names!" Lucas spouted, his sweaty face red from anger. "Don't even think about them!" He swung open the door with hostility, and before storming off, he looked back, ready to share a few nice parting words. Rage was coiled up inside and convulsing him. Laia approached Lucas and wrapped her arms around him. She tried to kiss him, but he turned his cheek. In that moment, Laia exchanged a sinister glance with Xavi. Anastasia butted in between them and bolted out of the storage room.

Xavi's gaze was encouraging Laia to keep it up, to at least hold Lucas under her spell for a bit longer. Judging by how Lucas was against every tactic they proposed, it didn't seem hopeful for him to remain in the organization for long. Laia looked away from Xavi and tried to kiss Lucas again. This time their lips met.

Hardly did Xavi leave the room when Laia and Lucas started kissing again. He pushed her against the shelf to show that he wanted it rough and to make her want it rough too. She wrapped her right leg around his waist. The heavy music from outside was pounding the walls. The sound of glasses clinked against one another, and one even fell and crashed to the ground. With unsettling desire mixing with fury, he grabbed her shirt and tore it off from the front. He kissed her neck and ripped off her bra and threw it into the sink. She moaned once or twice that she liked it like that, and that she wanted it that way, rough and hard. He then unzipped her jeans after unzipping his own, pulled them both down, and went inside her, thrusting vigorously, until someone took the closet for a bathroom and walked in on them. It was Moco from Bile Helmet. "We're on in five minutes. What are you doing *now* that you can't do after the show?"

* * *

A surplus of buzzing electricity, fists hammering the air, and the slaps of amped up strings. Lucas, however, felt nothing but his icy, numb face sloughing off like dead skin. In front of the stage was Paco, who had arrived a few minutes before Lucas walked out of the back room. A few more pills brought by his pal, booze to wash it all down, and the volatile and vulnerable boy was stripped down to his tank top, pants, and one shoe. Sweat was gliding off his body like rainwater. He quickly learned how to enjoy "dancing" full-body contact with the anarchists as the loud and heavy music pushed and pulled him around the mosh pit. Deep down inside he hated them and wished they'd all drop dead, just like how he would drop dead any minute now.

When he found himself on stage with Frank the Machine, the two of them—both tanked out of their minds— held screaming matches in each other's faces while the band played their hit songs. Xavi stood behind the bar with his arms crossed, glowering at Lucas from a distance, ready to come down on him like a ton of bricks, the dead man he was. Laia stood behind him, her head down and hair in disarray. She managed to knit up the shirt he had ripped off her, mending it back in a way that seemed suitable for the lowbrow event.

Lucas leaped off Superman-style from a speaker, and when he belly-flopped onto the crowd, he was quickly let down and given a bottle of vodka. He tipped it high in the air and took it all down. His world started spinning out of control. But Lucas didn't collapse onto the bar's cold and dirty floor—he plunged into water, or better, into the clay pit where he had made friends with a dolphin.

* * *

The gentle animal waved its tail and swam in a circle. Lucas finally buoyed up to the surface and gasped for air. The sunlight was unable to break through the thick clouds. He looked around in a panic and saw nobody on the clay pit's beach, none of the families that came at weekends to while away the summer heat. That was when he saw his father, mother, and Thiago floating face down on the water. He desperately swam over to try to rescue and resuscitate them, but when he popped his head back under, he saw the dolphin swimming around and playing with something. This time it was prodding with its snout and whacking with its tail a large mass. When Lucas got closer to the dolphin, he realized it was pushing around the Catalan's lifeless body.

16
Meeting with Noguerra

Lucas awoke to a cold splash of water jarring him. He wiped his face and focused his eyes on the figure across the table— it was Noguerra, the city's top cop, lowering the glass he had just emptied. His thick, aged frame sunk in his chair while he smoked calmly, thinking, rubbing his thumb over his lips, enjoying his cigarette and Lucas's unraveling. His foot was propped up on a chair pulled close to him, and an elbow was planted on his bent knee. One or two buttons from his shirt were undone.

Lucas looked himself over. Blood and vomit stained his tank top, and there was a pee stain around his crotch. His knuckles were bloodied. One bare foot and one boot, shoelaces untied. He felt a swollen lip in the same vicinity of a throbbing tooth.

Burning his eyes right into Lucas, Noguerra went from all smirks to anger and disappointment. He put his cigarette out in the ashtray, leaned forward, and punched Lucas in the face. The impact of fist on face blew Lucas back, then sprung him forward. "You know, I'm sorry for doing this," Noguerra said, leaning back in his chair. "One of my guys is posted at the door, and he's expecting me to rough you up a bit over an incident."

"An incident?" Lucas turned his face to the side to spit out blood.

"Told me you guys didn't play very nicely after the protest."

Lucas looked up, squinted at the door, and when it came into focus, he saw in the narrow sheet of meshed-glass an officer with a black eye and a bandage around his head. The cop was peeking through and smiling his sour smile, hoping the chief would let him in on the fun.

"That's him, all right," Lucas agreed. "Didn't want to be beaten up or dragged back here and thrown at your feet for you to do it. Had a lot of those lately. Let's just say that compared to some of the meatheads at the Arrow, your guys' punches are substandard in force and accuracy."

"How's her punch?"

"Whose punch?"

"Your lady friend's."

"I couldn't say."

"I could. She could deliver a mean one. She's small but Jesus she's feisty. Probably could put me down. I remember when she was once in the holding cell here, the beginning of the long and outspoken mess she's currently in. She got into it with a busty Corsican prostitute who had just stabbed one of her Juans who'd taken out his anger on her in bed. Well, let's just say the Corsican was transferred on a stretcher after Laia laid hands on her."

"She asserts herself when she has to."

"I heard about how things are progressing, by the way," Noguerra said, changing tones and topics. "Or not progressing...I got my foot soldiers telling me things."

"What are they telling you?"

"I'll give you sixty seconds to tell me first. If not, I'll have to stick one on you again." They both glanced over at the cop standing at the door, still grinning and waiting for Noguerra to wave him into the room.

"Warming up to Laia has worked so far, but the relationship is strained, to say the least. I've gained her trust, and we have a relationship loosely based on sex and similar political convictions. I've successfully infiltrated the group, but my days are numbered—they're starting to put two and two together. More disturbing is that she is starting to go ape shit in her tactics. I believe Xavi is calling the shots, though. But Xavi is another story. He's a bit more suspicious, and he wants me to plant the device again as he believes it's the only way I could prove I'm not a mole."

"This needs to end," Noguerra said firmly.

"I need to get to him first."

"Get it done, or I'll be sending you back to the Skulls. They've been asking around."

"And what has been said?"

"Nothing. There's no trace of you in Barcelona."

"Good. Because if you force me to go back, they'll kill me," Lucas emphasized with a deadpan expression on his face. "At least let me go back knowing that the Catalan is dead."

Noguerra lit another cigarette. "If you ever find him." He sympathetically tossed Lucas the pack. Lucas lit up and took a few quick puffs. "The Arrow is pushing the boat out too far,"

Noguerra said. "If this bomb doesn't explode a second time, they'll probably hang you by the balls, but if it does, we'll be inheriting another huge mess."

"I won't plant it and I'll make sure it won't be planted," Lucas assured. "I'll have enough on her to lock her up by then." Lucas leaned forward, put out his cigarette, and rested his arms on the table. "Do you think I was a lousy cop?" he asked. "I was a rookie…but my rookie mistake was being a good cop."

"I only care about what you do here, not there. In fact, I don't even care about you at all."

"I got into the police force before my whole family was wiped out by cops and robbers, and only God Himself knows who is who. Policing where I'm from," Lucas reinforced, "is done differently than policing here. There is impunity and a sense of lawlessness back home. But me … I will always follow my gut feeling. The squad that came down on my brother, those Skull bastards got what they deserved. I'm glad some of them will be sharing a cell with the same people they locked up from my brother's gang."

"You must have known what was coming to him. You could have stopped him, right? He had a splendid left foot, I heard, but a private militia at his disposal. And you want to defend scum like that?!"

"Like everybody, he deserved to have his day in court, and even though I'm not religious in any way, I'm sure he had to stand before God on the day he was gunned down to answer for his actions."

Noguerra gestured to the door and in came the vengeful officer with a glass of water. After holding it for a few beats, the officer finally placed it on the table. Lucas looked up at him. He could see both black eyes and a bandage around his head. A busted lip and broken blood vessels in his left eye. He looked like he'd been mauled by a tiger and lived to tell the tale. The officer and his wounded pride stared Lucas down with hostility.

Lucas looked at the glass and desperately crinkled his parched lips. He picked up the glass and brought it up to his face. "Is there a shortage of water here too?" The officer grabbed the cup from Lucas's hand, aimed his lips over it, and let fall a gob of spit. He placed it back on the table and smiled like the Joker.

"I don't want a red carpet laid out," Lucas said, "just something a bit less contaminated."

"Seeing how you went off last night, I should be sticking a fire hose down your throat and blasting you with water." Noguerra pushed his cup to Lucas, who grabbed it and flipped it head over heels, letting the last drops fall with gusto right into his open and dry mouth. "You hear from Ricardo?" asked Noguerra, waving the cop out of the room.

"He's the least of my worries," Lucas said, placing the cup back on the table. "Something tells me that he'll rear his ugly head sooner or later. He calls me and makes empty threats. Tries to get me to hand the Catalan over to him—he wants money from him and is looking for him too." Lucas leaned in and looked at Noguerra. "She'll be behind bars soon, mark my words, and the Catalan, his ending won't be a happy one, either."

"It shocks me how well you wear all these hats," Noguerra said. "Anarchist, ex-cop, drug dealer, photographer..." He took a puff of his cigarette. " ... Brazilian, Polish, punk rocker, *chatarrero*... murderer."

17
The Tsar's Snow Globes

Alba picked up her office phone and began dialing. After she pressed about four digits, her right eye started twitching, she bit her lip, her hands got sweaty, and her breathing increased. She quickly hung up, thinking that it probably wasn't the best of ideas to call the number on the business card. She leaned back in her chair and crossed her legs, then crossed them again. She didn't know if she was calling Lucas to set up another meeting, or if she was calling the number to demand answers for all the questions she had about the photo she had found. It certainly didn't make things better that the photo of the girl sat on her desk in front of her. For how much it burned in her thoughts, and how severely she had been tormented by its existence, the girl might as well have been sitting right in front of her, taunting her to find out who she was and why she was so important to her.

Alba slid open her desk drawer, about to drop the photo and the business card inside, when she stopped and put them both into her handbag. She pulled out a real estate brochure for properties in Mallorca. She wanted to buy Amelia and Martin a house as a wedding present. After looking at a few beachside villas, she became irritated that none of them had a tennis court—Amelia was once an under-eighteen tennis champion. She was also annoyed that the photos of the swimming pools were bluer than in real life.

She got up from her office chair and walked across the room, folding up the brochure in her hands. She dropped it into the trash bin and stopped to look out the window. Just the other day the plaza had been full of angry protesters demanding that she burn at the stake or serve a very long prison sentence. Today, the square was empty, apart from a few city workers sweeping up discarded posters and picket signs, and a small group of tourists following a guide who was holding the Chinese flag over her head.

Alba checked her watch and realized that it was time for her lunch meeting with Bet, an old friend from college who was the head of a law firm, and who was also helping her in her legal case. Alba wasn't looking forward to the meeting, as Bet mostly bragged about the hot and young Andalusian men she was fulfilling her fantasies with down on the Gold Coast. In the end, she decided she would go, but would stay for only a single alcohol-free cocktail.

* * *

On Via Diagonal the traffic was appalling, and Alba was losing her patience. The drivers in the city lacked audacity and fearlessness, she thought. Crawling in and out of lanes in her Mercedes, she got fed up with the road conditions and thoughtlessly whipped the steering wheel around to turn into the nearest side street. She didn't know what compelled her to react this way, yet it was better to be moving slowly in a fast-moving machine than sitting completely idle in one surrounded by clunkers fit for the scrapyard. No sooner did she make the turn, than she saw Lucas and a girl walking in and out of a shop. Surprised by the sight of him, she quickly pulled into an empty handicap space.

Apart from the worries the photo brought her, there were also thoughts of Lucas that had been pleasantly running in her mind all day. It was a real treat, and total coincidence, to see him in the flesh rather than in her fantasies. She looked at the shop he and the girl were going into and shifted her eyes up to its sign. She took out the business card from her handbag and was surprised to see that its logo was the same—Horst's World of Antiques.

Laia and Lucas were picking up boxes from a truck parked out front and carrying them into the shop. They were dividing their attention between carefully walking with the heavy load and arguing. Alba could tell they were fighting, even though she couldn't hear, because their faces were quite expressive, with Laia furrowing her brows and her face getting redder than Lucas's. Had their hands been free they might have pantomimed their anger. She put the window down a bit to hear them, and to light a cigarette.

"Of course, it's from the police," Lucas said, referring to the photo Stachu had shown him. They passed through the shop's door carrying brassware from the Ottoman Empire. The items inside were rattling a dull metallic chime. "Xavi shouldn't have thrown that Molotov cocktail. What was he thinking? I didn't sign up for this."

"They're looking for you because you attacked a pig," Laia retorted. "And about the protest—you didn't run with us to the safe house but chose your own path. I didn't make you attend the political rally. Standing up for your community requires tremendous effort and commitment. And besides," she continued, "it might be fake. I checked on their wanted database and there's no picture of you there. There are pictures of all those criminals who have committed crimes out of necessity, people who steal food just to provide for their families…but the corrupt white-collar criminals who steal millions are—"

"Enough!" he yelled out, at which point they dropped a medium-sized box that crashed to the ground. They heard glass break and looked at each other, realizing what they'd done. Lucas knelt and opened the box. Inside were snow globes; Horst had even written, "Be CAREFUL with THIS box, Please," on its lid.

"Were these the ones Horst told us about?" Laia asked with regret. "The ones he dreamed the Tsar of Russia giving him?" Lucas nodded. A few were broken and their stale water started to soak through. Horst appeared in the shop's door with a hot cup of tea, holding it with two hands and sipping thoughtfully. When he saw what had happened, he wasn't even angry. He waved them back to the garbage bin on the sidewalk, telling them to dump the ones that were broken but to keep the ones still intact. They walked over to the bin holding the soiled box in a way that prevented it from ripping apart. The box falling had been the full stop to their argument.

As they were removing the broken dome shards and placing the pieces into the trash bin, Laia let out a painful hiss and began sucking on her thumb. Lucas removed a tissue from his back pocket and offered it to her. She wiped her finger with it and threw the tissue into the garbage bin before Horst came out of the shop with antiseptic and an adhesive bandage.

* * *

Lucas plopped down on a chair in the back room of the shop. He knew the photo of him was a fake, but he still tried to get the Arrow to react, after which he would catch Laia off guard. He was exhausted but more confused as to why Stachu made him out to be a wanted criminal. He was starting to suspect something, that maybe Stachu was working for the Catalan, either contracted to steer Lucas away from the drug baron or to bring Lucas right to him.

It was quiet for a moment as he contemplated several different solutions to this problem. Finally, he came up with an idea that wasn't exactly perfect, but which would at least produce a net result, one that could potentially open other doors or offer up other clues to his whereabouts.

Lucas watched Laia wipe clean the last snow globe. She looked at her watch, grabbed her coat in a hurry, and kissed Lucas goodbye before leaving the shop. Lucas picked up the snow globe, ready to launch it against the wall. When he realized he was getting angry for no reason at all, like his father used to, he sat back down in the chair and began staring into the dome's snowy, fake world. Lucas knew Laia was going to Xavi's house. He also knew she was cheating on him with Xavi, but he never really cared to bring it up. She probably knew Lucas was also not being honest with her. *Time is running out,* he thought. Laia would soon start to see things more clearly, if she hadn't already. He had to act and find the Catalan before the Catalan found him.

Laia left the shop in a hurry and started down the street. Still sitting in the driver's seat, Alba followed her with her eyes, even when the young, rebellious girl walked by her car, staring right into it. But Laia couldn't see anything or anyone since Alba had tinted windows. Alba, however, was astonished by Laia's familiar face. She tried remembering where she could have seen the young woman, but nothing came to mind. As she was now certain where Lucas worked, Alba thought she should try calling the shop to get a hold of him. She called the number on the business card.

The phone next to the cash register started ringing and Horst, who was polishing a fancy wooden picture frame of a replica of da Vinci's *Lady With an Ermine,* gestured to Lucas to pick it up.

"Horst's Antiques, how can I help you?"

Alba hesitated. "Umm," she sat up and brought the phone closer to her ear. "Hello, my name is…"

"I recognized your voice," Lucas said, cutting her off. Lucas glanced around at Horst, who was now rearranging a few books. "Did you get your knee fixed up?" He spotted a white cat at the shop's door pawing at the window. He would have chased it away but it was Horst's. He pulled out a carton of milk from the small fridge under the cash register, walked around the counter, and crouched down near the door to fill an empty bowl.

"Yes, I did," she answered, feeling her face turn red. "Nothing too serious." Alba hiked up her skirt and looked at her knee. She delicately ran her hand over the bruise, but then moved her hand up and began fingering a run in her stockings up to her thigh. "I was wondering if…"

"Where are you right now?" Lucas asked, straight to the point. He opened the door to let the cat in.

"Where am I? Um, I'm just at—" she looked around, "— still back at the office."

As Lucas stood up from feeding the cat, he saw Alba sitting in her car. She was smoking a cigarette and ashing outside. He looked at her and thought: why is she calling and what does she want? The feeling of a warm surprise came first, then one of curiosity as to why she had lied, followed by a sense of disquiet that her car parked in front of the shop, with her inside, was beyond coincidence.

"Why don't you come by my place after work?" Lucas said. He peeked out the window once more from behind the counter and saw her looking at her watch.

She agreed without any forethought. After hanging up the phone, she called Bet to tell her that she still had a stack of reports to read on her desk. Coincidentally, Bet too was still back at her office.

Lucas hung up the phone and glanced at his watch. He saw that the cash register was open. It showed a few hundred euros in notes. Horst had a customer that day who bought a renaissance marble table that was pretty expensive. He shut the cash drawer and quickly finished sweeping. He thought how lucky Laia was to be running the Black Arrow bar rent-free because the basement in which the bar was located was Horst's other property in Orwell. He, too, had been an activist once before becoming a professor, a rebel who took a sledgehammer to the Berlin Wall. He even had a few pieces of the wall at home on his mantel. The offering of his property to Laia for free was because he saw in her what he used to be. To express her gratitude, Laia came by the shop weekly to help arrange books, dust old collectibles, and feed the cat. In recent months, Lucas took over as Laia was too busy.

Lucas went into the back room to pick up his camera bag as his shift had come to an end. While he was picking out a few books to read for the night, the doorbell chimed and two police officers entered. Horst greeted them politely and asked what he could do for them. They inquired about Lucas.

Lucas dodged out of the doorway. The shop's door and the backroom entrance were directly across from each other separated by a long hall full of bookshelves. He stuck his head out and saw one officer pull out a photo of him. *What's going on?* he thought. Since only Noguerra knew about Lucas, it would only make sense that regular street cops were looking for him, perhaps for Ricardo's fake credit card business, which might have connected Lucas to the crooked Panamanian. Maybe they wanted to question him about his involvement with the Arrow. He realized that it was the cop he'd had a fight with, the one from the alleyway. He was looking for Lucas to administer a proper beating of his own.

Lucas looked around for another way to escape the shop. He found a window, opened it, and began climbing out, but suddenly he overheard the end of their conversation. He returned to the door frame and peeked out. Horst was shaking his head with a bewildered look on his face. The cops asked him if he knew Lucas Brodowski, and if he ever worked at the antique shop. Horst was an old, little German man but he spoke perfect Spanish—a level he had reached by reading and re-reading Don Quixote—and with a Castilian lisp that made him sound even more convincing, he said, "No, officers, this boy you're asking me about does not work here and, to be honest, I've never seen him before." When the officers finally left, Lucas walked out of the back room and went straight to the window to see if they had gone. He breathed a sigh of relief and turned to Horst.

"Why did you say you didn't know me?" asked Lucas. Horst continued counting the till. "This is for the hourglass," Horst said, sticking out his hand. "I managed to sell it." He handed Lucas one hundred percent of its price—three thousand euros. Lucas was taken aback. He humbly accepted the money from the old man, said thanks, and left the antique shop.

18
Quijotic

Alba looked up at the balcony and saw a rusting exercise bike, a salon hair dryer chair, but no washing machine. She wondered if the washing machine had already been brought to the scrapyard, or if Lucas had repaired it and included it in his inventory of other salvaged washing machines. With five washing machines cluttering up his loft (she remembered as she had counted last time, just to be sure), she was sure he was able to wash his dirty clothes in a different one every day of the week but wear nothing on weekends when she came around. She also spotted a tapering *matrioshka* of broken flower pots, all springing an ugly tangle of withering stalks. When Alba looked down at her hands, a smile appeared on her face—she was giving Lucas something fresher, an already sprouting bamboo in a wooden box. This, she thought, could add a bit of color, if not life, to his dusty and disordered loft.

Will he come out to greet me? she wondered. She even closed her eyes and imagined it, yet Lucas didn't appear. She was overthinking the visit, and it was foolish of her to have such high expectations for somebody she'd met once. She only wanted him physically. But still, even if he were standing there, she wouldn't be able to see him because of the daylight's glare in the window's glass.

The truth was, Lucas *was* standing there. He even took a close-up photo of Alba's face staring up at the balcony. He zoomed out and got her standing in her stylish beige coat, red heels, brown satin hair and that wooden bamboo box in her arm. Around her shoulder was her purse and, in her hand, a shopping bag. Since she didn't lock her things in the trunk of her car, the items inside the bag, he thought, must have been expensive and not worth the risk for the local smash-and-grab thieves who targeted the occasional luxury vehicle parked in the neighborhood.

With his eye still in the viewfinder, Lucas tilted the camera upwards and focused across the building. Startled, he lowered the camera when he saw a woman standing on Esme's balcony, looking down at the street. She was observing Alba. Lucas stepped back from the window but continued gazing at the girl. She wore ripped jeans and had on a black spaghetti strap tank top. He raised the camera to his eye once more to have a better look. To his shock and surprise, it was Anastasia, the girl who ran Berlin's sister organization of the Black Arrow. Lucas lowered the camera, completely bewildered, and thought about this strange coincidence, but stopping him from puzzling over it way too much was Alba walking towards the main door.

Alba pressed the button under his apartment number and the buzzer sounded, loud and long. The door unlatched and she entered, braving several flights of stairs as the elevator was out of service, again. When she came to the door, she thought she was about to pass out and that she might have mistaken his apartment. But it was indeed the right one, and the knocker was something of a cast-iron hand holding what was supposed to be a crystal ball, also cast iron. It was very medieval and mystical looking, as though she were entering the home of a fortune teller. She thought about having something similar on her door despite it hardly complementing her home's style, which she was very particular about, a carbon-copy model taken straight from the pages of a luxury real estate brochure.

She passed the bamboo box from one hand to the other, and right before she lifted the hand to drop its heavy ball, Lucas swung open the door with a welcoming grin. He looked at her, then at the bamboo box, and then down at her knee. He stared at the bruise longer than usual, more than on the gift she came bearing. Embarrassed, she thought he was staring at the run in her stocking, so she discreetly pulled down the skirt with the hand holding the shopping bag.

"No damage?" he asked enthusiastically.

"No damage," she said, sticking it out and bending it. "This is for you, by the way. A little 'thank you' for helping me out the other day."

"Will go with my Japanese divider," he said. "I could definitely use some color in here too."

"Color and air. It's also self-regenerating."

"What does that mean?" he asked with a funny smirk. "Things are dying in my loft?"

"It *is* a graveyard … for electronics," she quipped.

Lucas grabbed the bamboo, moved out of the way, and asked her to come in. He asked to take her coat but she politely refused as she could stay for only a short while. He ushered her to the familiar couch on which sat Apollo, a permanent accessory to a temporary piece of furniture. Lucas placed the box on the washing machine that had been on the balcony earlier, while Alba placed the shopping bag and her purse on the armchair next to the couch. She sat down, crossed her legs while keeping her posture straight, and started petting Neymar.

"I have coffee or wine," Lucas yelled out from the kitchen. "Which do you prefer?"

"I thought this was a coffee break?" she asked loudly.

"I never said anything about a coffee break," he said. "I'm giving you an option, though…maybe to make it a wine visit, something more exciting." Though she couldn't see, she knew he had said those words with a subtle smirk on his face.

"Wine is fine," she said.

"Great choice!" Lucas said, already coming out of the kitchen with two mugs on a tray.

"I thought you said wine," she said, smiling.

"Yes, wine," he answered with a puzzled look on his face. "Do you want coffee instead?" He placed the tray onto the table. She looked down and saw a light red ring around the inside of both mugs. It was wine, and she tried not to laugh. It was also not the standard wine serving as the mugs had been filled almost to the brim, like it was grape juice. She found his lack of sophistication endearing.

"Oh, I see," he nodded slowly. "You only drink from wine glasses, right? With your pinky finger held out like this? Rinsing it in your mouth and spitting it out? Little fancy nips?"

"No, no," she said, laughing. "This is fine. I'm not a sommelier or anything."

"A what?"

"Never mind."

"Well then, *saluti tutti bello i brutti*," he said in a jovial manner.

"Italian, too?"

He shook his head. "My friend, Paco, taught me a few things in Italian. It means, 'cheers to the ugly and the beautiful.'" She looked at him with knit brows. *What a weird thing to say,* she thought. "It's something the Italians say, apparently. Something different than *Salud!*"

"Okay, I get it," she said, hardly convinced.

"The Spanish are so boring," he said sarcastically.

They both took a sip of the wine—she winced inwardly while Lucas exhaled with satisfaction. The wine was atrocious, and she wanted to spit it back out. Lucas took another sip and smiled. She didn't look at him for fear of being asked what she thought of Don Simon, if her refraining from any sort of commentary was already enough for him to figure out that it wasn't the kind she had in her cellar at home.

"Lucas," she said, "you should be drinking good wine— there's plenty of it out here." She grabbed her purse and took out her wallet, then removed a business card and handed it to Lucas. He grabbed it and froze. The business card's background was the same picture da Silva dropped when he made the death notification—the stone chapel in the vineyard.

"You didn't like the wine?" Alba asked, an embarrassed look crossing her face. "Our flagship product is ranked the best *tempranillo*." Lucas didn't say anything. "Well," she said, breaking the awkward silence, "it's not my company anymore as my husband took it over." Alba cleared her throat.

"I remember now," he finally said. "I think I've tried this brand before. It wasn't bad at all." Lucas was concealing his shock while engaging himself in a bit of mental arithmetic, trying to figure out how the photo connected Alba to his parents' murder. "Very tasty," Lucas lied, but he did to play it cool and to keep the conversation going.

Alba pulled out her smartphone and started showing him more photos of the vineyard while telling him about the company. She mentioned how many hectares they had, awards the company had won, and locations to where the wine was exported. She mentioned that its biggest customer was a Brazilian restaurant chain in Rio de Janeiro.

"Impressive, really nice," he commented with a note of absence in his voice. "The land, beautiful and…fertile," he said, hardly paying any more attention to the photos, replaying in his mind the day he'd been visited by the detective.

Alba put her phone in her purse and leaned back. She drank some more of the bad wine out of courtesy. To diffuse the awkward moment, she said she needed to use the bathroom. After she left the living room area, Lucas shot over to the bookshelf and began rummaging through some magazines, where he found the photo in question. Now he was positive—it was the same image. When he heard the toilet flush, he returned to the couch and sat back down.

"Was it really that bad?" she asked, coming out of the bathroom and taking her seat.

"Bad?"

"The wine?" she clarified. "By the look on your face… maybe it wasn't your preference, I guess."

"No, no, sorry," he snapped out of the trance. "There's just a similar place where my family and I once went on vacation. It was like a clay pit, like a massive pond where people bathe."

"What's this?" she asked, changing topics.

An old and large book sat on the table. It was so old that all vestiges of identifying marks had been rubbed off by time and overuse. It wasn't until Alba picked it up and flipped through the first few pages that she knew it was a classic. Inspired by how well Horst spoke Spanish, an old German man whose proficiency had been mastered in the few years his shop was set up in Barcelona, Lucas had found his old copy of *Don Quixote* and asked to borrow it. It was marked up everywhere, and the only thing that made it look like it was still in use were the little fluorescent markers sticking out, indicating that the book had been not only enjoyed but thoroughly dissected in detail, of every bit of old vocabulary or outdated grammar.

"I wanted to ask you something," Lucas said, leaning into Alba and flipping through some pages. "It's about my pronunciation." He cared very little about his pronunciation but wanted to buy some more time as his head was still reeling from the revelation. He grabbed the book from her lap and placed it on his. With his finger he found a particular passage.

"*'The clear waters of the brooks are my mirrors,'*" he began reading, "*'and to the trees and waters I make known my thoughts and charms. I am a fire afar off, a sword laid aside. Those whom I have inspired with love by letting them see me, I have by words undeceived....'*"

She noticed how he accentuated certain sounds and how he moved his lips. His lips, she thought, how she wanted them, how carefully she watched them. She leaned back as he continued reading, admiring him for reasons she couldn't pin down. His youthful beauty wasn't subtle but a crude machismo with a touch of suppressed sensitivity that attracted her.

"You have to try pronouncing things better," she said.

"Of course," he agreed. "I guess to be taken seriously here you have to try to sound like the locals, right?"

"That's why you should be practicing your Catalan too."

"Catalan, huh?"

"So, what's your story anyway?" she finally asked.

"What's my story?" he repeated, reluctant to say. Right when he was about to make up a lie, Alba's phone rang. She excused herself to answer it, gave a few stern orders, then quickly hung up.

"So?" she continued prodding.

"Come, I want to show you something," he said, standing up and grabbing her hand. He gently pulled her off the couch towards the curtain. The book fell off his lap onto the floor, arousing Neymar, who was sleeping in an empty rattan basket on an old record player. "This is where I told you I develop my prints," he said. "A dark room."

"A dark room? Looks more like a…I see now—a crystal ball on your door. So, this is your magical portal, huh? To the past or to the future?"

"To both," he said, trying to be funny. "Do I look like a wizard from Hogwarts to you?"

Lucas grabbed the curtain and whipped it around them. It was suddenly dark in the space between the door and the curtain. They stood listening to each other's breathing. He could vaguely make out the contours of her face, the lines of her nose and cheeks. He opened the door and they walked into another curtain. He whipped it out of the way and finally they entered the dark room.

The room plunged into a blood-red color that was emitted by a special bulb fixed against the wall above an old bathtub. Inside the tub, which was filled halfway with stagnant water, lay a stack of plastic trays. In the topmost tray were old photos curling up. The room gave off traces of a harsh, vinegarlike smell. It was quiet and eerie inside, and Alba felt uneasy as she couldn't see where she was stepping. Lucas pulled her towards him and told her that she'd trusted him once before so she could trust him again.

They now stood between a small table, on which sat an enlarger, and a bigger table, on which lay trays next to a sink. Running from one corner of the darkroom to the other, right over their heads like a zip-line, were a few strings to which were clipped hanging sheets of drying photographs. Like on the wall outside over the broken television, the photos were mostly of people from the neighborhood.

"Maybe it's not *my* story," he said, "but you were talking about stories, many stories, weaving into each other to make one bigger story."

Alba stepped in a small circle, in whatever space she could navigate, and peered into the photos one by one. Upon laying eyes on Laia, Alba lost her breath, and a cold feeling washed over her heart. Seeing her reaction, Lucas unclipped the photo and let her hold it. There were no chemical stains on it, and it offered a clear picture of Laia talking with a friend. Alba brought her other hand up and touched Laia's face with her fingertips. Lucas raised his hand and placed his fingers on top of hers. He liked that she didn't pull her hand away from Laia or from his touch.

"She looks like you," he said, confirming what she had been thinking all along.

Their eyes locked in a deep gaze, and as Lucas's hand now moved away from the photo and up to her face to caress her cheek, Alba slowly lowered Laia until she let her fall into a tub sticking out from underneath the table. With chemical residue still left behind in the wash, the image of Laia gradually started overexposing, turning her portrait into a blank piece of paper. Lucas brought both hands up and continued caressing Alba's cheeks, moving a strand of her hair behind her ear. In the back of her mind, Alba the mother and Alba the wife was condemning her desires, lashing out at her impetuous willingness to have and to hold Lucas, but Alba the woman felt like she needed to remember how it felt like to be touched, what it felt like to be desired and wanted and loved.

She moistened her lips and explored his face with her fingers. They both closed the space between their bodies and began kissing when suddenly the loud voice in her head won her over—she stopped, lowered her head to avoid his gaze, and pulled away. "I'm sorry, Lucas, I can't do this." She walked back to the curtain and entered it. She closed her eyes and gently placed her forehead on the door. The torment, the indecisiveness, the feeling of wanting and of hating to want so much. She began opening and closing her eyes rapidly, blinking as fast as she could for no reason at all, and while blinking, she couldn't tell when her eyes were open or closed. It all seemed the same to her, darkness over darkness, uncertainty over uncertainty, naivety merging with shamelessness.

Lucas came from behind and grabbed her affectionately. She cocked her head back, then reached down to place her hands on his thighs. He wrapped his arms around her waist and held her close to him. Alba turned to him, and as they began kissing, their bodies melting into each other, they spilled out of the dark room and fell onto the bed, impatiently undressing each other. They made love while the darkroom's door remained open, with the curtain drawn to one side, permitting ambient light to enter and damage all the photos of Laia that Lucas had recently developed.

19
The Blue Room

"It was right down here," Lucas said. They turned off the main avenue and entered a filthy back alleyway. Even at night he recognized the stench, the way the bins stood, and the archipelago of trash heaps.

"Looks like the kind of place the mob would dump their victims," Paco said. He lit a cigarette and accidentally kicked a glass bottle. Lucas told him to keep it down while looking around for the brothel's door.

"Don't they give them cement boots anyway?" Lucas asked, his eyes roving the wall. He found caged windows and the back doors of restaurants, but no brothel. "Or the necktie?"

"Those were the Colombians," Paco said, "It's called the Colombian necktie."

"Yeah, right," Lucas said. "You're always talking about the mob, cartels, and gangsters—have you ever killed anyone before?"

"Yeah, sure, I kill three hundred million every night," Paco answered with a stupid smirk. "When I log on to my favorite porn site and—"

"I get it," Lucas said. "Thanks for that. You plan on killing three hundred million more when we find the place and get in?"

"I thought that's why you invited me here, *amigo*? Hookers and blow."

"Just be nice to my *amiga*, *amigo*. She went beyond her duties to get me solid intel."

"I think this is the place," said Paco, looking over the wall.

"Sure looks like it," added Lucas.

They were standing in front of an alcove oozing of thick darkness. From his pocket, Lucas pulled out a small flashlight and turned it on. The shock of light scattered a few rats and illuminated used needles, broken beer bottles, and garbage bags. When he shined the light at eye level, he found a thick, studded door covered in stickers, logos, and other urban art. The door was without a handle, made from sheet metal, and resembled an impenetrable armored suit.

Lucas hesitantly looked back at Paco, stepped forward, and took a deep breath. He turned off the flashlight and banged on the door loudly three times.

No answer.

Paco threw down his cigarette, walked up, and gave the door three sharp raps with the butt of his Zippo lighter. They glanced at each other, wondering if they would get in.

"Real hidden this place, huh?"

"Uh-huh," Lucas said.

"Doesn't look like the place for a—"

"Guess not."

They waited seven seconds before a hatch slid open and a pair of psychotic eyes appeared in the slot, gleaning the surroundings before landing on Paco and Lucas. The background to this deep and murderous stare was bathed in a dull, blue light—The Blue Room.

Lucas waited for the doorman to open the door but instead, he slid back the hatch, ignoring them completely.

"Must have had different management the last time I was here," said Lucas. Frustrated, he banged again with the steel toe of his well-worn boot. The hatch opened quickly.

"Fuck off!" the doorman said. The hatch closed and it was silent again except for loud music pounding from inside, a distant police siren, and a few cats caterwauling in the distance. Lucas glanced at Paco, a look saying they had to try harder.

"I think today will be three hundred million and one," Paco said, flashing with anger.

A chaotic din coming from inside made Lucas and Paco step back. They had to jump out of the way to avoid being crushed by the swinging door. Sauntering out of the raunchy establishment was a tall woman in very high heels, a trench coat, and a ginger colored wig, her arm hooked tightly around the elbow of a pudgy man with a hideous face. Paco was immediately taken by the man's coat, fedora, and white shawl, which made him look like a crooning love ballad singer from the eighties or a mobster, maybe even Italian. Or maybe he was just an elegantly dressed office worker paying a visit to his favorite lady friend after hours. Lucas was confused by the big grin on Paco's face; either Paco admired the outfit and wanted to strip it off the man, or he thought the buffoon parodied the mob's threads most egregiously. The man pushed Lucas aside and continued walking down the alley towards the main road.

"Hey!" Lucas shouted. "How do we get inside?"

The man turned around and looked at what Lucas was wearing, then at what Paco was wearing, and answered him with a snobbish simper and a "go away" wave of the hand. He turned back, pulling on his lady's waist, and they went on their way.

"I need to get in there," Lucas yelled. He bolted after the couple, then grabbed the man's arm and spun him around. "Hey!"

The man knocked Lucas's hand away and scowled at him. "Pub round the corner," he said. As the couple walked off, he muttered something about the homeless problem in the city.

Lucas bristled at the remark. He caught up to him again, pulled out his gun, and pushed it into his back. The moment the man felt the gun's tip touch his body, he put his hands up and froze. The beauty queen jumped back and started screeching, but Paco grabbed her from behind and covered her mouth with his palm. He told her to keep quiet, and that if she started yelling, he would cut her throat. This threat was conveyed by a highly comical gesture of passing his finger along his neck, the "Sicilian way," he said, feeling compelled to clarify.

"Now, let's start again," Lucas said into the man's ear. "We're going to go inside this club, and you're going to take us. Got it?"

Paco released the woman and took a step back. He lit a cigarette and took a few pulls while observing her beauty, wondering how she was leaving with that beast.

"Okay, please! Don't kill me! I will help!" He turned to his lady friend and said, "Wait here," while motioning downwards, as though he were testing out a mattress's softness. He turned back to Paco and Lucas. This time it wasn't a look of admonition but of careful deliberation. He took off his fedora and put it on Lucas's head. He then removed his shawl to wrap around Paco's neck. He finally stepped back and signaled a "please, go ahead" with his hands. Paco knocked again after examining their new threads, which only slightly improved their shabby looks, better suited for two after-work carpenters rather than an ex-cop and his nefarious sidekick.

The hatch slid open, and without even looking out, the doorman yelled his neighborly greeting. But this time, realizing the grave mistake he had made, the bolt came off the door and the doorman welcomed them inside most hospitably after a round of apologies.

They entered the corridor, which was pulsating with an array of seizure-inducing blue lights to go with its characteristic moonlight ambience. Other strange motifs decorated the bar area, like a picture on the wall of a boy sitting in a moon's crescent and fishing; a clock shaped like a moon; drinks named after the planets; and high-tech strobe stars light-stenciling the entire brothel. It might have appeared large and infinite, but this was because of the mirrors that covered almost every inch of wall, fooling you to believe that it was a colossal gentleman's club on a spaceship. Around the walls were side-by-side plush booths, a circular table in each with ice buckets full of vodka bottles. On the left side was a bar currently accommodating half a dozen men on stools, either with their heads down on the bar top, negotiating the price of their rendezvous with a lady, or discussing confidential business matters with a colleague away from recorded minutes and boardroom anxieties.

Women of all shapes and sizes were everywhere, some dressed in nothing or in very little, some looking for company, still others beating men off with the help of a few bouncers.

Some paced back and forth in the entryway looking to pounce on cleanly-coiffed and well-dressed hedge fund playboys or real estate moguls. The non-sex workers walked around in high heels and mini-skirts, adeptly balancing trays of test-tube shots over their heads, a ruffle of bills held like *farfalles* between each finger or behind the straps of their halter tops.

Apart from cigar smoke, sweet perfumes, and musky colognes, there also hung in the air an overabundance of unfettered hormones that no perfect marriage could rein in. But Lucas and Paco didn't fit that profile at all, didn't enter the adult playground as if they were the biggest bullies on the block. Admittedly, they were hardly loadstones and didn't ooze sex or money, which was why no lady approached them to solicit business.

"One Jupiter," asked Lucas at the bar, embarrassed to be ordering a drink named after the largest planet in the solar system.

"We ran out of Coke," the bartender said. Lucas glanced down at the bartender's tie and wondered how all the planets could fit on it. "Jupiter is made with Coke and lime," the bartender said indifferently. "We also ran out of lime."

"Just get me a whiskey on the rocks, will you?" said Lucas. The bartender rolled his eyes.

"You got beer, *amigo*?" asked Paco. The bartender shook his head and gave up.

"Hey there, sexy boy! You looking for a good time?" said someone at Lucas's back in a heavy French accent.

"Yes, as a matter of fact, I am," he answered, turning around.

She had a honey-brown pixie cut, eyes like the color of autumn, and her upper arms abundantly filled with freckles. When Lucas looked over at Paco, his friend was already in deep conversation with a gorgeous lady of African origin, purposely lying to her about his ties to the mob yet ingratiatingly admitting to Italy's wrongdoings in Ethiopia during World War II. But she was not Ethiopian and was hardly offended, since most of her Juans and Joses believed Africa to be a country anyway.

"So, what's your name, *mon amour*?" Lucas asked with a lewd grin on his face.

"That doesn't matter," she said, then, irritated, grabbed Lucas by the hand, pulled him away from the bar, and led him to the back of the brothel. They took the stairs to the second floor and entered a smoky, upstairs corridor. Loud banging and sex sounds permeated through the thin walls wallpapered with a sixties flower pattern. The woman opened a door and shoved Lucas into a suite that looked more like an actor's dressing room. She closed the door behind her, locked it, and told Lucas to take a seat. She threw her tiny purse onto the dresser and let herself fall onto the mattress, either exhausted or just blasé. She then cocked her head and propped herself up on her elbows. She didn't say a word, just lay there staring at Lucas, legs bent like a schoolgirl in the pasture, her heels cutely fondling the air. Lucas sat down on the edge of the vanity and watched her, amused by her childish behavior.

"How did you get in here looking like that?" Anita asked. "You look like you're homeless."

"Almost homeless," Lucas said, "and Paco had to role-play being a bad guy with an imaginary knife."

"Oh! That sounds fun," Anita said, titillated by the thought of dangerous excitement. She got on her knees on top of the mattress, wanting to hear more. "I like pain, Lucas. Pleasure and pain. But I mostly like what we call in French," she tried to get serious, "*le petit mort* [little death], the orgasm of all orgasms, and then passing out."

"I remember you being aggressive once," Lucas said. "When you pulled your arm back and punched me in the eye."

"I am usually like this with anyone who pays for it. What's with the stupid hat, by the way?" Lucas came over and sat down on the bed with his back to her, facing a wall full of French movie stars from the sixties. "You disgust me, Lucas," she burst out. "Why don't you return my calls?"

"You know I've got a lot on my mind."

Anita got up and went into the vanity's drawer. She pulled out a photo. It was taken by Lucas from his balcony at a distance and developed in his darkroom.

"This guy who calls himself Stachu," she said, placing the photo down on the vanity. "His real name is Roman Radzinski, a Pole who works for the Catalan in one of his brothels. His plan of taking you to Warsaw, which in turn would take himself there in a suitcase, was going to land you six feet under. He came up with this asinine idea to make you believe he was a harmless and stupid guy in desperate need of help." She jumped back onto the springy mattress and began taking off Lucas's coat and feeling up his chest and shoulders. "The moment you would have taken him off the baggage claim belt—" she said, kissing him on the neck and sucking on his earlobe, "—you would have been greeted by his driver—" She grabbed his funny fedora and whipped it across the room like a Frisbee. "—and killed in the airport's parking lot."

"I'm astonished as to how much information you can get," Lucas interrupted, "just for getting these men drunk and making them happy."

"Actually, I had to put in some overtime with a very important client, one of this Catalan fella's ex-bodyguards, which, by the way…" She stuck her hand out asking for more money. Lucas pulled out a few bills from his pocket and placed the wrinkled papers down on the mattress. "Now that you have this information," Anita said, pulling him back softly but roughly pinning him down against the mattress. "How about a little something for me, *mon chouchou?*" She held her face over his and winked. She stuck her tongue out and lashed the air with it. "Do you like snakes, Lucas?" Lucas was confused and partly disgusted. "Or butterflies?" She brought her face closer to his and started blinking her eyelashes over his eyelashes. "Snakes or butterflies?"

"I like wanted photos," he said, evidently not in the mood. "Particularly the one of me."

"Alleyway camera." Anita leaned forward and tried slipping her hand under his belt.

"So, I should watch my back?"

She stopped and looked at him like he'd be stupid if he didn't. "Or maybe you should walk right into the lion's den." She giggled and Lucas whacked her hand away from being inside his pants for too long.

Lucas pulled out some more cash. "Thanks, Anita," he said, grabbing the string of her thong and letting it snap against another bill. He got up, grabbed his fedora, and walked over to the door.

"Oh, and by the way," she said, "that Laia girl of yours." Lucas turned around with his hand on the handle. "I'd be a bit more careful with her if I were you."

He nodded a bleak goodbye, opened the door, and walked out. While walking down the corridor, he passed a door behind which he heard Paco moaning about how he wanted to visit the continent someday, how beautiful it could be, and how amazing she was.

20

Exclamation in Blood

Moved far away from her desk's regular orbit, Alba sat motionless in her leather chair, facing the window in the dimly lit office. Her coat was lying on her Chesterfield and papers were scattered everywhere. A half empty bottle of whiskey stood on the carpet next to her feet. From the many times she'd poured herself a drink that late afternoon, circular crease stains formed on the topmost court filings in the pattern of the Olympic rings, though in total disarray, just as how she felt that day. Exhausted, she gazed out at Rocafort Plaza, which had resumed normal activity. Pickpockets were out and about; vendors were selling postcards of Gaudí's architectural wonders; *chatarreros* were rummaging through garbage bins; a smartly-dressed Jehovah's Witness was handing out religious propaganda. A few loiterers were doing card tricks for tourists, a suspicious bunch who very well could have been pickpockets.

Valentina knocked three times and entered. She had stayed late as Alba had given her a last-minute task. "You could call Dr. Bustos at this private number," she said. She held out a piece of paper and a cell phone. Alba didn't move. "Ms. Partagas?" No reaction. Alba finally swiveled around in her chair. Valentina could make out in her hand a glass with a sherry liquid inside. She saw that Alba's eyes were moist and red.

"Thank you, you're free to go," Alba said, reaching out her hand and collecting the number and phone. As Valentina was heading for the door, Alba called her back.

"Yes, Ms. Partagas?"

"Can you turn off the lights, please? The whole floor?"

"Certainly, Ms. Partagas."

The entire office was plunged into darkness, except for the red exit signs and the ambient light entering from outside. Alba nervously played with the paper in her hand while staring at the bus stop across the street, watched as passengers got off and boarded every fifteen minutes or so. Only when an ambulance sped by with its sirens blaring and blue light flashing against her face, did she realize she hadn't looked at the phone number since Valentina left the office, about three hours earlier. Her mind was unresponsive and her body ached from inactivity. She could see her dark silhouette in the window. She could see that her shirt collar was loose and her hair was a mess. She could not see the fading bruise on her knee but when she straightened her leg, she did feel it a bit more since it was raining earlier in the day.

Alba swigged the rest of her drink, placed the glass down on the carpet, and turned on the phone. She had finally found the courage to call. After three rings, Dr. Valeria Bustos picked up.

"Hello Alba, I'm glad you called."

"Thank you again, Doctor. This really means a lot to me."

"Well, I looked through the archives and, unfortunately, I couldn't find anything. At this point, the best way to proceed is by doing a DNA test."

"A DNA test?"

"Yes, that's correct. That way we could establish a ninety-nine percent match."

"Are you sure there's no other way, Doctor?"

"Well, I could set my whole team on the task, but I'm doing this alone, as you requested. I do trust my workers, but I wouldn't want this to come out in the press, especially since they haven't been very good to you lately."

"Thank you for understanding, Doctor."

"I'll have another look in the neonatal department's records and will let you know if I find anything or not."

"Thank you, Doctor. By the way, how is Leo doing? Last time I saw you was at your fifteenth anniversary."

"Leo passed away last year."

"He what? Passed away? I'm … I'm terribly sorry. I had no idea."

"A blood parasite," she said, "while we were on vacation."

"I … I'm sorry," Alba repeated.

Alba hung up and thought about Leo and the horrible death he had suffered. She looked over at her desk and saw a blue light blinking on her cell phone. Amelia was probably worried sick about her and wondering if she was going to make it for dinner with the Abaroas, Amelia's future parents-in-law.

Alba could call back and just make up some lie, as she often did. Maybe she might have to.

A thought suddenly came to her and she scrambled for the phone. "Doctor, it's me again—about the test. Can blood be used from, say, a piece of fabric or a—?"

"Of course," she interrupted, "provided there is enough blood on the sample that could be taken out for testing."

Alba hung up, collected her briefcase, and dashed out of the office. She wished Angela a good night and made way for the elevator. In the basement, she got into her car and exited the parking lot, tires screeching against the pavement.

She drove down Via Diagonal, almost getting into an accident not once but twice. With one hand on the steering wheel, she used the other to reach into her handbag and dig around for Horst's business card as she had forgotten the address. Hardly did she find the card when she looked up and passed the street. She made a quick U-turn, hung a left, and parked right in front of the antique shop. She turned off the car and took a deep breath while sitting in silence, thinking and wondering if this would work. She opened the glove box and took out a pair of leather gloves, untouched since last winter. She put them on and got out and walked over to the garbage bin. It was still full, and despite her always complaining about the city's inefficiency, she was thankful the waste collectors hadn't picked up the rubbish that day.

Holding a small keychain flashlight and pointing it down into the bin, Alba started picking trash out and throwing it into the street. The noise of cans and plastic hitting the pavement at night was jarring and inescapable. Suddenly, a window opened above the shop and a man stuck his head out. It was Horst, and he asked Alba to keep it down. He also said it was etiquette for *chatarreros* not to work so late in the evening so as not to disturb the neighbors. She was breaking the rules; the old German emphasized crassly, "*Ordnung muss sein!*" She glanced up at him but didn't say anything, ignoring him until he stuck his head back inside and closed the window, loudly, in frustration. She finally got to the bottom of the bin where the glass from the snow globes was and found a piece of tissue with a bloodstain.

21

Wine Tablets

Gelsomina's was not a Michelin starred restaurant, but in the hearts and minds of its loyal patrons, it must have been the best Italian eatery outside of Italy. Its dishes were reasonably priced, considering the massive portions, while its presumptuous waiters made you believe you were not walking through a rickety wooden door into a family restaurant but striding proudly into a Medici palace's dining hall. It was a loud and busy place with many tourist patrons in attendance, the most enthusiastic of them having relied solely on word of mouth to be easily convinced of its excellent reputation and delectable menu, which changed by the day.

There was never an evening when the ailing matriarch didn't come out of the kitchen to greet her guests. Despite bequeathing all skills and business operations onto her entrepreneurial sons, her appearance always caused a frenzy, with praises lauded and selfies taken, and sometimes a ceremonious standing ovation. Dozens of waiters in bow ties, white shirts, and black vests ran around the dining hall balancing Quattro Formaggi pizzas over their heads, or tucking numerous bowls of Gnocchi di Ricotta or Ravioli into their bodies like linebackers holding footballs. On that night, it seemed even busier as the rain scattered everyone out of the streets and into the restaurant's Etruscan-designed indoors, preferably to the tables closer to the stone ovens.

When Alba walked in, the host quickly ran over—not to grab her wet coat, or even to greet her, but to shut the door behind her to prevent the restaurant's unique aromas from seeping out. It was, one could hardly believe, part of strict company policy to enhance the dining experience and to make guests feel that God was in the next room, wearing an apron and toiling away in front of a saucepan. After securing the door and ensuring its rubber skirts were straightened, the host then turned to Alba and finally grabbed her coat.

"Good evening, Señora Partagas," he said insipidly. "Let me check the list to see where your party is seated this evening." As she followed the host to the lectern, she spotted Amelia's hand up in the distance.

"Mr. Ludevici, I see them over there." The host smiled and nodded before rushing over to the opening door again.

"Sorry I'm late, everyone," Alba said in a tired voice. She pulled out a chair and quietly sat down as she didn't want to interrupt Miquel in the middle of one of his infamous jokes. She whispered her hellos to Santiago and Fernanda Maria, the founders of Abaroa foods, Spain's biggest tin food manufacturer. She waved to Amelia and Martin across the table. She then nodded gruffly to Fernando and Duarte, Miquel's two closest associates, who sat in their seats like two stone effigies, their muscles bursting through the seams of their tight shirts. She then took a good look at her husband.

Miquel was flushed yet still far from slurring his words. His hand gripped the wine glass hovering in the air, ready to take a sip, but not before the joke's fast-approaching punch line. He didn't look over to greet his wife but continued to revel in being the center of attention.

"... and that's why the *campesinos* call grapes 'wine tablets!' And a thermometer? — 'mercury cigar!' And when anyone ever jokes about the size of my belly, whenever they say I'm a bit too wide around the waist these days, I tell them that my wife irons my shirts on watermelons!"

Fernando and Duarte broke out in rehearsed laughter while the rest of them chuckled. Miquel finally gulped down his wine and greedily grabbed the bottle, the one which he took the pleasure of personally minding. He poured himself another glass and brought his ear close to its rim.

"It's telling me that we should savor it by breathing it in, to invite its wholesome goodness unceremoniously and suck in the sweet air of those forgotten, hot summers. Hmmm, and when those bubbles pop," he gloated with greed, obviously overdoing it, "that sound is the sound of a bill counter shuffling the banknotes of my retirement."

The Abaroas were saving face and would do nothing to jeopardize a nice evening, despite being in the presence of a vulgar big shot. But try as they might, they could hardly ignore how disrespectful he was to his one and only, to the woman who wore his wedding ring on her finger. The Abaroas, when all they could do was listen and smile, also noticed that Alba wasn't herself. At least it was easier to attribute her look of numb resignation to the ongoing court battle. They had no idea Alba was still privately wallowing in the memories of her first incredible yet short sexual encounter with Lucas.

"Friends, let's turn to the blood of Christ," Miquel said, urging everyone to drink up while sloppily filling whoever's glass needed to be filled. "They say a toast without wine is like a nuptial bed without the bride…" Amelia smiled bashfully and looked around the table. *When is this torture going to end?* she thought. "A sweet elixir and a great year," Miquel said, going off on a tangent and forgetting to finish the toast, "—and a very expensive bottle, might I add, but free of charge coming from the bride-to-be, the manager of my company."

"I even checked my harvest card," Santiago said, assuring everyone that what they were drinking was truly the best. His eyes met Amelia's and she thanked him for the kind words.

"These 'wine tablets,'" Fernanda Maria joked, "are indeed quite superior to all the other 'wine tablets.'" Everybody finally laughed, not at the stale pun itself, but because somebody else had finally made an attempt at humor.

"Nowadays, we have a phone application to check on harvests and wine qualities," said Martin, suggesting his mother was a bit old-fashioned when it came to vintage appraising.

"Don't be such a smart ass," Santiago answered back. "Let's see you drive an ox, collect olives by the barrel, and run the kind of mom-and-pop shop we got our start on."

"Times have changed," Martin said. "It's all technology… startups, innovation, e-commerce."

"You are right, young man," Miquel interrupted, "that's exactly why I chose you as my son-in-law. You can help take our wine business into the twenty-first century, and I can also help in getting your canned goods to other parts of the world. India? Brazil? China? The Far East is on the up and up. They're even counterfeiting our famous *jamón* and selling it for a pretty penny." Miquel's mood suddenly changed, and he became thoughtful and emotional. "You know, Martin, having you around will be a good thing for our family...will take the edge off a bit. And I suppose to be happy in life one needs to be a little less serious...like those *campesinos*!" They raised their glasses and drank to the toast that had long ago been forgotten.

The Abaroa family finally lightened up, convinced that despite Mr. Partagas being a happily excessive drinker, at least he wasn't a hostile one. Miquel raised his hand to the waiter in the distance and called for another bottle. Alba looked over at her husband and tried to hide her embarrassment. She hadn't said a single word to him since arriving; she preferred to watch the jester perform for the dignified guests. Miquel returned the look, although it wasn't the kind seeking approval, but rather to say that he was in charge, a powerful businessman. In fact, he knew it and felt it deep down inside, that he was even more powerful than her, and that he could do whatever he wanted. Alba found Miquel's competitiveness pugnacious. His frivolity to serious matters, like pre-wedding dinners with the groom's family, was also humiliating and tarnished the family name. For this reason, she found her husband to be unbearable, and in recent months this had evidently put a huge strain on their relationship.

It was momentarily quiet when Miquel placed his elbows on the table and intertwined his fingers. His heavy head hung low yet the rest of his body spoke gleefully even before the words left his mouth. He looked over at Alba, almost as a pre-warning of sorts. She was staring at her wine glass, embittered, rolling its stem between her fingers. He noticed that something was wrong but, like always, wanted to take it up with her at home rather than in public.

"Mela," Miquel said, looking at her from across the table, "now that the whole family is here and we have their undivided attention, I suppose it would be the best time to share the good news."

On hearing *news*, Alba stopped twirling the glass's stem and shifted her gaze up in subtle shock. The waiter had brought the bottle and handed it to Miquel, but Alba grabbed it and started pouring herself a glass. She filled it almost to the top and took a big sip; she then poised herself for the *news*.

"Martin and I are going to have a baby," Amelia said with a huge smile on her face, looking around the table for whoever would congratulate her first. "I'm six weeks pregnant!"

Alba almost spat her wine out. She looked at her daughter with incredulity. Only after the shock wore off could she show her true emotion—indifference and bitterness arising from the fact that Miquel knew about his daughter's pregnancy and had kept it a secret from her.

Alba stayed silent for a moment, thinking deeply about the matter while sipping her wine, until she realized she had already finished her third glass. "Can you pass some more?" she said. Anger spread across Miquel's face, not only because he saw she wasn't as happy as everyone else but also because she was drinking too much and way too fast.

"Congratulations!" said Santiago.

"Oh, my dearest Amelia, that is great news!" rejoiced Fernanda Maria, reaching her hand across the table to affectionately clutch her future daughter-in-law's forearm.

"That is wonderful...sweetie," Alba finally said, unconvincingly, pouring herself another glass. "I'm really proud of you," she added drily.

Miquel looked over at his wife with a dissatisfied sneer. He wiped his mouth with a napkin and threw it onto the dinner table. Had the Abaroas not been present, then Miquel would have reminded Alba in his usual manner the importance of family and not only lunch dates with her girlfriends. Seeing how upset her mother was, Amelia's smile slowly collapsed.

"I'm sorry," Alba said, looking at everyone at the table. "It's been a really long day." Martin and his parents were embarrassed. Even though not a single word was said about what was going on behind the scenes, it made them uncomfortable that the dirty laundry of the Partagas family was being aired out (or acted out) in real time. "This case is … really, um, taking a toll on me." She looked at her daughter, finally showing a note of genuine happiness. "I'm really proud of you, sweetie. I really am! Let's make a toast." While raising her glass and beckoning everyone to do the same, she looked across the room and saw Mr. Ludevici walking Lucas and Laia over to a table. She lowered her eyes in embarrassment and forgot what she was about to say. In her thoughts, her little secret suddenly appeared without invitation, stealing from her a breath and quickening her heart rate. But to everyone at the table, Alba simply froze up amid her toast because of stress, character assassinations at work, and her bank's volatile stock price. Nobody knew that Lucas was what her sore eyes needed at that moment, that he was the object that fueled her little addiction to something sweet and different and bad. Lucas helped her take in this absurd spectacle called love, which she knew would quickly dissolve and fall apart in the coming years.

"Alba? A toast?" Miquel nudged her with his elbow.

"To the new addition to the family," she said, finally looking up and raising her glass.

"To the new addition!" everyone said, clinking their glasses. While everyone showered Amelia with attention, asking her if it was a boy or a girl or what names they had decided on, Alba kept glancing over at Lucas. When Lucas got up and excused himself from the table, their eyes locked momentarily, a quick alluring exchange, but Lucas pretended not to know her and walked out of the dining hall as if she never existed in the first place.

Looking back at the wine glass, Alba smiled mischievously. Suddenly, she grabbed her purse and stood up slightly off-balanced, almost knocking into a waitress who was carrying a carafe of water. She apologized and excused herself from the table most cordially and said that she needed to visit the ladies' room.

Meandering through the noisy tables full of happy families, Alba entered a hall, and after taking a few steps, she felt a hand grip her arm and her body tugged out of the restaurant and into a back alleyway through an emergency exit.

No sooner was she embraced than they began kissing and groping each other. Lucas stuck out his foot and kicked the door shut. They whirled around and stopped behind a dumpster. She placed her purse on its lid and was spun around with his strong and impatient hands. Her back was now to his chest, and she was hiking up her skirt and pulling down her panties. He undid his belt and slightly lowered his pants and pushed inside a few times, deeply, passionately, until he finished and held her in an embrace. They leaned back against the wall, not letting go of each other until his phone started ringing. The sound suddenly made Alba realize that she was being unfaithful, and brought to mind all the offensive labeling that would come with the territory. For Lucas, the phone ringing meant that his master plan was afoot.

Lucas grabbed his belt and zipped up his zipper while Alba adjusted her panties and fixed her dress. She wiped her bottom lip with her finger and grabbed her purse. She leaned back against the brick wall and looked at Lucas, wondering what all their meetings amounted to. Lucas's mind, on the other hand, was occupied by death-dealing questions and concerns. When he finally answered the phone, a man on the other end said that everything was ready.

"Do we just sink him in the Vistula River?" Lucas asked. "Maybe a waste of a human belongs in the dump, right?" Lucas could sense that Karol, his cousin from Warsaw, was grinning from ear to ear. Lucas turned around and didn't even notice that Alba had left. She walked back into the restaurant and went to the ladies' room, where she locked the door. She threw her purse onto the counter and stood in front of the mirror. She rubbed her face and nervously shoved her hands into her hair until tears started running down her cheeks.

Alba was exhausted. She pulled out a long leaf of toilet paper, almost too long for any kind of acceptable use on the body, crumpled it into a ball, and dampened it under running water. She placed the tip of her heel on the toilet seat, hiked up her skirt, and put her hand gently into her underwear to clean her crotch. She then changed her mind and decided to take off her underwear, slipping it through her heels and placing it deep into the trash bin. She tore some more toilet paper from the roll just to be sure and stuffed it inside the bin, covering up the evidence of her infidelity. After fixing her skirt and adjusting her earrings, she pulled out a deodorant stick from her bag and applied it to her underarms. A spray of perfume on her wrist was rubbed onto her neck. The sudden knock on the door from an impatient patron threw Lucas out of her thoughts and grounded her back to the moral reality of a marriage on the verge of dissolution. A second knock on the door and she rushed to put on a fresh layer of lipstick and to fluff her hair. She returned to the dining hall rehearsing the excuse that she was feeling unwell.

* * *

Alba was leaning back in a chair with her legs thrown on top of the kitchen table. She hadn't bothered removing her heels, or even her raincoat for that matter, as she'd gone straight to the wine fridge to grab herself another bottle. In her hand was a half-empty glass just barely tipping off her thigh.

For as long as she was drinking in solitude, she was staring at another face, one which, like Lucas, she couldn't get out of her mind. Miquel walked into the kitchen not expecting to find her there. He stopped and glanced at the photo, puzzled that Alba was looking at it. She didn't even bother hiding it anymore when she heard him come in.

"That's a great shot," he said sarcastically.

"I found it on a desk at work," she said, a lie, which she knew wouldn't stick, yet it didn't seem to matter anymore. "It was just lying there."

"Was it the security guard's desk?"

"Security guard's desk?" Alba brought her legs down and turned around. She was stunned, and his remark sobered her up in an instant. "What do you mean?"

"You honestly don't know who that is?"

Alba was too embarrassed to say anything. Miquel shook his head with disappointment. He walked around the table to where the printed media lay in a basket on the bay window's sill.

"You really are oblivious these days," he said, "even to those who are trying to destroy us, our family." He sifted through some magazines and started throwing them, with a touch of restrained hostility, off to the side, until he found the one he was looking for. He flipped through some pages until he found the story. He threw it down onto the table. Alba leaned forward and read and gulped nervously. She placed her glass onto the table, grabbed the magazine with both hands, and brought it up to her face. It was an article about Laia Requena and her political ambitions. Complementing the feature story was a picture of Laia standing on a trash bin holding up a sign that said, "Down with Alba Partagas!"

"Tell me that *this* is what has been bothering you and nothing else the last few weeks," he said, holding back the anger bubbling inside. He bent over her in a threatening manner, bringing his face close to hers. His left arm was straightened against the table's edge and his right hand gripped the chairback. Alba didn't look into his eyes, as much ashamed as she was frightened.

"Tell me the truth!" he yelled. In a fit of rage, Miquel raised his left hand and squeezed Alba's face. She tried to wrench his grip, but he pushed her back and watched her fall onto the floor. He stood over her as she begged and pleaded for him to stop until he stormed out of the kitchen.

22
Freddie Chopin

Lucas stood in front of the carousel and watched edgy passengers clamoring for foot space. Some argued over who grabbed their cart first while others moaned about the conveyor belt taking too long to bring luggage out. The atmosphere was so tense that should a live wire have been thrown in, the entire baggage claim area would have gone up in flames. What made it even worse was that the longer he stood there waiting for his single checked-in item, the more he was putting himself at risk of being caught.

Lucas tried to think happy thoughts from when he was a kid, when his parents and brother were still alive. He recalled the first time setting foot in Poland in the fall of '88. He remembered old ladies in headscarves and buckskin leather boots, the autumn leaves, soup served in bread bowls, distilled vodkas and old clunky cars. It was so different from growing up in Brazil. The following summer, another vacation, when they'd spent time camping out at lakes and trekking through natural parks. Now, as he stood in the airport, everybody still ogled him and pointed their fingers, as he looked a bit out of place. Luckily, nobody could pull back the curtains to see what was really going on inside his head.

Maybe Stachu, the man who had ill-devised the most shortsighted assassination attempt in the history of assassination attempts, had surrendered to the airport authority. Perhaps he was snitching that very moment and handing over Lucas's name to border officials like a buttery bribe to a corrupt politician. The nightmarish scenario didn't make any sense at all, he thought, as luggage inspections usually occurred at the point of departure, not at the destination. He was sure to be in the clear. But maybe. There was always that ominous "maybe" that hung around, which said that something had gone wrong when, in fact, someone was doing something wrong. Maybe the trunk started shaking and alerted security to it. Maybe it fell off the luggage cab and broke open to reveal a trafficked human. Maybe.

He glanced around and saw a tourist information booth managed by a young girl with heavy makeup handing out pamphlets of Old Town tours. Next to her was the currency exchange kiosk in which sat a long-in-the-tooth man with drowsy eyes and bushy eyebrows. He was grumpily counting stacks of foreign currency bills. Then Lucas spotted border guards with Kalashnikovs patrolling the area, combing through the recent arrivals and leveling glances at those most suspicious looking.

The luggage chute finally expelled the large leather trunk through the curtains onto the conveyor belt. Lucas steeled himself, watching it come around at the pace of a snail. He stared at it, hoping he could make it move faster with his eyes.

There was no way to back down, however unthinkable and outrageous the plan was. In due process, he and his cousin, Karol, had certain designs on the luggage. Its current occupant would get the kibosh because of the current occupant's plan of putting the kibosh on Lucas. Adding equal parts forgiveness and compassion into fate's crucible wasn't part of the killing recipe.

He checked his phone to see if Karol had sent him a message, asking if he needed to stall or to speed things up, but none flashed on the screen. He put the phone away and finally lunged forward grabbing the trunk's handle with both hands. He hoisted it off the belt and onto a luggage cart he had torn away from the other carts. He heard a loud, muffled moan but wasn't sure if it was Stachu. He looked around and hoped nobody had heard his hidden passenger. After balancing the trunk on the cart, Lucas looked around one last time before pushing it towards the exit. He looked down and observed the trunk's faded leather exterior and the studded buckles that wrapped around it for extra support. There was no way you could tell a human being was inside, because the human being was either expertly immobile or dead.

"Excuse me, sir, is this your piece of luggage?" asked a man in a hoarse voice. It was obvious, Lucas thought, as he was the only one pushing it towards the doors, something he wanted to say out loud but decided not to. He turned around and saw a border guard with a gun on his belt and a leather notepad in his hand. His top button was undone, revealing a white undershirt. A coffee stain had found its way next to his badge, which was pinned on but hanging at a downward angle.

The officer looked at the trunk, raised his hand to examine an item he held, then looked down at the trunk again just to be sure. Though he kept his cool the entire time, Lucas felt like he was coming undone. If the guard said something like: "Please, come with me, sir," or, "Can you open your luggage?" then Lucas would have had to make a dash for the exit. Or, if other guards with bigger weapons closed in on him, he'd be forced to grab the gun off the guard's belt, turning the guard into a hostage.

"I think this came off your luggage," the guard said in a trusting manner. He stuck out his palm, on which rested a baggage tag.

Lucas breathed a sigh of relief. "Yes, it did, thank you, officer," he said, feigning appreciation. Truly, he didn't know if it came off his trunk, but he grabbed the tag anyway and tried looping it around the leather handle. He couldn't get it to snap, so he just stuffed it into his pocket instead. He then smiled nervously at the nice guard and continued for the exit, pushing his way through the large and heavy doors.

It was a ruddy day with thick clouds poking along in the sky. He took a lungful of crisp air and shivered. He zipped up his jacket, but soon zipped it back down as he remembered that he had to keep it open for Stachu's driver to identify him by the soccer jersey he was wearing.

He walked up and down the taxi rank passing a bunch of Opels, Fiats, and one Mercedes oddly out of place. He stopped and lit a cigarette. He looked around and bluffed the excitement of a tourist ready to explore a gray and drabby city in winter.

"Some player, that Pelé was," someone said at his back. Lucas turned around and saw the man who was to pay him for transporting Stachu. Lucas, however, was fully aware that the man was going to shoot him, execution style, very soon.

The driver stuck out his hand to greet him. Jesus Christ, Lucas thought, how massive, a wrestler's grip, five sausages dangling from a pork cutlet. Lucas stuck out his hand for the greeting and watched it get devoured by the driver's hand.

"I am your chauffeur today," he said in a formal and rehearsed manner. "My name is Bogdan, but you can call me Bog. I will take you to a safe place to take out Stachu from the luggage and pay you for transporting him." Bog suspiciously looked down at the trunk and then up at Lucas.

"Cigarette?" Lucas asked while pulling out a pack from his coat's inner pocket. "Was it Bog? Or Bóg [God]?" he added, trying to be funny while lighting up. Bog didn't say anything. He was, however, amused by Lucas's broken Polish.

Bog might not have answered such a question, but he certainly stood with a steadfast godliness. He was a tall man with a square-shaped head, a tight and shiny part down the middle that looked like two black tsunamis rippling away from each other. He had round and intelligent eyes, and a thin moustache.

"You wait here," Bog commanded. "I will clean the car to make space."

"Precious cargo," Lucas remarked, taking a full-lunged toke of his cigarette, panning his head side to side, hoping Karol would come very soon.

Lucas threw down his cigarette and glanced quickly at Bog. He was still awed by the size of his hands. A farmer cum hitman, Lucas thought. When Bog finally waved Lucas over, Lucas pushed the confined Stachu towards the back of the car. Bog hurried to grab the cart from Lucas, pulling it as close as possible to the trunk, but not too close to avoid scratching the paint. He said he had to be careful not to damage the car as it wasn't his. Where the hell is Karol? Lucas thought, shivering in the cold.

Bog grabbed Stachu, hefted him up, but struggled to put him inside the trunk. For such a large-sized man, it was funny to see him unable to lift another man half his size. He asked Lucas for help but Lucas was smoking another cigarette and nervously scouring the parking lot. When he glanced back at Bog, he finally saw Karol standing next to him, poking a newspaper into Bog's rib cage. Lucas realized it was the Warsaw Daily wrapped around a gun firmly held to the big chauffeur's meaty flank.

"Like speed dating," Lucas remarked. How fast his cousin and Bog became acquainted wasn't at all impressive; he knew his cousin to possess quite the talent when called upon for dirty jobs.

"Prepared for our fishing trip today, aren't you?" Lucas yelled out.

"Got the rods and reels in the back," Karol answered. "Catch us some bottom-dwelling carp for Christmas?"

"Not staying that long, cousin. By the way, I have a present for you, and I'm sorry to say that it's not a crate of wine or a leg of ham." Lucas gestured towards the trunk now secured in the back of the car.

"Yeah, me too," Karol said, flicking his eyebrows to the car behind him.

Lucas looked over Karol's shoulder. It was an old Fiat 125p, also known as *kredens* for its uncanny resemblance to the sideboard found in almost every Polish household in the eighties. It was maroon with a pee-yellow racing band running along the doors, from headlights to trunk, passing over a constellation of rust holes, a missing gas cover, and finally wrapping around the broken tail lights. Two of the four tires, from what Lucas could tell, were spares unsuitable for cold and slippery road conditions.

"I see you brought the Ferrari," Lucas joked.

"The Audi is in the shop and the wife has got the Lamborghini," Karol said.

Inside the *kredens* were two men. One of them, a young boy who went by the name of Perch, got out of the car pell-mell and made a beeline towards the Mercedes' driver's side door. The swiftness of his reaction and the look on his face suggested that it was time to be serious, that operation rip-out-Stachu's-teeth-with-pliers was in progress.

Perch opened the door, sat down, and started the Mercedes. With the trunk in place and a gun on Bog, Karol gestured with the wink of an eye for Lucas to get in. Lucas threw down his cigarette and got in the passenger seat while Karol shoved Bog into the back. The driver of the *kredens*, Hubert, waved his hand out of the window to signal that he was ready. He would tail the Mercedes, just in case.

"If you've ever thought of a kidney transplant from all the boozing, well, now is the best time," said Karol, "because if you move a muscle, I'll shoot them out with the same bullet." Perch put the car in gear and they sped off.

"How is Grandma, Karol?" Lucas asked.

"Soon, soon…she'll be with the angels in heaven, nothing more to do but kneel in the confessional…what the man to my left should have done yesterday."

"So, you never answered me," said Lucas, turning to Bog. "Was it Bog or Bóg?" Bog held an ice cold look on his face. "If you're really Bóg, are you All-Knowing and All-Seeing?" They laughed. "I guess not, since you failed to see the tables turn, no?

Can you get out of this mess and save Karol's grandmother, Bóg?"

"If it were up to me, I'd have pulled the plug on her a long time ago," Bog said.

"What was that?!" Karol lost his cool from the offhand remark. He nudged the gun deeper into Bog's side and snarled at him like a pit bull chained to a fence, telling him what he would do to him, but because of the nice car they found themselves in, he resisted the temptation to send him up. "Take it back," Karol spat, "before she even touches heaven's stairway, the devil will be casting you into a lake of fire."

"Relax, Karol!" Lucas shouted, checking his phone.

"I can save myself—always," Bog said in a casual and confident manner.

"What was that, Bog?" asked Lucas, putting away his phone and fixing a gaze on him. "What was that?"

"I said that I can save myself," Bog repeated sternly, "and my kidneys. Not your poor grandmother."

"Yeah, and I'm Saint Nicholas," piped Karol. "Not with this burner trained on you, buddy."

"So, what were the plans going to be?" Lucas asked. "The Catalan must have paid you quite a bit for the job, no?" Bog sat quietly, staring out the window like a child on his first road trip.

"The plans *are*," Bog finally said, "that I'm going to take this gun off of this mama's boy and shoot you both with it. Then I'm going to collect my forty thousand euros from the capo."

"That's how much I'm worth?" Lucas asked. "At least a bounty that could help anyone stay afloat these days." Lucas's unusually chipper mood quickly subsided when he saw Perch's face.

Perch was a young kid in his early twenties with light blue eyes and a sharp chin. He had a shaved head and wore a tracksuit under his parka. Judging by his getup, one would not be wrong in pegging him as a hoodlum. In fact, he was what people in Poland called a *dresiarz*, a sweatsuit hooligan. Barring the stereotypical criminal outfit, he did look like an unstable guy: a nervous tick rippled through him occasionally, along with the incessant habit of cracking his knuckles against his thigh. He chain-smoked for a good twenty Hail Marys the moment they passed a sign that said Warsaw, though slashed across, indicating they were exiting city limits.

"What's with the driver, Karol?" Lucas finally asked. "What's *his* drug of choice?"

Though Perch seemed overly excited to have a front row seat, he paid little attention to Lucas or to Karol and just sat crouched into the steering wheel, shooting glances into the rearview mirror, worried that Bog was up to something.

"He's a deaf mute," Karol finally answered. "He reads lips. Don't pay too much attention to him." Perch grinned and Lucas spotted the blank space of a missing front tooth. "We call him Perch," Karol added, "because of the deer-in-the-headlights look on his face. He's a little off, but he's as good as gold."

Suddenly, a tussle broke out in the backseat. Bog started wrestling Karol for his gun, but when Karol pulled the trigger, and the gun didn't fire, Bog took the chance and enveloped his massive hands around Karol's neck. Lucas contorted his body around and started wailing punches at Bog, but it was as good as punching a sack of potatoes. Perch slammed the brakes. From his coat's inner pocket, he pulled out a hand cannon, a massive Dirty Harry Smith & Wesson. He turned around and shot Bog in the head. Bam! Just like that. Bog's body flopped over onto Karol's lap. Brain matter was splattered against the rear window and blood caked half of Karol's face and body. For a few seconds, there was church silence.

"What the fuck did you do that for, Perch?" Karol shrilled, looking at the gaping hollow in Bog's head. "Are you out of your fuckin' mind?!"

"Why do you have that thing?!" Lucas screamed.

Perch jumped out of the car with the huge gun dangling from his hand. He lit a cigarette and started pacing nervously. Karol looked over his defective gun with disappointment. He pushed whatever was left of Bog away from him, rolled down his window, and threw the gun into the bushes. They were in a residential district in the suburbs, on a road with colossal palaces and stonewall fences that looked more like medieval fortifications. No doubt the police patrolled such a posh neighborhood, and in no time the pigs would be around to find a band of hoodlums in possession of a body missing a head in a luxury vehicle missing its real owner.

Lucas jumped out, opened the trunk, and started pulling out Stachu. Luckily, the *kredens* pulled up behind them, driven by Karol's aide-de-camp, Hubert.

"What the hell happened?" Hubert asked, sticking his head out the window. "Let's get the fuck out of here, Karol!" Lucas yelled, panicking, heaving the trunk up and letting it fall out of the car onto the snowy road. He started dragging it towards the *kredens*.

After transferring Stachu from one car to the other, Lucas jumped into the passenger seat. He banged the roof of the *kredens* and yelled out, "Come on! Let's move!" Perch quit pacing and waved Hubert out of the driver's seat with the gun.

Karol was still taking in what had just happened, grabbing his head and gasping for strangled gulps of air. After picking up a handful of snow and rubbing it into his face and hands, trying to cool down as much as wash Bog's blood off him, he finally got into the car and they sped off through the countryside, driving over potholes as big as moon craters.

* * *

"We are here," mouthed Perch, puffing his cigarette smoke into the rearview mirror.

"We could have cleaned up the ride and sent it to the Moldovans," lamented Hubert, who was sitting in the back seat with Karol. "Maybe we could've stripped it for parts," he added. Lucas took off his seat belt and said nothing. He grabbed the cross from around his neck and stared out the front window.

"We could have somehow swindled that forty grand, too," said Karol, an exhausted afterthought.

"They were going to kill me!" Lucas yelled out. "Do you not understand that?! That was their plan!"

A vast swathe of hilly, snow-covered land sprawled out ahead of them. A few seagulls wheeled and turned in the sky, and a bulldozer was flattening a fresh load of trash. A wrought path led away from the pit and a dump truck could be seen driving off into the horizon. A stone chapel, in the most unusual of places, bordered the pit and clanged its single bell plaintively.

Perch killed the engine and placed his shaky hands on the steering wheel. Lucas continued holding the cross. It was a familiar place and he felt a strange déjà vu coming on, like he had been there before. Karol, Hubert, and Perch all glanced at each other and waited for Lucas to say or do something.

"The guy is a homeless man, *man*," said Karol sympathetically.

"Street musician, like my old pops," added Hubert. They obviously hadn't been correctly informed about who Stachu really was. Perch grabbed the gun and placed it on the dashboard. They all stared at the massive weapon. He then lit up a joint.

"You have to smoke that now?" asked Karol. Perch turned around. His face was pale and he was sweating profusely. "I ju- kill- a ma-," he stammered. Karol forked his index and ring finger and asked for the roach. He took a hit to calm his nerves. Suddenly, with rage in his eyes, Lucas opened the door, reached across and grabbed the gun on the dashboard, then bolted out of the car. "Fucker…rip out his…" he mumbled incoherently. He rushed to the back of the car and planted himself in front of the trunk.

"It's not going to open itself, now is it?" he yelled out, shifting his body weight from one foot to the other, waving the gun around, pantomiming his panicked state. Nobody budged and they all pretended not to hear him. "Open the goddamn trunk!" he shouted.

Perch removed the keys from the ignition and got out; Karol and Hubert followed his lead. After Perch opened the trunk of the car, Hubert grabbed the piece of luggage by its handle and threw it onto the ground. It broke open, and when Stachu spilled out, Lucas stomped on him with a hefty foot. Rolling around and moaning, Stachu grabbed his head in pain, cursing Bog for taking so long. He took off his sleep mask, threw the portable oxygen tank off to the side, and pulled off the breathing apparatus. He began hyperventilating and coughing. The sedative he'd taken was starting to wear off.

Lucas waited for him to finish squirming and when he did, he bent over at the waist and took a good look at Stachu's face. After Stachu's sight adjusted to the daylight, he was shocked to see that Bog was not around, and that Lucas had taken his place with the addition of a big gun pointed at his head.

"Where is Bog?" Stachu shouted. "Where is he?!"

"The next words that are going to come out of your mouth will determine whether you live or die," Lucas said, sticking the gun in Stachu's face.

"Lucas?! What are you doing? It's me—Stachu!"

"Or Roman Radzinski?" said Lucas, pulling out a photocopy of Stachu's Polish driver's license from his back pocket, crumpling it up, and throwing it at him. Stachu uncrumpled the paper and brought it up to his bleary eyes. "*O kurwa*! [Oh, fuck!]" he yelled. "Are you gonna kill me?"

"Wrong answer," said Karol, kicking Stachu in the ribs. "That was a question!"

Stachu folded up from the blow, grabbing his stomach. Lucas crouched down and put the gun's barrel into Stachu's mouth.

"You've held a nice disguise for way too long…following me, asking people about me, sitting near my building and pretending to be genuinely interested in trying to help me find—"

"The Catalan, right? Okay, okay, okay. Le' me ekplay'n," he tried to say as Lucas pushed the barrel deeper into his mouth. "The capo hire' me," he said. Lucas removed the gun to hear him out. "The Catalan knew you were looking for him." Stachu cleared his throat and spat. "He hired us to kill you. I work at one of his brothels, where he takes his customers for meetings. I'm the guest liaison."

"Fancy job title ... for a guy who...travels in his luggage," mouthed Perch, leaning against the car, his arms crossed. Karol and Lucas glanced at each other, a look that said, Where did this guy come from? Seeing that the interrogation was getting them nowhere, Lucas kicked Stachu in the chest. He then smashed him in the face with the butt of the gun.

"What is his name?" Lucas asked.

"Who?!" Stachu yelled.

"Who? What are you, an owl now?! Give me his name!"

"The Catalan!"

"No, you imbecile! His real name!" Lucas smashed him again with the butt of the gun, splitting his lip and opening a gash over his right eye.

"His name is ... Miquel," Stachu finally said. "Miquel Partagas." He started weeping, because he knew that giving up the Catalan's real name was the end of him.

"How do we get to him?" asked Lucas.

Stachu didn't answer and Lucas pistol whipped him again.

"Oh, God, no!" cried Stachu. "Stop! Please!" He wiped the tears from his eyes and begged them not to kill him. "Miquel was talking about going to watch a soccer game. Barcelona against Bayern. He sits behind the team's bench. Can't miss him."

"Team's bench?"

"You'll see what I mean."

"How do we get to him?"

"That's for you to decide and figure out, I can't give ..." Lucas pulled back and smashed Stachu again. He crooned from the blow and started spitting out more blood. "He enters through the VIP doors," Stachu said in a gurgly voice, "but leaves out the back…access door twenty-one leads to a conference room where he usually stays behind to talk with some players. He's a big shot, throws money at the team like it's nothing."

Perch was still leaning against the hood when he threw his cigarette down and came over. He began gesturing angrily and pointing towards the church in the distance, then back to Stachu.

"What the hell is he saying?" Stachu asked. Lucas looked over at Karol and asked him the same question.

"He says for you not to use God's name in vain in front of the church," Karol interpreted. "He says for you to get on your knees and touch your forehead to the holy ground."

"Holy ground? What holy ground?! It's a fuckin' landfill site, for God's sake!" Perch's eyes widened reading blasphemy on Stachu's lips a second time. Karol and Lucas exchanged glances. Stachu saw the garbage scattered everywhere but succumbed to Perch's demands. He turned his body and got on his knees and lowered his head. With his eyes fixed on Perch the whole time, he brought his face down to the snow-covered dirt.

Angry that Stachu wasn't taking him seriously, Perch walked up, grabbed the gun from Lucas's hand, pointed it at Stachu and pulled the trigger. Bam! Stachu flopped over. Perch stepped closer. Bam! Bam! Bam! He reached down and took out Stachu's wallet and put it in his pocket. Bam! He pushed Stachu over the cliff's edge with the help of Hubert, who made the sign of the cross. Stachu fell onto a large piece of ice on top of a small body of water. Perch looked over the edge, spat with contempt, and peered at him lying there flat on his face. He then mumbled something incoherently.

"He says, 'Welcome back to Poland,'" Karol translated.

They all went back to the car, except for Lucas, who continued looking down at Stachu's body. He had landed in a clay pit, like the one Lucas's family used to visit during summer vacation to idle away those hot and boring days. He looked up at the stone chapel. The seagulls. The landfill site. The bulldozer was still flattening all the city's waste in the distance. He finally got back into the car and they left.

23

Bayern vs. Barça

L ong and narrow hews of streetlight cut into Lucas's darkened loft. Like an incurious spectator, he sat in his armchair and watched through the blinds; it was not perverse interest anymore, just habit. Esme's naked, glistening, and tattooed body rocked back and forth over Anastasia's. In the hot amber glow of their lamplight, a slow, erotic, and beautiful display of affection was deepening, nothing like the previous encounters of snuff filmmaking for fast cash.

Because of how exposed his private "wonderbox" was (a source of entertainment that required no coins or much personal investment), he was starting to suspect that something was not what it seemed—it couldn't have been this good and for so long and for free. The whole out-in-the-open of a little in-and-out seemed to mock more than stimulate him these last few days. This was also compounded by the fact that he was struggling with himself and in finding him, and in trying to close this chapter in his life. In a city known the world over, Lucas would be no stranger to its criminal underworld and nothing more. He'd be a mad person in a metropolis, a gangster trying to exact revenge on another gangster. A city of vice was squeezed into a single person who himself was no moral beacon.

He got up from the armchair and took to his routine, which would continue every night until the memory of a complicit murder was out of his mind—shadow boxing in the shadows and then a few rounds on the bag. He slipped, ducked, and swayed in unison with the leather teardrop, strategically launching his rag-strapped fists ... a toothless street kid flashed in his mind ... a ferocious left hook pitting a hole, then the bag's chain bunching up in a twine ... an unscrupulous brothel employee who rolled the dice and put on a hired-gun persona ... an uppercut buried into the bag's canvas cavity the floor creaking under him and bowing from his soft footfall ... sweat lashing out from his rapidly torquing body ... trash mounds ... a stone chapel.

Despite finding it hard to ignore the reality that could not be undone, it was during training when he could put his mind on autopilot, when he felt more alive and more conscious of his place on earth.

After a long ten-round session, he dropped his hands and plopped down on a chair. He looked at the bag slowly returning to a hang-still, watched its shadow on the wall shrink and stretch grotesquely. He leaned forward and rested his elbows on his knees and looked over his fists. He watched the sweat drip from his face and pool on the parquet. He might have been out of shape but still had it in him. He knew the muscles in his body were tightening up too quickly, yet they were in no way forgetful—it would all come back to him upon returning home to a proper gym. But while unwrapping his gloves, he was suddenly hit with the realization that that day may never come.

He balled up his fists, got up, and started punching the concrete wall next to the bag. Maybe he was as strong as an ox, but mentally he was as weak as one breathing its last dying breath. The undid straps flailed like streamers and blood soon appeared on his knuckles and the wall. Holding them back as much as he could, tears coursed down his cheeks, but he kept punching and wincing from the pain. Amid this sudden discharge of rage, the phone started ringing, but he kept pounding away, watching cement crumble off the wall as loud thuds reverberated throughout the building. After a few more rings, he finally stopped and dropped back down in the chair. He looked at his hands and didn't feel a thing. There must have been a few broken bones in there, he thought. He finally picked up the phone.

Alba wanted to meet with Lucas at his flat that night, but he said that he was busy. She insisted on a special romantic evening together in the coming days. Lucas numbly agreed.

"'Okay, sure?'" she said. "What does that mean?"

Lucas stood up, walked over to the window, and glanced down at the street. Paco's car pulled up. Eager to finish the phone call, Lucas reassured Alba that he too missed her, and that he was fine. She asked him what was going on, but he said there was nothing to worry about. Right when he hung up, a camera flash went off in Esme's flat. He peered across into her window but saw nothing, only silhouettes of bodies moving in the dark. That much of an expert he became with cameras, he wondered why they were using such bursts of flash in a room plunged into darkness.

He undid his gloves and added them to the sweaty pile of dirty clothes. He opened the window, passed a towel over his body, and wiped the blood from his hands. He applied some bandages to his split knuckles, took a few swigs of Don Simon, and put on some clothes. He left the flat in a rush and stole down the stairs, slipping into the night. Before getting into Paco's sedan, he looked up and saw another camera flash go off.

* * *

When fans started clamoring into the stadium and making their way to their seats, it occurred to Lucas that they would soon cease being individuals and transform into a large, flowing, and frenzied mass, mad about the beautiful game. The stadium's bright lights illuminated the green pitch perfectly. From nosebleeds to sidelines, cameras flashed while a steady stream of uproarious chants filled the air along with club flags waving in support of the home team. Children's faces were painted with the team's logo, and some even wore the team scarves around their necks or held them up over their heads. A sellout crowd of more than eighty thousand fans would soon be watching men who occupied the hierarchical space between priests and gods kick leather orbs into each other's nets. It was the final game of the European championships—Bayern Munich versus FC Barcelona, the game at which, according to Stachu, the Catalan—or Miquel—would be in attendance.

Lucas stood motionless in the stands while his eyes roved behind the bench. Around him bodies jostled en route to their seats, squeezing in on his flanks, bumping into him and stepping on his boots. He couldn't be taken out of his concentration. Paco squeezed through with a sheepish smile on his face. He was bringing back a tray of stadium food and seemed more in the festive mood than Lucas.

"This is pure madness," said Paco, handing Lucas a greasy *bocadillo*. Lucas reached out and grabbed it. That was when Paco noticed blood seeping through a bandage over his hand.

"What's pure madness?" Lucas asked, taking a few bites, not noticing the sudden attention to his injury.

"That the stadium is packed," Paco said loudly, almost shouting.

"And nobody even stopped us when we scaled the fence to get in," said Lucas.

"You should take care of that," Paco said. "You look like a leper loose out of the colony." Lucas looked at his hand but said nothing. "It'll be impossible to spot him," Paco added. The Andalusian took quick and large bites of his *bocadillo* to get rid of the sloppy mess. "Difficult, especially from up here," he added.

"Not unless you got some good glass," Lucas said, pulling out a set of binoculars from his jacket pocket. "I found these," he said. "Guess where?" Paco smiled with a mouthful of cheese and a dollop of mayo clinging to the side of his mouth. Lucas raised the binoculars to his eyes and started focusing the Soviet-made glass on the field.

Despite their creative dribbling, which Lucas likened to samba dancing during Carnival, the home team seemed to be moving the ball around with difficulty, repeatedly losing possession. "They're running around with their heads up their asses," Paco said. Lucas nodded in agreement.

Before a few calculated tackles that hammered the ankles of the team's midfielder, Barcelona got unlucky and turned over a one-touch pass into a scoring opportunity for the Germans. The away team quickly made it one-to-naught and momentarily, the collective spirit of the crowd sank and the *blaugrana* wave died down. But the world's greatest football team, with their slogan *mes que un club* [more than a club], had one secret weapon—the most venerable of football gods reincarnated in elfish proportions. With the ball trotting along the sideline, he would turn and drive down the middle, deceive a defender, fake left, then right, and then smash the ball through the hands of the goalkeeper into the top right corner of the net. Amid the eruption of fanatical cheers, Lucas sedately nudged Paco.

"That's him," said Lucas. The seats trembled under them and the stadium shook, but Paco and Lucas remained focused, thinking and plotting how to take him out. "I remember that face," Lucas said. "I remember the first words he said to Thiago: 'You got potential, kid.'"

24
The Best Team in the World

In a country where football is faith and players are profitable prophets, Thiago must have been the golden child set on the highest pedestal with a foreseeable golden boot in his future. But instead, he chose drugs, jewelry, fast cars, designer clothes, and a customized golden glock, which he stuffed behind his crocodile skin belt like some Libyan dictator.

Some might say he was a victim of the Escobar effect. Whether he deserved his mausoleum to be torn down or for cops to spit after saying his name was a matter of debate. And those debating such matters probably took sides according to who received his gifts or help and who didn't. Regardless, one could say the cards were stacked against him even before the *abandonado* became the city's most hated—and most loved—gangster.

* * *

One day, Gregorio was walking home from watching a game on the big screen at a local bar. Palmeiras had lost to Flamengo. Two to five. A wager which won him a few extra beers and a mildly spinning head. Soon after leaving the bar, he was quickly lured away from the road by what sounded like a wailing child. There, under a highway overpass, a boy in soiled clothes was sitting in the dirt between an oil drum and a pile of trash. Unable to ignore his crying, Gregorio picked him up and held him like the boy was his own, letting himself be spellbound by those big and brown eyes full of tears. He took him home to meet his wife, Rafaela. It would be unthinkable to leave a child in a dangerous and disconsolate part of the city without proper care and attention.

Walking home with the child now sleeping in his arms, Gregorio wondered how the boy ended up left like a dog in the first place. Nobody was around to tell him that his father was serving a life sentence for murder. The police found his mother under the very same overpass a few days later behind a dumpster with a needle stuck in her arm.

Lucas, who was a young boy at the time, greeted him by kicking a ball to his feet. While they played, Gregorio watched the abandoned boy chase the ball around exuberantly, demonstrating a natural talent for Brazil's national sport. A few years later, Gregorio decided to put Thiago on the Flamengo Juniors, a feeder squad that he coached ever since he had finished his illustrious career as a player for the Series A team.

Over time, with exceptional physicality, sharp intuition, and a firm grasp of the rules of the game, Thiago would become the smart bruiser up front. While he played with extraordinary panache, fulfilling the role as the team's main striker, Lucas, became the passing marksman who'd set up his brother for almost every goal. Everyone on the team called Thiago Pitbull, not only because he was short and stocky, but also for bearing a hard-bitten look on his face. But things quickly went downhill as he came of age, when the ball at his feet was soon replaced by the pistol in his hand.

The attempt at early delinquency not only absorbed him into gang life and attracted the head *soldados* on the hill, but it exhilarated him to be a criminal as much as score hat tricks and dance around his opponents on the pitch. He would keep this up for as long as he could because, as far as he understood, his circumstance was not mutually exclusive—he could rob and play soccer since fate had allowed him both gifts. Eventually, in the end, one would end up the gift and the other the curse.

With violence and drugs all around him, Thiago soon learned that your actions in the streets dictated whether you lived or died, whereas your actions on the soccer field determined your transfer fee, signing bonus, salary, and what kind of supermodel you'd be dating. And many were the Bündschens and Ambrosios in his arms, for Thiago got called up to play for the Series A team very early on in his career. Comfortably living a double life, it would be a matter of time before he not only became the club's star player but de facto general manager after strong-arming the club's proprietor, turning the club into his private money laundering empire.

Though the lifestyle of a professional athlete appealed to many young boys from the favela, for Thiago it wasn't rugged or daring enough, as he believed that he wielded what he called real power from the armchair he often referred to as his throne. "Let me consult the throne," or, "Let me think things over on the throne," were just some of the things he'd say before ordering a hit on a corrupt cop or contemplating which routes he would use to traffic arms through an enemy's territory. There were also drugs, of course, and Flamengo's position in the ranks was the perfect barometer to selling cocaine or heroin: when they were in the bottom half, conversely, he'd move more weight to bolster his ego; when in the upper half, drug dealing became secondary to celebrating his team's path to a cup victory.

Despite only playing half of his season's games, Thiago ended up as the team's highest goal scorer. It would come to the point where his feet would be blessed with holy water before matches to protect him from injuries and get him to score as many goals as possible. Lucas, who had decided to take another career route after an injury, often went to the stadium to watch his human highlight reel of a brother embarrass his opponents. And his swagger while doing so was enough to cause some of the opposing players to tackle his teammates out of jealousy. God forbid they start hammering at Thiago's ankles as they all knew who he was and what he could do. If he did so much damage on the field with just his foot and a ball, then imagine what he could do with an AK47 off the field.

During police academy, Lucas would only meet with Thiago on what he called "visiting the witch doctor, Raimunda," where he and his brother could trust to be out of the crosshairs of his enemies or members of the Pacification Unit. Since Thiago's phone lines were tapped, this manner of speaking was, of course, code language for Thiago to hide his gun and put his three cell phones into his drawer, and escape the city whenever family matters needed to be discussed.

"Visiting the witchdoctor, Raimunda" consisted of driving up the coast in Gregorio's beaten-up Volkswagen Golf Trek, where they would talk, or better, where Lucas would try to be big brother and talk down to little brother. For a power-hungry little brother, this didn't sit very well with him.

Lucas witnessed over the years that a number of issues subtly preyed on Thiago's conscience, issues which found expression in not-so-subtle ways, such as violence or using the drugs he was pushing. Lucas would do his best to try to appease his brother's anger and bitterness from being abandoned as a child. He would also show sympathy whenever Thiago expressed guilt and shame for not reciprocating the love his adopted parents showed him.

Despite Lucas, Gregorio, and Rafaela doing their best to steer Thiago clear from this predictable path of perdition chosen by many young and tormented kids in the favela; despite managers and trainers reinforcing his good behaviors on the field with countless sports accolades, Thiago showed no interest in severing ties with the hardened criminals he associated with from the neighborhood. Should he have decided to tear himself away from the "Children of God" who were anchoring him down, then perhaps he would have started to dedicate more time to listening to his trainers and fellow teammates. But no, that was out of the question—those with whom he robbed and dealt drugs were his brothers and sisters. Even Thiago's girlfriend could do nothing to help him change, as she'd been jumped into the same gang at the same time he was.

"Either you fall off the fence and land on the side of Carandiru's yard," Lucas said, driving along a paved, sun-drenched coastal road in a rich area outside the city, "or land on the other side, where you find a swimming pool next to a beautiful garden protected by a high wall with security cameras."

Despite Lucas's best efforts of persuasion, his brotherly words always fell on deaf ears as Thiago sat quietly in the passenger seat. He was forced to listen to Lucas, tolerating the unwanted sermonizing just because they were in the same car together.

Thiago wore a dismal look on his face and was staring out at the blue ocean and the waves crashing against the rocks, willfully blocking out all that talk about "tottering on the brink of self-destruction." Deep down inside he was furious and obviously bothered that he let his brother drag him out to "visit Raimunda" in recent weeks, because it wasn't like two brothers talking about girls or funk, but a stern-faced lecture given by somebody who himself was no angel.

Tired and indifferent, Thiago reached his hand down and pulled the seat lever. He reclined so far back that the seat belt, which remained in front of him, looked like a rope strung crosswise. He started playfully punching the air on one side of the rope, then punching the other side, alternating like the slip-rope drill in boxing.

"Still box?" Thiago asked, trying to change the somber mood in the car.

Lucas didn't answer, keeping his eyes fixed on the road. His knuckles clung white to the steering wheel and his foot was flooring the gas pedal. Lucas's head was still in the original conversation, and he was getting angry that his brother was trying to change the subject.

"They say you're not supposed to drive like that anymore," Thiago said.

"Like what?!" snapped Lucas.

"One hand at ten and the other at two. That was before we had power steering. Better at nine and three."

"You must have a lot of experience," said Lucas bitterly, "practicing your driving skills on those sports cars you steal before selling them on the black market, huh?"

Thiago kissed his teeth and checked his pockets to see if at least he brought one phone along. He was waiting for Lucas to start preaching again, like the evangelical pastor he had become lately. It was silent for a while, and then Thiago put on the radio. Lucas occasionally glanced over at him, seething in quiet rage, trying to find the words to drive his point home. He turned the radio off and tried again.

"Those mansions," Lucas said, gesturing to the beachfront property on golden sand facing the glistening sea. "You see this when you wake up." He timed it so that Thiago would also catch a glimpse of a sailboat heeling on the horizon and the Petrobras businessmen driving home in their luxury cars.

"Man, why don't you quit it with that foolish talk," Thiago finally said. "And besides, they tore down Carandiru a long time ago—you should know that cause you're a pig now!" Lucas looked at him angrily. "A few from the gang were even killed during that prison riot—your guys did the killing, not mine!" Silence. Lucas started footing the brakes, turned onto the shoulder, and stopped the car. He wanted to settle this sensibly.

"What do you want out of life, Thiago?" Lucas pleaded, yanking the handbrake as they were on a slight incline. "You have talent on the field, and it gives you honest options. It's the kind of freedom every boy grows up dreaming about—to have at least one option out of his misery."

"Every boy? You mean, what you grew up dreaming? I have everything I need up on that hill—money, women, drugs, a crew. Most of all, I have power. With one phone call from my throne, I could have the city under siege in less than an hour."

Lucas couldn't take it anymore. He thrust his arm at Thiago and grabbed him by the collar. "You know what I don't understand?" Lucas yelled in his face, pushing him up against the passenger door. "I don't understand how the fastest and most skilled striker in our city becomes addicted to the drugs he peddles, abusive towards his pregnant girlfriend, and a *soldado* in a local favela gang named the 7th Street Commandos!"

"You and your hypocrisy," Thiago responded, hardly fighting back his bigger and stronger brother. "So typical of a lawman communicating with anger and aggression." He laughed. "You guys are all the same, using violence when you're frustrated. The only difference is that I'm not ashamed to use violence, while you do it for the heads of state who steal from the poor, and then hide within the comfy confines of the law."

"My days are numbered at the academy," Lucas said. "They think I'm protecting you! They think I'm one of you!"

"Get a grip, Lucas. It's only a matter of time before you become an animal like the rest of them, before you kill and maim with that badge over your heart."

Silence.

"To kill or maim, huh?!" Lucas bellowed. "To kill or maim?! You'll be *killed* or *maimed* without your pistol! Without your crew! Dad should have left you under that bridge for *you* to be killed or maimed!"

That was the last straw for Thiago.

They started throwing hands in the car but stopped, got out, and met in front of the hood, saying what they would do to each other along the way. But before Thiago could punish his brother for his last remark, the one which dug the knife deeper into his heart, Lucas connected with a jab and a hook, knocking him flat on his face.

"Without your guns and your posse, huh?" Lucas repeated, standing over him. "That's how you end up—on the side of the road, in the dirt!" Thiago touched his face; it felt warm. Blood welled up in his mouth and he spat. "And if you keep up this lifestyle, you'll end up six feet deep in the dirt!" Lucas walked back to the car and sat down on its hood, regretting having taken it this far. He lit a cigarette to calm his nerves and turned to face the sea. The breeze was blowing off the water and the sun was setting. A sports car sped by honking at them for no reason.

"You don't even know the kind of blessing you've been given," he said, exhaling smoke, eyes fixed on the cruise ship passing by. Thiago pulled himself up from the ground and wiped his lip and nose. "He sure knows what He's doing though," Lucas added, refusing to look at his brother.

* * *

The next day, Thiago finally agreed to hear what one team's manager had to say. In the past, he'd always agreed to meet with representatives from big-name teams but in the end, he would cancel the meetings. This time he was genuinely interested in an offer to play across the Atlantic. He even invited Lucas to come along and see what it was all about, how much it would cost to buy Flamengo's best player.

After Lucas hung up the phone, agreeing to go with Thiago, he went into his closet and found a shirt and tie he could give his brother to wear for the meeting. He then took the Volkswagen and picked him up on the side of the highway's entrance. They drove to a beach resort on the outskirts of the city to meet a man by the name of Miquel Partagas, some bigwig club manager from Europe, Thiago mentioned.

"You got potential, kid," Miquel said as they all sat at a table on the pool deck, drinking fancy drinks with umbrellas coming out of them. At an adjacent table sat two of Miquel's associates, Fernando and Duarte, who were present for the meeting, but were obviously distracted by the bikini-clad ladies in the swimming pool. "That's why I invited you to have a talk," Miquel said, "try to get you to come play for the best team in the world, where all the young stars are proving themselves." His greasy spiel was nothing new and seemed overly contrived, Lucas thought. And neither did Thiago react, since he had been hearing those same fawning lines ever since he'd been a star player with the tykes.

Wondering where to take the conversation, Miquel pulled out the napkin from under his drink, clicked the pen that was inserted in his Ralph Lauren shirt pocket, and began writing numbers on it. Lucas unseated his bottom from the chair and craned his neck to see Miquel write down a large sum of money. Lucas went agog seeing all those zeroes, as he took this as the salary per season. It was more money than he had ever seen in his life. Thiago, on the other hand, wasn't too impressed. He seemed a tad bit too proud and negotiated with the kind of seriousness that one wouldn't expect, especially when he would be striking it rich in the golden foot lottery.

Miquel unclicked the pen and inserted it back into his pocket. "A player like you, Thiago," Miquel said, pushing the napkin across the table and then leaning back in his chair, "is born once every fifty years, but the hoodlums from Rocinha are shot dead in the streets every fifty minutes."

"Shot dead in the streets?" Thiago asked with a puzzled look on his face. Lucas saw his brother get angry.

"You decide for yourself your own fate," Miquel added. "It all lies in your hands, and not many people even have that."

Fernando stood up and walked over to Miquel and whispered something into his ear.

"Ah, yes," Miquel said, aroused by the reminder. "A little gift from me to you, Thiago." Lucas and Thiago glanced at each other, wondering what Miquel was talking about.

The sound of a faint sputtering engine started growing when suddenly an airplane appeared at a low altitude flying over the ocean. Thiago shaded his eyes and looked up. Lucas repositioned his chair to catch more shade from under the umbrella, but moved his head out to see what all the fuss was about. Miquel was now arranging a date with the supermodel in the chaise lounge closest to their table, but she stopped flirting to look up at a banner the airplane was pulling. Miquel took the napkin and crossed out the sum he had written down. Under it he wrote, "No deal. Call Lula," and handed the napkin to Duarte.

The banner read:

And one fine day the goddess of the wind kisses the foot of man, that mistreated, scorned foot, and from that kiss the football idol is born. He is born in a straw crib in a tin-roofed shack and he enters the world clinging to a ball. —Eduardo Galeano

25
Day of Thiago

It was the moment when an officer from a special task force stopped the vehicle Thiago and Lucas were driving at a random and rarely occurring checkpoint. They had changed places; Thiago wanted to show Lucas how to drive, but Lucas fell asleep and was out cold.

Thiago's lookouts had failed to notify him of the impromptu checkpoint. With possibly devastating consequences, the very sensitive regulation to check every car was authorized by the chief commanding officer, Lula Oliveira.

Lula set up the checkpoints, which he exploited in his favor, as something that had to be done "in order to rid society of the most reprehensible types." In the end, this checkpoint was manned by cops with cold guns and was set up to finally take down Rocinha's biggest drug dealer and arms trafficker.

When Thiago pulled up to the officer, he noticed a familiar face. It was the cop who had killed one of his street soldiers in a shootout a few weeks back. It happened in a rural area outside the city. A small army in civilian clothes had entered a meth lab and shot up the place. The cop was asking for an increased thirty-five percent of profits on top of the initial rejected offer of fifteen percent. It was a reasonable and fair amount that would continue funding their look-the-other-way policy. This cop, in the end, turned out to be a police detective carrying out the dirty work for Lula Oliveira. His name was Detective Hector da Silva, also known as Hollywood Hector.

Thiago saw a grin on da Silva's face, one showing that he remembered Thiago escaping through the back door during the ambush. At present, the look communicated wordlessly that Thiago's dead body would finally fulfill the unofficial quota for the night, the kind of unwritten rule that allowed for pending case files to be burned up after rendering certain individuals "disappeared" from society.

Thiago hit the gas and busted through the oil barrel barricade. Lucas woke up and started yelling at his brother, asking him what the hell he was doing and if he had lost his mind. He ran over the officers who stood in front of the car. A few rounds of gunfire shattered the rear window as they sped off, perforating the trunk and fender. They escaped unharmed, but while racing down the street at full speed, the car nearly lost control veering into oncoming traffic.

Lucas begged Thiago to stop the car, but he didn't listen and kept speeding, telling Lucas that they would kill them if he stopped and surrendered. When Thiago made a sharp turn on an unpaved road, he lost control, crashing through a shop's front window and coming to a stop in aisle four, with baby formula and milk powder bags thrown off the shelves. Luckily, no parents were shopping at midnight.

The car's front was heavily damaged. Smoke was escaping from the hissing engine. Da Silva and the special task force crept in through the broken windows with their guns drawn and began circling the vehicle. Both boys were moaning in pain—Thiago had a deep cut over his cheek and glass lodged in his arm. Lucas was bleeding from his mouth.

Thiago looked over at Lucas, a glance that haunted Lucas for many months after. "I told you so, brother," he said. No sooner did Thiago reach under his seat, than the police opened fire. He was killed in seconds. The object he reached for was a CD of Jorge Ben Jor's greatest hits.

Many weeks later, when Lucas's legal team pulled out a large chart paper with the bodies of Thiago and Lucas drawn on for shock value, the revelation took everybody in the courtroom by surprise: twenty-six red stickers clung to Thiago's body, indicating point of entry for each bullet. Only two were stuck to Lucas's body in non-life-threatening places—one in the leg and one in the stomach. Apart from his wounds being a "sprinkling of lead" to remind him that he'd sworn an oath to the force, the disproportionate number of red holes between both brothers stated more than the obvious: this was not the police doing their job but a gang of murderers doing some very powerful people's bidding in the streets.

When Lucas finally raised his hand to the Bible, his testimony resulted in several prison sentences and expulsions of members of the Skulls, the special task force. Not only did he claim that Thiago didn't have his gun with him that day, he also divulged a history of violence and ongoing corruption in the force, which he'd learned about first-hand as well as through his brother. This useful information—with hard evidence in the form of photos capturing money handoffs and audio recordings discussing murders and drug deals with the corrupt cops—would be something Lucas could fall back on if Thiago would one day be killed.

It was also Lucas's testimony that sought to publicly denounce the Skulls and put them under greater scrutiny. The police, however, counterclaimed that all evidence was fabricated, and that they were trained in urban warfare, their only tactic being, as emphasized at a press conference, to "shoot to kill the barbarians that were overrunning the city." They had lost way too many of the boys in black (the Skulls wore black) on the front lines, and there was, according to one cop interviewed with his face covered with a balaclava, no other scientifically proven social remedy.

"Prison is university for criminals," the anonymous cop said, "and makes them smarter and braver for when they are released." One sociologist agreed, and even claimed that they came out with the knowledge in committing crimes equivalent to an MBA at Harvard. Another sociologist who testified at Lucas's hearing fought in his defense, stating that what was happening in society was "social and ethnic cleansing," unfairly targeting minorities.

The police never made a public apology that Lucas being hit was an accident, despite the press doing some digging and finding out that Lucas was not one of those "reprehensible types." Still, he was made redundant in the force. "The psychological trauma that he suffered," said police chief Oliveira, "would make him unable to carry out his duty as an officer." The irony was that after Lucas's parents were also killed, Lula took him back and sent him to Spain on a manhunt to collaborate with Barcelona's police and to arrest the alleged killer.

A few days after Thiago's death, Lucas called Miquel from his hospital bed to inform him that his manna from heaven would soon be ashes scattered into the sea. Though Miquel heard the news, he was not saddened at all to hear that his recruit would not be playing for the best team in the world. Instead, Miquel proposed to finance the building of a mausoleum for Thiago in the favela at a children's park.

A few weeks later, Lucas placed a statue of Our Lady of Aparecida inside the mausoleum with Thiago's ashes in an urn—Miquel convinced Lucas to keep the ashes and not scatter them out to sea. An old team photo stood next to the urn, in which you could find Thiago and Lucas taking a knee next to each other in the front row, a soccer ball between them. At the end of the row in the picture stood Gregorio, the man who had done his best to raise Thiago, on and off the field.

Not too long after the mausoleum's construction, a special task force—outraged that criminals were being glorified and memorialized—entered the favela on the pretense of rounding up a few gang members, but instead they stood around with guns while officers in balaclavas took sledgehammers to the shrine. They reduced it to rubble as fast as Thiago had been wiped off the face of the earth. The community stood by and watched in horror, yet the gangsters closest to Thiago vowed to take revenge, which they did, even before dusk of the very same day.

A phone call was made and a riot broke out in a prison called Little Carandiru, leaving seven guards dead: they were all decapitated and their bodies were thrown off the roof of the prison. But that wasn't all. Later that night, some boys from the gang threw rocks at government buildings, flipped over a few cruisers and lit them on fire. There were also three officers who were ambushed in their service jeeps and shot dead before their vehicles were set ablaze. The few protesters who opted for peaceful means of expressing their grief camped out in the park, in front of the razed shrine, banging pots and pans for five minutes every hour until the early morning. The small rebellion would be remembered as The Day of Thiago.

26

The Ambush

The announcer boomed his long and protracted "Gooooool!" followed by, "What a work of art," and, "A sign from God," praises which brought everyone to their feet and Lucas out of his reverie. Fans went ballistic, jumping and cheering and kissing their Barcelona scarves. Some strangers even embraced each other out of pure joy. But Lucas stood with an indignant look on his face, uninterested in the beautiful game he'd once loved.

"The worst thing, Paco," Lucas said in a calm and bitter tone, staring blankly ahead, "is that I'm starting to forget." Paco glanced at him but couldn't hear what Lucas had said over all the cheers and celebrating. For the first time he saw in his face something that made the hair stand on his neck: his sense of revenge was real and bloodcurdling; his faith to rid the world of Miquel was clearly defined and unshakable. It was madness, a violent state of mind previously bottled up but now ripe for expression.

Twenty minutes before the game ended, they shoved their way out of the stands and exited down the ramp to the northeastern gate. They rounded the stadium until they reached access door twenty-one facing the parking lot. They waited through the different stages of fans trickling out: those who were confident that Barcelona would keep the lead and preferred to duck out earlier so as to avoid traffic; those who waited until the whistle blew as a sign of loyalty regardless if they were winning or losing; and the few drunken stragglers who left with the previous group yet lingered around for longer to continue drinking and maybe spot a player drive off in his sports car. Lucas and Paco fit neither of those categories, as they were waiting patiently to kill a man.

As they stood against the concrete buttress near access door twenty-one, sharing a cigarette, a somber yet tense quiet fell upon them. Garbage lay scattered everywhere, with a few stadium workers in the distance sweeping up the mess. The air was sweet and cool, the pavement sleek from rain, and the sun was just starting to set. Lucas was making smoke donuts, puffing out his anxiety, and running through the imminent course of action in his head. He held the cross around his neck and occasionally looked at his watch.

"You keep playing with that gold cross," Paco said, looking over at him, blowing smoke.

Lucas looked down at the cross, then at Paco. "What? What's so funny?"

"Like it's a nervous tick or something."

"I'll tell you a little story."

"Shoot."

"My mom was a pretty lady when she was younger. All the boys liked her in the neighborhood and would give her jewelry like gold chains, silver watches, diamonds and pearls. But before she married my dad, she took all the gold, melted it, and made a single gold chain. It was supposed to be a gift for my confirmation. My father wanted me to be confirmed in some Polish church in the south of Brazil, in Curitiba.

"She wanted to have a boy, one boy, and no more kids. But when they adopted my brother, my mother took the chain, melted it again, and made two gold chains—one was given to my brother and the other one is this one, around my neck."

Paco took a puff of his cigarette and thought for a moment. "I wish I had a mother like yours," he said. "Mine died when I was eight. They said it was a heart attack, but they also said my dad had something to do with it. He was a cop, a corrupt one who spent more time in brothels doing favors for gangsters than at home raising three kids." Not knowing what more to say on the subject, Paco changed topics. "Are you sure that Stachu, or Roman or whoever, was telling the truth?" He flicked the cigarette away and ran his hands through his hair. "We've been waiting around for what? An hour? Maybe Miquel left with the players? Took a cab home? Maybe we were sold a lie?"

"He'll come out," Lucas said. "Better get ourselves ready." Paco walked ahead about forty feet, hoisted himself up onto a garbage bin, and reached his arm inside. Sifting through trash, he finally pulled out a bowling ball bag, got down from the bin, and brought the bag back to Lucas. They removed two guns from the bag, racked their slides, and jammed them into the waistbands of their pants before covering them with their jackets.

"It's your job, remember that," Paco reminded. "I'm here just in case things get out of hand." Lucas didn't say anything. Paco reached into the bag and pulled out a three-hole balaclava. Lucas looked at him blankly. "For when you go back to Brazil," Paco said, "and I'm left here with a bulls-eye on my head." Lucas agreed to wearing one too.

They waited until Miquel was supposed to walk out of access door twenty-one, but he didn't. Instead, the doors of access door twenty-three flew open a few feet away. Miquel stepped out holding a cell phone to his ear, talking loudly and uninhibitedly. Seeing him exit the door, they crouched behind the buttress and watched him light a cigarette. They were ready to jump out but waited to see if he was coming out alone or with his bodyguards.

Suddenly, a Mercedes came into view, sped across the wide and open lot, and stopped, tires squealing. It flashed its high beams. Miquel threw down his unfinished cigarette, closed his phone and inserted it into his coat pocket. He checked his watch, fixed his Barcelona scarf around his neck, and started walking towards the car, passing the dumpster along the way. He didn't have his bodyguards with him, but Lucas and Paco were sure the car had at least two armed men inside who'd get out and engage in a gunfight if they had to—if they had time to react.

Lucas hurtled forward drawing himself up to full height. Without breaking his stride, he drew his pistol and pointed it at Miquel.

"Miquel!" Lucas called out.

As if he knew what was coming, Miquel stopped and slowly raised his hands and turned around. They stood facing each other, a few feet of space between them. Lucas could now have a good look at the man who had murdered his family in cold blood—not a single reaction, a calm killer's face, and a fraction of time and space separating his life from his death.

After looking Lucas up and down, Miquel shifted his eyes to Paco, who crept out and walked in line with the dumpster so as not to be seen by Miquel's men.

The balaclava was soaking up Lucas's sweaty brow, its fabric itching his cheeks and forehead. His finger over the trigger started trembling. "When you kill someone," Lucas said, "they say you usually die with them." He pressed the trigger ready to fire, but let go when an SUV appeared racing towards them from the opposite side of the parking lot. It stopped and its black, tinted windows rolled down. The barrels of two high-powered assault rifles stuck out like medieval cannons jutting through embrasures. It was an ambush on top of their ambush.

A rapid fire of bullets started cutting through the air with flashes and smoke coming from two muzzles, then flashes and ricochets against the dumpster's exterior, then bullets hitting and pockmarking the stadium's wall. Miquel dove for cover behind the dumpster. Lucas fell back, thinking he was hit, and started crawling his way towards a car parked a few meters away. Paco hid behind the buttress and returned fire.

Amid the ceaseless volley of gunfire, Lucas peeked out from behind the car. Miquel was sitting against the dumpster, desperately trying to dial someone's number on his phone. He was grabbing his thigh in pain as he'd been hit. He slid his body to the other side of the dumpster and peeked out from the edge to see if his men were shooting back. The gunfire finally stopped and the SUV circled around and sped off in the direction it came from.

Miquel stood up wounded, hissing and moaning from pain, breathing deeply. He walked as quickly as he could to get away, and when he came to his car, he made a grim discovery: Fernando and Duarte were dead. Fernando lay face down in a pool of blood in front of the open passenger-side door. Duarte had keeled forward against the steering wheel. He went around to collect their guns and then grabbed Duarte, pulled him out, and let him drop onto the pavement. Before getting into the car, he turned around one last time and made eye contact with Lucas; he wanted to know who he was but his balaclava made identifying him impossible.

Miquel got into the car and sped off, driving over Fernando's dead body with his back tire. That was when Lucas turned around and made his own grim discovery: Paco had been hit in the chest and was bleeding. He was gone.

27
High Time

He sat on the edge of the heart-shaped bed, slouched forward with his elbows on his knees, an unlit joint wedged in the corner of his mouth. A strip of bedding lay over his crotch, hardly concealing the rest of his naked and sweaty body. Dozens of cheesy decorative pillows lay scattered around the bed like a fluffy fortress. Damp towels lay strewn over the bar in the dining room. The smell of sex hung in the room, and patches of condensation had formed on the ceiling mirror above the bed.

Lucas played connect the torn-off-clothes-in-the-heat-of-the-moment on the hotel carpet floor with his eyes: expensive lace panties and a bra closer to the bed; a one-piece dress and stockings; dirty jeans, moth-eaten socks, and a T-shirt, all forming a trail from the bed to the door. Her heels were missing, kicked off somewhere as they'd entered the suite, embracing and kissing each other, grabbing at each other's throbbing private parts. His underwear was draped over the lampshade as though it was drying from the heat the bulb was giving off. He was still too hungover to try to remember how it had ended up there.

After the euphoria of the moment had died down, Lucas was brought back to reality. He raised his hand and put it on his chest, where Paco had been hit. It felt like his chest had caved in. He couldn't believe that his best friend and partner in crime was dead. Staring morosely at Paco's zipper lighter, he couldn't resist opening and closing it. *Like another one of those nervous ticks?* he thought. Every time he flicked it open, the ambush played on the screen of his mind, and every time he closed it, the ambush rewound until he opened it again to replay it. He paused and ran his hand over a freshly-shaved head, a different look altogether, a symbol of his coming undone. His face was pale and his eyes had rings around them.

The ambush was botched, he reconciled, sighing. But who wanted him dead? Was it Ricardo? Or who wanted Miquel dead? Naturally, many people in the business wanted to see Miquel fed to the pigs. Lucas only wanted to do the job and be on his way out of España. He just wanted to put out the fire that was lit inside him. He hadn't even been to the running of the bulls or seen a Flamenco dancer waving around her floral-printed hand fan in sync with her feet poetically punishing a wooden floor. He didn't intend on Paco being sent up; he didn't think it would go so horribly wrong.

After falling out of the vivid trance that illuminated quite clearly the possibility of one of those bullets having his name on it, he gently slapped himself to stop thinking about the tragedy. Ruminating over all the what-if scenarios would get him nowhere. He accepted what had happened and finally lit the joint he'd been holding in his mouth. He took a few puffs and tried to relax.

In the large and spacious room sat a lavish futon on which were Alba's shopping bags, an errand she had made before meeting Lucas in the hotel lobby and coming up to the twenty-third floor of the W, Barcelona's most luxurious hotel. A half-empty bottle of wine sat on a marble table with two glasses, one tipped and the other standing. Next to it was a small stack of binders containing legal documents she had to study for her case.

Lucas had never been amid such gloss and swank before, in such an extravagant albeit kitsch suite with a bed designed for honeymooners. What made the boudoir even more out of place was the mirror on the ceiling. This accessory made Lucas feel as though he and Alba had been having an audience, even though it was only him looking past her when Alba was on top of him. Safeguarding the further spoiling of his mood was the view from outside, something he could also glimpse in the ceiling mirror.

As the room was a corner suite in the shark-fin-shaped building, the eastern balcony gave an unobstructed and expensive view of the rippling Mediterranean Sea. The other balcony faced the city and a length of beach that receded in the distance towards France. Pushed up against the balcony rail were only three items: two steel chairs that looked like Z-shaped Tetris blocks and a small table, also in the same style, wedged between them.

He restlessly fell back onto the mattress and looked over his shadowy outline in the mirror. He tried to spot the left ventricle and imagined the bed like a real heart, beating and bulging and swooshing, unlike his heart which didn't seem to be working at all anymore. He then thought about Alba; she didn't know that his mind was in a worse place, darker and colder than before, where no decent person dwelled. She finally turned on the shower.

Lucas puffed on the joint, closed his eyes, and envisioned water gliding over her every curve. He saw her hair turn into a streaming waterfall of black oil. He opened his eyes again and looked over at the right atrium, where an open book lay bookmarked by a photo. The photo was of Amelia, Alba's daughter. *She's pretty,* he thought. The book was by Paulo Coelho. To impress Lucas, Alba was even trying to read it in his native tongue. This could explain why many words had their Spanish equivalent penciled in the margins.

Lucas stood up, letting the cover fall off his groin area, and walked to the balcony window. He placed his hand on the glass and looked out at the city. A few hundred feet high up in the air offered a different view than down below, where the streets looked of grime and decadence, where he often drank in the gutters with some of his *chatarrero* friends. Being in the lap of luxury was much different than living on the poor side of the tracks. He looked up into the night sky and imagined flying over Sagrada Família in a helicopter. Its unfinished spires stabbed into the bellies of fat rainclouds ready to burst. He wondered if helicopter pilots held their steering wheels at nine and three. He was far away from his birthplace and would be a lonely passenger looking down at the city, seeing nothing but a water frontier merging with a coast of medieval squares and soulless cathedrals.

He returned to the bed and finished the joint, then put it out in a wet ashtray. Before turning off the lamp, he reached over and removed his underwear from the lampshade. It warmed up his loins when he slipped it on, the warmest feeling he had felt that day. He then lay back and grabbed the book to give it another try. He read an underlined passage while lighting a cigarette. He flipped through some more pages and read another quote that Alba, to his surprise, had translated perfectly. Restless and bored, he threw the book onto the left ventricle and kicked out his legs along the septum. He then caught a glimpse of her purse sitting on the bed.

Lucas pried into her wallet, where he made a bizarre discovery: looking at Alba's driver's license, he noticed she had the same surname as Miquel. *How did I not know her surname?* he asked himself, scratching his head. He snooped around some more until he found a family photo in the bill slot. The surprising realization burst upon him seeing Alba standing next to Miquel, Amelia, and Martin on the patio of their villa in Calella de Palafrugell.

He shot up from bed and paced up and down the room, consumed by anger and confusion, grinding his teeth and clenching his fists. He stopped and cast looks at the bathroom door—Alba was still showering and humming a song. *What do I do?* he thought. He looked at the photo in his hand and tried to figure out what was going on. He sat back down on the edge of the bed and couldn't believe that the woman he was sleeping with was Miquel's wife. A flashback. He vaguely remembered seeing Miquel and his henchmen at the Italian restaurant, but at the time he'd made nothing of it. As far as he knew, two of Miquel's men were killed a few nights ago. Their white and cold bodies were lying in a morgue with nothing but a toe tag distinguishing them apart. Paco was there too and Lucas couldn't come to terms with the fact that they were sharing the same fridge.

He put his hand inside her purse once more and found something even more perplexing: it was a photo of Laia, one he had taken with his vintage camera. How did Alba get a photo of Laia? And why was it in her bag? When Alba turned off the shower, Lucas put the photos back in her bag. He returned to lying down, wondering what he had gotten himself into. He was angry with himself that he'd failed to connect Alba to his parents' crime scene via a photo. But now, by a strange twist of fate, everything made perfect sense.

She finally opened the door, and after the bathroom expelled the last of its steam, her slim and scrubbed body appeared in the door. Lucas studied her in the ceiling mirror while she studied herself in the bathroom mirror. She turned her body sideways, scrutinized her buttocks, patted her tummy. She then went back inside and grabbed two towels, one to wrap her body with and the other to wrap her hair.

"Tell me about your husband," Lucas said without introduction. The question threw her off.

"My husband?" she asked, her voice inflecting upwards, catching the question on its heels. "Why do you want to know about my husband?" She came out of the bathroom and stopped in front of the dining table with a blow dryer in her hand. She wiggled out a cigarette from a pack lying on the table and put it into her mouth. She lit it with an electric lighter while keeping her head still and face forward, as though her neck was in a brace, balancing the towel turban on her head.

"Just curious," he said. "I saw him once." They resumed the conversation now in the ceiling mirror. She took a puff of the cigarette, wondering how to navigate through the imminent interrogation. She put the cigarette in the ashtray to free her hands. She then unraveled the towel turban, placing it over the chairback, and turned on the blow dryer. "I saw him after a game," he repeated, a notch louder over the dryer's whirring, "coming out the back door."

"Back door? He's one of the club's premium sponsors. I don't see why he should be leaving through the back door given the amount of money he throws at them."

"You said he was a … ?"

"He's a sponsor. Our wine business, remember? We invest in the organization's youth club." She changed her mind and resorted to blotting and squeezing her hair with the towel rather than blowing hot air at it. "The business has been good to us, but it has almost turned him into an alcoholic."

"I thought he was a recruiter or something…"

"A recruiter?" Alba laughed. She changed her mind and started again with the dryer. "No, he's not in any manner affiliated with the team's recruiting staff, not at all." Upon saying those words, Alba became self-conscious. She sat down on a chair facing the sea. Thinking with her hands, she turned off the blow dryer and carefully put it on the table. A feeling of sadness came over her as she realized where the conversation was coming from, yet she didn't want to acknowledge where it was going. She hung her head in shame and her mood changed. For the first time in her life, she realized there was no way out of this by lying. "He's very controlling," she said, "and he's unfaithful." Lucas adjusted his pillow and sat up against the bedstead. "He's abusive," she added. With her back to him, Lucas could only make out her expression in the balcony's window. She was devastated; she was falling apart. "He's done some very bad things," she said.

"What kind of things?" Lucas asked.

"He's killed people." She dropped her face into her hands and started sobbing. "He made people kill people."

She gathered herself for a moment but couldn't bear the pain, couldn't hear herself say such words. "I once overheard him talking on the phone...some deal that went bad...and a young man paid for it with his life..."

"Do you remember the person on the other end?"

"It was a long time ago. Come to think of it, his name reminded me of the moon."

"The moon?"

"The way it sounded ... Luna?"

"Lula?"

"Yes," she said, turning around. "That's it! Do you know him?"

Lucas put out the cigarette in the ashtray, sprung from the bed, and started gathering his things. When Alba saw him getting dressed, she got up and walked across the room to try to stop him, ashamed to even look him in the face. She then walked over to her bag and opened it, pulling out a pill bottle. She undid the cap and shook out a pill. When another pill dropped into her palm it wasn't enough, so she tried knocking out another, but as it got stuck against the cotton ball—she kept them in a Tylenol bottle so as not to raise suspicion—she banged harder and out came eight pills. Right when she was about to pop all of them into her mouth, Lucas grabbed her. She put up a stubborn fight against his stern grip and even tried to slap him but she missed his face. The pill bottle fell and the pills from her hand spilled onto the carpet. She dropped to her knees like a desperate addict, cursing Lucas while picking them up one by one. Lucas didn't allow her to lose her self-respect, didn't want her to drag her dignity through the mud. He yanked her up from the carpet and pulled her into a straitjacket hold. She was now sobbing in his arms.

"It's all because of him," she muttered, her face pressed into his chest. She looked up at him. There were tears in her eyes, too many tears. "He came up with the plan to defraud my bank and steal from so many families…he manipulated me… ruined my career—he ruined my life!" Drunk from sadness and despair, she slid down and dropped to her knees. Lucas sighed and sat down on the edge of the bed. He looked into her eyes and caressed her moist cheek, circled a lock of hair around her ear. She fell into his lap and embraced his midsection, but after holding onto him for a short while, she straightened up and looked pleadingly into his face. "Will you kill him for me?" she asked. "I will give you money, property—anything you want!"

It was her foolish naivety and trustworthiness that angered Lucas, the fact that she thought Lucas would be there when her husband was bound to fall from grace. Listening to her, he couldn't come to sympathize with her desperation in wanting to be taken away from the mess Miquel was the architect of. As much as he was visualizing Miquel's death, his rage was now growing even more, especially after learning that it was his very own boss at the precinct who had a hand in his brother's slaying.

Alba stood up and wiggled her waist to make her towel fall off. He looked up into her eyes as he was still seated on the edge of the bed, then dropped them down to her breasts and navel. He hugged her tummy and started kissing her, moving his lips down to her thigh.

After they made love, it was Lucas's turn to wash up, and while he was in the shower, Alba's mood hardly changed as she lay in bed. In fact, it worsened when she thought about how she had come to be with a criminal her whole life and had given birth to his daughter, who was put up for adoption only days after. There was also Amelia, robbed of knowing her father's identity. Worse was that Alba had just made a pact that would end her career and destroy her family, but at least put an end to all the lies and deception.

They both got dressed and went down to the lobby for a drink, but it was Alba who returned in no mood to drown her despair. When she opened the door, she entered the suite and removed her shoes and neatly placed them by the bed. She took off her coat and threw it onto the dining table. She was tipsy as she had left Lucas at the bar all alone. She undid the bracelet from her wrist and walked over to the book she had been reading and replaced the picture of Amelia with it. She looked at the photo endearingly and walked back to her coat, inserting it into its pocket, giving the photo one last glance. She got fully undressed and walked over to the balcony door.

When Alba slid the door open, the wind began howling and blowing violently into the suite, streaming her hair and scattering the pages from her court files. She looked back one last time at the room and placed her right foot onto the table, then stepped with her left foot onto the wide handrail before steadying herself. She looked down and saw boats bobbing on the sea. From the moon's aura the water looked like diamonds scattered over black silk; from its delicate shimmer, her naked body was blanched to a white, angelic glow.

She said a prayer and was ready to jump when suddenly her phone started ringing. And with every ring, her fragile state of mind petered out. She stepped back down and, crying, went back inside. One could even say it was that moment that saved her life because on the other end of the phone was Doctor Valeria Bustos, giving Alba a reason to live.

28

Revenge

Thirty kilometers off the coast of Barcelona, the only land in sight a few small but barren islands cropping out of the water, Miquel was standing in his underwear on the sun deck of *The Secret Investment*. His pants were down to his ankles and his Tommy Bahama shirt was blowing in the breeze. In one hand, his gun hung limply by his side; in the other, a satellite phone held up to his ear. His doctor struggled to keep crouched behind him. He was forced to use the outriggers of his arms for balance every time the luxury yacht swayed and surged on the precipice of a wave. A bottle of antiseptic wobbled on the deck near his feet whenever the boat swooped down and the waves crashed into the hull. The bag of cotton swabs had been long ago swept away into the Balearic Sea by a strong gust of wind.

With his head at the level of Miquel's buttocks, the doctor was carefully looking over the bullet wound his patient had suffered from the shootout. Most of the bullet, as it had broken apart inside his body, was taken out, yet the wound still needed to be cared for. By the end of the examination, or when the doctor began applying the antiseptic for the third time and dabbing the wound with the last cotton swab he had in his hand, Miquel was given a most disturbing bit of news that distracted him from hissing painfully: Ricardo, the Panamanian drug lord, was holding Alba hostage. He lowered the phone and pressed it into his chest, unleashing a profanity-laced tirade.

"That lowlife son of a bitch," he snarled, gritting his teeth, jaw muscles quivering. "The audacity to mess with me and my family! He's got to be out of his mind!" He looked towards the horizon, breathing in and out, trying to relax. His face turned red and veins bulged on both temples. His doctor looked up and gave him a serious look, indicating that he should calm down.

Miquel moved the phone away from his chest and raised it back to his ear. "What does he want, *cariño*?" he asked. "Does he want money?" He pulled up his pants sloppily with the hand holding the gun and shooed away the doctor. He managed to slide the end of the belt through the buckle; it was a surprise the gun didn't go off. He began limping from one side of the deck to the other, discomposed by the unsavory news.

Alba continued stammering on the phone. Unable to tolerate her crying, he gestured for one of his men to make him a drink. There were two of them around, new but young guys whom he could trust with his life. The other one fetched a line of coke and Miquel snorted it up quickly.

"Ricardo said for you to cooperate," Alba cried, "and that he wants to make an agreement."

"An agreement?!"

"He says—" Alba stopped talking. Confusion, a muffled exchange of words, and what sounded like her hand covering the phone. "He says he wants the corridor." She gave this demand as though reading it off a piece of paper. "For his trawlers to offload in your port."

"He what?!" Miquel snapped upon hearing the absurd condition that would wipe him out of business. "That's putting a bullet in my own head."

The words stunned him to silence. Miquel lowered the phone and pressed it into his chest again. He then raised his other hand, the one still gripping the gun, and checked the temperature of his forehead with the back of his palm. He was sweating profusely. Through a chink in the clouds the sun seemed to have been beating down on him and nobody else.

He put the phone back to his ear and said, "This guy has some big brass balls to be calling me out like this."

"Please, *cariño*," Alba begged.

"Does he know who he's fucking with?" asked Miquel, steel in his voice, a screwed look on his face. There was confusion and crying on the other end. "Stop crying, *cariño*, and put him on the phone." No answer. "*Cariño*, please!" No answer again. "Put him on the phone!"

"He doesn't want to talk about this over the phone," she bawled. "He wants to talk in person." Miquel pushed himself away from the rail in a fit of anger. What normally took six strides to get from one side of the deck to the other now took fifteen as a gimpy invalid. The choppy waves also added to his drunk and disabled footing.

Stubborn and foolish, he returned to the bench starboard side and tried to sit down but couldn't from the throbbing pain in his ass. He stood against the rail instead and leaned over, trying to take pressure off the compromised cheek.

"In person?" Miquel asked, considering the option. "You wait and see what I do to him in person—"

"Alone," she cut him off. "No guns, none of your men, or—"

"Or what?"

"Or they'll kill me."

"Kill you?"

"Do it for Amelia and her newborn, for the baby's future, put an end to these wars between you and Ricardo, once and for all."

"Tell me the address," he capitulated.

"It's 173 Tamarit, top floor."

"173 Tamarit," he repeated so that one of his men would remember. "173 Tamarit."

Right after Miquel hung up, he emptied his entire clip into the water. He then swigged back a whiskey and blew his nose, *campesino*-style.

"Put on your floaties and load your guns, gentlemen," Miquel said, wiping his hands on his shirt. "We're heading back to land."

* * *

The buzzer sounded and the main door unlocked. Before Miquel stepped inside, he glanced at a car parked down the street. He wondered what good it was for his men to sit and wait for his command, but in the end he decided to settle this with words and not guns. He looked ahead and saw an older lady scuffing towards him in the corridor. It was Doña Alvarez pulling Juanita on her leash. She greeted Miquel with a *buenos días* before brushing him aside and exiting the building. He looked back at her but hobbled inside with more important business to take care of.

He took in the squalor but headed straight to the elevator. He pressed the elevator's button and waited. In the meantime, he ensured his collar was neatly folded and that his tie hung nicely. "Let's talk business, Ricardo," he said to himself, "man to man, leave my family out of it." He pressed the button again, but the elevator didn't come. If the elevator didn't work, he thought, then maybe his plan wouldn't work. He postured up and cracked his neck to the left, then to the right. He leaned his body over the rail of the staircase and looked up to be sure nobody was looking down or pointing a gun at him. He struggled up to the top floor and noticed the door ajar.

Miquel pulled the gun from behind his belt, gently pushed open the door, and crept inside. He heard stifled moaning and the sound of a body writhing on a wooden floor. He followed the sound through the corridor until a cluttered living room opened up. That was when he saw Alba on the floor hogtied with a strip of masking tape over her mouth. She had a look of panic on her bruised face. Blood was running from her nose.

Rather than run over and try to free her, Miquel looked around the room, leading with his gun. It wasn't the kind of room Ricardo would put his men in an ambush, he thought. When he took a careful step forward, thinking that any minute somebody armed would start shooting, a gun slowly appeared from behind the darkroom's curtain, poking out until the barrel touched the back of his head. He jarred from the contact and knew right away it was him.

"Let's talk business, Ricardo," Miquel said, putting his hands up. "Man to man, leave my family out of it."

Lucas quietly came out from the dark room and took the gun out of Miquel's hand. He patted him down and checked his leather boots. "They're Fendi," Miquel scoffed with his back still to him. "I wouldn't want to ruin them by inserting a piece down there. I'm sure you've got a pair yourself ... I'm willing to make this problem go away. Name your price. Let's put this beef to rest once and for all."

Once Lucas finished patting him down, he pulled his arm back and answered him with a pistol-whip to the head. Miquel dropped to the ground, shrieking and grabbing his head in pain. He looked at his hands and was enraged to see blood on his fingers. He looked up and realized it wasn't Ricardo standing over him but a young, grizzly-looking boy with a gaunt face and shaved head.

"Your wife told you to come unarmed, you lying sack of shit," Lucas said, carefully stepping around with his gun pointed at Miquel. "I suppose that's the first sign of a failing marriage—when you stop listening to each other."

"What the fuck do you know about my marriage?" Miquel spat, looking Lucas up and down with a confused look, wondering who this punk was. After his indignation subsided, familiarity emerged on his face. "Do I know you?"

"Yeah," Lucas answered. "Let me refresh your memory." Lucas sprung forward and kicked Miquel's head like a soccer ball. "Goooooool!" he yelled, putting up his arms like a player after scoring a penalty kick. Blood burst from Miquel's mouth and he spit out a tooth. "Wait, the ref called for a retake. The other team's player got in there before the whistle." Lucas's eyes bulged and he licked his dry lips. He ran up and kicked

Miquel with his good foot. "Gol! Gol! Gol!" Lucas cut off his own celebratory dance. "Sit there on the floor!" he spat, transforming the cheerful look on his face psychotically.

Miquel dragged himself up from the ground and staggered over dizzily from the blows. That was the cue for Alba to stand up from the uncomfortable position she was in and brush the ropes off her hands and feet. She grabbed the tape around her mouth, pulled it off with a quick rip, and cleaned the dust off her legs. She stuck her hand out, into which Lucas placed the gun he had taken off Miquel. She gripped it like a beginner, raised it, and pointed it at her husband. Lucas offered her a tissue from the tissue box. She accepted it and wiped the bloody makeup off her face.

With tough rope he had found scrapping, Lucas started tying Miquel's hands behind his back. Miquel didn't dare move as Alba warned him not to. He was distraught by the mere sight of his wife not doing anything about him being tied up and imminently tortured.

"Alba?" said Miquel, more husbandly than usual. "Is this really you?" Alba didn't answer, holding back her tears. Her hands were trembling nervously, shaking the gun, making it impossible for her to aim it properly. "This is me...Miquel, your husband." Lucas punched him in the face and told him to shut up. Alba shook her head as she couldn't believe what was happening.

Once his hands were tied up, Lucas returned to the couch and sat down like he was about to watch the television, or Esmeralda and Anastasia amid their love-making in the window across from his building. Alba walked over and sank into the couch next to him, putting her face in her palms. Lucas took the gun off her, said she did a good job, and placed the gun on his lap. She didn't look up or react.

Lucas lit a cigarette and took a few nervous puffs. He stared at Miquel for a while, thinking about how to do it, how to inflict as much pain and suffering as possible. He plugged up his mouth with the cigarette and pulled out a piece of paper from his back pocket. It was an obituary.

"Thiago Brodowski," he started reading, clearing the thick mucous welling up in his throat, "number twenty-seven from Flamengo … .Mother, Rafaela Brodowski … and father, Gregorio Brodowski.…" He stopped reading and looked up at Miquel. The smoke from his cigarette was going in his face and stinging his eyes, or maybe he was tearing up. "Do these details ring a bell?"

Miquel started pleading with Lucas. Lucas waited for an answer but when he didn't get it, he grabbed the gun from his lap, pointed it at Miquel, and shot him once in the leg. Miquel shrieked and started writhing and twitching like a worm impaled on a fishing hook. Lucas placed the gun back in his lap. He looked over and saw Alba turn to the side and retch. He started reading the clipping again, both hands returning to the paper, ignoring Miquel's cursing and crying and begging.

"…Thiago Brodowski, gunned down on—" Lucas paused and looked at him again. "I too was collateral damage," he said, lifting his shirt and showing Miquel a bullet scar. "Or maybe I was targeted?" Miquel didn't react as he was still coiling in agony on the floor. He pushed himself up with his feet, smearing blood all over the floor, and was now leaning against the bookshelf.

"Did you order the killing?" Lucas asked. "Did you kill my parents and my brother?!" Lucas grabbed the gun and raised it once more and pointed it at Miquel.

"I didn't kill anyone!" Miquel gasped, shaking his head. "It was Lula ... Lula Oliveira did it ... he killed everyone." Lucas didn't say anything and lowered his gun. "I was supposed to sell Thiago a large shipment of guns ... Lula found out and wanted to intercept the shipment, link the charges to your brother, and put him behind bars. He would then keep the guns for himself and sell them off later...but Thiago flip-flopped on the deal; he called it off last minute. This angered Lula so he set up the roadblock and decided that Thiago's time was up."

"And this recruiting business?"

"We weren't negotiating his salary that day." Miquel leaned over and spat out some more blood. With his hands tied behind his back it didn't even look like he had arms at all. "We were negotiating the price of the guns."

"Why did he send me here?"

"Lula didn't want you sniffing around. That is why he put you on me...he started working behind my back with Ricardo. Maybe they wanted me dead, to get rid of the competition. Maybe because I owed Lula some money and he sent Ricardo to find me to collect it. I don't know. He also knew you would try to get revenge and he knew you'd go after me ... tell you just enough to set you on the right path. Wind you up like a toy soldier and watch you go. That's why I tried to get Roman to steer you away from me."

"To kill me?!" Lucas yelled.

"To kill you," Miquel admitted. "What would you do in my shoes? There was no other way. Roman used to clean my boat. Then he became a manager at one of my brothels, but then he said he wanted a *real* job. Can't you see this is all Lula's plan? He wanted to put the bite on me, deflect attention away from him."

Lucas placed both guns on the floor next to the couch. He thought about everything Miquel had said but wasn't satisfied with his explanation. Overtaken by rage, he shot up from the couch, marched over to Miquel, and started kicking and punching him. Miquel moaned his apologies and begged him to stop. He asked Lucas how much money he wanted, but the proposal infuriated Lucas even more. Lucas saw a bowling ball and an empty aquarium, but he picked up a microwave instead. He raised it over his head and dropped it down on Miquel. Alba was still crying on the couch, covering her eyes as she couldn't watch the beating.

Lucas returned to the couch, grabbed both guns (inserting one into his belt) and went back to Miquel. He grabbed a tuft of his oily hair and pulled back his head. He then stuck the gun into Miquel's mouth and pressed the barrel against the back of his throat. Lucas's hand was shaking and sweat appeared on his forehead. Miquel was looking into Lucas's eyes mercifully.

"Don't you … find it strange … that you were sent here right after your parents were killed?" Lucas removed the barrel and let him talk. "That a photo connecting me … to my wine business was … placed at the murder scene? Lula killed your parents because they found out about Thiago…Gregorio and Rafaela had evidence that connected Lula to Thiago's murder. It was a recorded conversation between Lula … and a senator … Lula was bragging to him about killing your brother."

Lucas stuffed the barrel back inside Miquel's mouth, even deeper than before. His finger started pressing the trigger. He couldn't take it anymore and closed his eyes, about to fire.

"Lucas!" Someone called out his name and he opened his eyes. Alba was holding a gun and pointing it at him. *How did she have a gun? It must have been in her purse,* he thought. "That's enough," she said with tears flooding her sunken and tired eyes. "I can't anymore ... please stop!"

Lucas knew she wouldn't fire the gun, so he closed his eyes again and was about to squeeze the trigger when a loud noise erupted at the door. He turned his head and saw a dark mass appear out of nowhere. It quickly broke apart in the corridor, stealthily and strategically, like a group of trained commandos. They wore black hoodies and their black boots glided over the parquet soundlessly. Guy Fawkes masks covered their faces. Their weapons were the kind of artillery used to pull off a diamond heist.

They all removed their masks except for one person, the last person inching closer with a shotgun trained on Alba. At a short enough range to fill her with just enough lead, that person removed her mask.

"Put down the gun, Alba!" Laia shouted.

Anastasia, Xavi, Frank the Machine (and his machine gun), and Esmeralda were standing in the loft with their weapons trained on Alba, Lucas, and Miquel. Even the Cristiano look-alike stood there with a handgun pointed at Lucas, his diamonds scintillating and polished to perfection.

"Put down your guns!" Lucas shouted.

"Lower it, Alba!" screamed Laia.

"Tell him to put his gun down," Alba said, referring to Lucas's gun still lodged in Miquel's mouth. Miquel was panicking, his beady eyes flitting around the room. Nobody moved. Nobody lowered their weapons. A standoff. Alba wiped her tears and moved a lock of hair away from her eyes.

"You wouldn't shoot your own ... mother, would you?" Alba blurted out, a desperate look peering through her anguish. Everyone looked at each other confused by the comment. Had she gone mad?

"What did you say?" Laia asked with a puzzled look on her face.

"I thought somebody at the hospital would take good care of you ... thought that you'd get to a good home." With the gun still on Lucas, Alba slowly reached her other hand into her pocket. "I left you alone ... all by yourself ... in this unforgiving world." She pulled out a piece of paper and handed it to Laia. "And now I have to suffer the consequences."

"This is ... I can't believe this ... it's ridiculous!" Filled with disgust as much as denial, Laia threw down the DNA test and stepped forward, releveling her shotgun on Alba.

"When you cut your finger that day at the antique shop," Alba said. Everyone looked at the children's Band-Aid on Laia's finger. "Lucas gave you a tissue, you wiped the blood with it, and threw it into the trash bin...I saw that. I was in a car parked next to the shop. I then used that bloodied tissue to check if you were my daughter. And you were ... are ... Your date of birth is October 13, 1988. Your blood type is B+. You have a birthmark on your right knee and behind your right ear ... you smiled when I ... when I gave you back ... because Miquel told me I couldn't handle motherhood, because I was too young, because we needed to live a little ... *he* said we had to live a little!" Alba started sobbing uncontrollably, her hand feebly holding the gun still pointed at Lucas.

"Shut up!" Laia yelled. "Shut up! Shut up! Shut up!" She couldn't believe what she was hearing, shaking her head not wanting to hear anymore. "This is not true!" Laia, in a state of shock, slowly lowered her gun. But she raised it again, enraged for other reasons. "Go ahead," Laia said. "Shoot Lucas! Shoot that swine! The informant from Rio." Alba stopped crying and looked at Lucas with knit brows. She shook her head, not understanding.

"Police officer?" Alba asked.

"A cop! A pig! And our little red-light setup," Laia said, pointing to the apartment across the street. "What made you think filming each other was the only thing we were doing?" Alba and Lucas looked over at Esmeralda, who smiled mischievously. Esmeralda finally spoke, asking Anastasia in German if she could just shoot the pervert right there. Cristiano butted in and said he would be honored to shoot Lucas in the balls. "Did you think he was with you because he loved you?" Laia said. "Or because he wanted to get close to Miquel by turning you into a victim. This is exactly what he wanted ... to get you to kill him!" Alba looked at Lucas in disbelief. "This was all part of his plan. He manipulated you!"

"Don't listen to her, Alba," Lucas said.

"Pick who it is you want dead," Laia continued, "shoot Miquel Partagas and—" Alba nodded, knowing what Laia was thinking. A disgusted look appeared on Laia's face and her grip of the shotgun slackened.

"Though this family reunion is as shocking as it is beautiful," interrupted Xavi, "that's not why we're here." He turned to Alba and gave her a strict ultimatum. "We have Amelia," he said plainly and to the point, "and in exchange for her healthy pregnant body, we want you to confess on air to the corruption case and to publicly denounce the evictions— or better, to stop them from happening. If you don't comply, well, you'll never see her and your granddaughter again."

"You're getting my…my daughter involved?" Alba stuttered hopelessly, choking back her tears. "My grandchild is a…girl?" Again, she was the last one to find out. "What was my crime?" she asked, lowering her gun. "Was it because I became the world's most hated banker? The victim of my husband's greed? A bad mother? Was it because I gave up my firstborn for adoption?" Alba looked up and made eye contact with everyone in the room. "I'm sorry," she said. "I'm sorry for all of this…for all of your grief and suffering." She looked at her husband. "I'm sorry, Miquel. Please forgive me and tell Amelia and our granddaughter I love them." Alba brought the gun up to her temple and before anyone could stop her, she pulled the trigger. Bang! She dropped to the floor and the gun fell from her hand. A pool of blood started forming around her head. It went quiet in the loft and the only thing you could hear was the ticking of the grandfather clock.

Laia lowered the shotgun and dropped her exhausted body down on the couch, lapsing into deep thought, wondering if it was all true. Lucas removed the gun from Miquel's mouth and ran over to Alba. He stood over her lifeless body and couldn't believe she had killed herself. He knelt, placed his gun to the side, and raised her head, putting it into his lap. He looked into her eyes, moved a lock of hair from her mouth and stroked her cheek. After gently caressing her eyelids closed, he grabbed her gun and got up from her cooling body. He walked back and stood over Miquel, who was shaking and pleading for his life. Lucas raised the gun, pointed it at him, and pulled the trigger. Bang! Miquel flopped over on his side. Dead. Lucas wiped the gun's handle with a dishcloth and put it in Alba's hand to get her prints on it. He then carefully placed it next to Alba's body. He stuffed his gun behind his belt and walked over to the window; he planted his palms down, sighing and shaking his head. He snuck a peek at Esme and Cristiano, who were standing next to the table, next to where he ate his ravioli every night. He couldn't believe they were in his loft, staring at him as if they wanted to kill him. *What a twisted world,* he thought.

A squeal of tires at street level aroused his attention. Ricardo and four armed men got out of a black SUV, the same SUV that ambushed Lucas. "Oh shit!" Lucas hissed. He snapped his gaze to the opposite side of the street and saw two other men in black leather jackets approach the car where Miquel's men were waiting. Silencers. Four shots in total. Broad daylight. When he turned around to warn the others the first thing he saw was a shotgun in his face. He had always underestimated her but now, staring down the barrel, he wondered if Laia would really do it.

"Move," she said, nuzzling him away from the window.

He put up his hands. "We've just started World War III."

"You still have a job to do," said Laia.

"A job? Alba is dead … Miquel is dead."

"The bank is not *dead,*" Laia said.

"You got what you wanted," Lucas said. "I got what I wanted…you just don't get it, do you? There will be another Alba Partagas, another Miquel."

"You were fucking around with the woman I've been working for years to bring down! You were doing this to shame me, to undermine me…to send me to prison?!" She pushed the back of his head with the shotgun's tip.

"Innocent people, Laia," Lucas pleaded, "people who just want to work and provide for their families; people who want to get on with their lives in this shitty crisis."

"They work for a corrupt bank," Laia said, "—they should know better."

"This is our statement, Lucas," Xavi interjected. "Our statement to the world."

"This doesn't make any sense at all!" Lucas shouted. "You're all sick in the head! You and your twisted ideology!"

Xavi approached and trained his gun on Lucas while Laia knelt and removed a bomb from her backpack. She set the detonator for twenty minutes and then placed it in Lucas's camera bag after removing his camera and throwing it to the side. She stood up and wrapped the backpack's straps around his shoulders.

"This one is tamperproof, Lucas," said Xavi with a grin on his face. "If you remove the batteries, you become a martyr."

"What is there to live for, Lucas, if not for the *cause?*" Laia said. "Your family is gone and now you just have the world... to defend the poor and the helpless. You've got your personal justice, how about social justice?"

Ricardo strolled into the loft with a gun in his hand, looking cool and calm in a flamboyant suit. Everybody stopped and stared at him, wondering who he was, like an uninvited guest arriving late to a party. He looked over the junk-filled loft and grimaced. He grabbed an umbrella leaning against the wall and turned to look at all the people, from Esmeralda and Laia to Lucas, making eye contact with every one of them. Soon he noticed that two people were not making themselves available for the visual greeting.

"Who is that?" Ricardo asked, pointing the umbrella at the person who failed to acknowledge his entrance. He walked over to Alba and poked her with the umbrella's tip. He hissed, a look of pain crossing his face upon seeing her head shot. He then walked over to Miquel and recognized him right away. When Ricardo pressed his foot into Miquel's round and lifeless body, and when he noticed that Miquel wasn't moving, his face turned red with anger. He threw the umbrella off to the side, annoyed that he now had to ask what had happened.

"What the fuck is this?" he said, gesturing his gun at Miquel.

"Excuse me, but who the fuck are you?" Xavi interrupted.

"Who the fuck are *you* to ask me who the fuck *I am*?" Ricardo snarled, with the question coming back and freezing Xavi. "You're telling me you don't know who the fuck I am? I am the guy who gave your crusty anarchist specific orders for this man right here not to die as he owes me a lot of money—but somebody fucked up because he's dead. Who fucked up?!"

A creak sounded in the corridor and in a fraction of a second a hail of gunfire erupted. Frank the Machine, already on edge and jittery from the drugs he had taken, pulled the trigger and started firing his leviathan of a machine gun at Ricardo's men, who walked into the living room with all sorts of guns drawn. In the exchange of gunfire, Anastasia, Esme, and Cristiano took cover behind the couch and started firing back. A salvo of bullets flew overhead, breaking windows and marking the walls and damaging all the photos. The appliances all fizzled and TV screens shattered and the clocks exploded. Ricardo jumped behind the washing machine. He was wounded by one of his own men from a bullet intended for Frank the Machine. Laia and Lucas jumped under the table, but when Laia stuck her body out to shoot, she got hit in her arm and chest. While the gun battle raged, Lucas crawled his way from under the table towards the kitchen and then out the door.

Aware that he had a bomb strapped to his body and that it would detonate any minute, he pulled the camera bag from his back and looked inside. Red numerals flashed on a digital clock. He had eight minutes to spare before it would go off. Where could he detonate it safely?

Comfortably outside the line of fire, he got to his feet and bolted down the stairs and out the main doors, heading straight to his motorcycle. He threw off the cover and prayed to God for it to start. He looked up and realized it wasn't raining anymore, and that the sun was peeking out from behind a cloud. He fished out his keys from his pocket and put them in the ignition and turned. The engine cranked and cranked. He tried to inject gas by pumping the starter but nothing. His luck hadn't run out just yet—the motorcycle finally started and off he went, meandering through traffic, averting fatal accidents by inches.

He rode around a routine traffic stop and remembered when his brother had done the same. He wondered if doing this would have the same tragic result. The traffic police called in for backup to pursue the mad rider flying down Via Diagonal. He passed the Rocafort Plaza, La Rambla, Barrio Raval, and finally entered Montjuic. He climbed its hill at a low gear, driving around a protest, and got up to the top. He jumped a curb and sped along a footpath under the leafy pergola. Strolling couples dove out of his way. He saw the cliff in the distance but when he slammed the brakes, he lost control. He dumped the bike and flew off. It spun in circles at a forward trajectory until it broke through the cliff's barrier and plunged hundreds of feet down the hill. As he too was about to tumble off the cliff, he managed to grab a part of the rail. Hanging suspended, he wiggled the straps off his shoulders and let the bag slide down to his hand. He dropped the bag and reached up to grab the rail with both hands. The bomb exploded right before it crashed into the scree at the bottom of the cliff. Lucas pulled himself up and rolled onto solid ground. A crowd surrounded him and asked if he was okay. He was coughing and gasping for air. A tourist approached and took a picture of him with his camera.

* * *

The Rock of Gibraltar began to shrink at his back the closer the ferry moved towards Tangier. He wore a light coat and underneath it a sling held his arm in place. His face was scarred and scabbed, and his black eye reached a stage of discoloration that could be taken for sleeplessness and stress.

The upper deck of the ferry was entirely empty of passengers. He stood near the bow, watching the hull part through the water. His healthy arm rested on the rail and his hand held a small stack of photos flickering in the breeze.

Lucas recalled the children from the neighborhood painting the abandoned car, the mothers smiling and pushing their strollers, and the seniors talking about the civil war. He looked back down and stared into the deep and mysterious water. It was at that moment he saw something he never expected to see in this corridor between Africa and Europe, in the space where the Atlantic and Mediterranean meet—a lone dolphin. Under the gentle sun its sleek and shiny body swam gracefully on the water's surface, rising and falling with the current until it dove down and never came up. Lucas smiled, slipped the photos into his jacket's inner pocket, and went back inside to the passenger area.

ABOUT THE AUTHOR

Marius Stankiewicz, a Toronto native, is a former international journalist, photographer, and documentary filmmaker who currently resides in Barcelona. His journalistic work has been featured on NPR and Al Jazeera, and in *Barcelona Metropolitan*, the *Toronto Star*, the *Globe and Mail*, the *Province*, and *Men's Journal*. Stankiewicz graduated with an MA in English from Jagiellonian University in Cracow and an MA in communication science & media from the University of Amsterdam. In his free time, he plays the drums, frequents dive bars, and trains in Muay Thai, an ancient combat sport originating in Thailand.